A New Beginning for Beth

Catherine Angelone

AuthorHouse™
1663 Liberty Drive, Suite 200
Bloomington, IN 47403
www.authorhouse.com
Phone: 1-800-839-8640

©2008 Catherine Angelone. All rights reserved.

No part of this book may be reproduced, stored in a retrieval system, or transmitted by any means without the written permission of the author.

First published by AuthorHouse 5/19/2008

ISBN: 978-1-4343-7855-2 (sc)

Printed in the United States of America
Bloomington, Indiana

This book is printed on acid-free paper.

DEDICATED TO

MY HUSBAND TONY AND MY CHILDREN,
MICHAEL, STEVEN, CHELSEA AND PATRICK.
YOU ARE NEVER TOO OLD TO CHASE
YOUR DREAMS AND CATCH THEM.

Chapter One

Mary stuck her head into Beth's office. Beth raised her eyes to Mary with curiosity.

"Yes?" Beth asked, wondering why Mary didn't use the intercom phone. Mary moved into the office, closing the door behind her. Her eyes darted back and forth. Not a good sign Beth thought. Mary moved closer to Beth's desk closing the gap between them. Beth sat back in her chair and watch as Mary planted herself in one of the leather chairs that sat across from her desk.

"Okay Mary. Now, you're scaring me. What's up?"

"Um, your husband is in the waiting room. He wants to see you." she coughed. The women sat and stared at each other then focused their attention at the closed door. Beth secretly hoped it was a joke and that James really wasn't sitting on the other side of her office door. Mary made no attempt to move from her chair.

"What shall I tell him?" Mary asked not knowing how Beth was going to react to the news.

Beth thought of a few good answers. Most involved sticking things in areas of James's body where the sun doesn't shine. Either way each idea seemed pleasing to Beth but would cause great pain as well as difficulty for James when performing the art of sitting.

"Give me five minutes then send him in." she replied.

Mary formed a slight smile on her lips and exited the office, closing the door behind her.

Beth poured herself a glass of water. Nervously sipping it, she checked herself in the mirror. She couldn't figure out what brought James here unannounced. It had been two months since they separated. Aside from a few formal phone calls, they really had not been in touch with each other. But one thing was for sure. She was still angry over all that had happened.

She was angry at the seven years she wasted on him. She was angry at how he, along with her mothers help, convinced her to change her career from criminal law to family law. But more than anything, she was angry how she caught him playing office desk mambo with his receptionist. Right on the desk she picked out and paid for. Right there in the office that she paid to have decorated for him.

She did a mental head slap as she recalled that fateful night when she caught them. Then he had the nerve to come by the next day. Not to explain, although there were no words to explain what she witnessed and what he had been doing for the past six months. But only to pick up his things and tell her that he was leaving because she had changed.

She had cut him short when he tried to blame her for the separation. It was one thing to be caught in the act of adultery, but it was another thing to try to justify his actions because she supposedly changed.

Beth brushed a blonde curl from her face and tucked it behind her ear. She ran her hands over her cream linen skirt and unbuttoned the top button of her white blouse. She took her place behind her desk and nervously fidgeted with the papers she was looking at before Mary brought her the news of the unexpected visitor. Beth buzzed Mary on the intercom phone. "Send him in." She calmly said. Mary replied with a yes and motioned James towards the door.

James stuck his head in the door and smiled a hello to Beth. Beth looked up at him and her heart skipped a beat. James had changed his hair to a younger style but she wasn't going to give him the satisfaction of mentioning it, although it suited him. Even his clothes seemed much younger than what he used to wear. Beth stood and managed a slight smile.

"What brings you here to my office?" She asked as she motioned for him to have a seat.

"What? No hello?" he replied with slight nervousness.

She grunted and rolled her eyes. "What do you want James?"

He studied her face. He could tell by her tone that his visit wasn't something she expected or wanted. He decided that trying to be pleasant wasn't going to work. "I came to talk to you about the house." He said taking a seat.

Beth nodded, sitting back down in her big leather chair. She leaned back in the chair, crossed her arms over her chest and studied his face.

She was a good family lawyer but an even better criminal lawyer. She knew all the facial moves that would indicate whether someone was lying to her or just plain nervous. But she knew James' facial moves even better. And his face was telling her that this was more difficult for him than it was for her. She also figured that Jill had something to do with this.

She remembered the Christmas party that she and James had thrown for his staff. She had commented on the house many times during that evening. Beth shuddered as she recalled that night.

There was a brief time that Jill and James were not around. It was much later when she found out that they had somehow managed to sneak away for a quickie in their upstairs bathroom. They did it right on her makeup table.

"Are you okay?" James asked.

"I'm good thanks. The air conditioning is a bit cool."

James nodded as if to know exactly what she meant.

"So, Beth, what are your plans about the house?"

"I'm not sure yet James. I may stay there." Beth knew that was a lie.

She hated coming home to that big empty house. But she hated giving it to James and Jill to share, even more.

"You know that I want the house and I'm willing to pay you top dollar for it."

"I know James but I'm not sure if I want to sell it."

James' eyes narrowed. "Are you unsure you want to sell it, or you just don't want to sell it to me?"

Beth felt her face flush. She wanted to scream but she kept her composure. "Tell you what James. I will look over your offer and if I do decide to sell it, I will get a fair market evaluation and then you can double that if you want the house."

She stood indicating to him that the conversation was over.

"You know that my offer is fair enough." He stood staring her down.

She felt small next to his six foot height. Just as she always had in her small five foot three inch frame. But she wasn't about to be intimidated.

"If you and Jill want the house bad enough, you will give me my asking price." She stood firm. "And from now on, James, if you have anything you want to discuss, I suggest you contact my lawyer. The next time you show up here without an appointment, I will have security remove you." She motioned for the door.

James' eyes widened at her words. "Are you throwing me out?" he asked.

"No James. I'm asking you to leave. Throwing you out would involve body contact and I wouldn't touch you with a ten foot pole."

James turned on his heels. "You better think about my offer Beth. I have a good chance of taking the house from you and you could end up with nothing." He growled as he headed for the door.

"You don't frighten me James. You forget how good a family lawyer I am." She growled back.

He stopped at the door and looked back at Beth. "Speaking of law, I hear you are going back to criminal law. Don't you think that is a dangerous thing to do?"

"Since when have you been concerned about my well being?"

"Beth." His voice softened. "I've always been concerned about you. That will never change. But going back to a career that almost cost you your life is crazy."

"One little death threat didn't cost me my life. And besides, it is part of the job."

James stood silently, shaking his head in disbelief. He knew it was pointless to argue with Beth. She hated family law and he knew it. Besides, it wasn't his call anymore. "Just think about my offer for the house." He left the office without closing the door. Beth moved towards the door and slammed it shut, scaring the hell out of Mary in the process.

She opened the door again checking to see if James was still there. When she didn't see him, she leaned out the doorway in Mary's direction.

"The next time he comes here without an appointment, tell him I'm not here." Mary nodded yes and Beth disappeared back into her office.

The sun was bright orange, and still high in the sky by the time Beth pulled her white Malibu into her garage. It was the end of June and summer had appeared with a vengeance. There had been three weeks of cold rain, followed by a week of intense heat. Welcome to Canada, Beth thought as she raced to get out of the heat of her garage.

There was no weaning from cold to hot especially in Ontario. There were two season in Ontario. There was winter and summer with a brief moment of frost and thaw, in between.

Beth had her blouse off and her skirt unbuttoned, by the time she made it up the stairs to her bedroom. Her shoes lay at the bottom of the stairs and her purse and brief case were placed on the laundry room counter.

She moved her naked self into the bathroom and flipped on the shower. The tepid water felt good against her skin. She scrubbed her face free of makeup and conditioned her hair. Wrapping her hair in a towel; she rummaged through her closet trading in her linen suit for a pair of grey shorts and a white baby tee. Beth brushed her blonde hair free of any tangles and tied it up into a pony tail.

She walked barefoot into the kitchen and glanced over at her phone. The light from the phone was blinking wildly. She sighed. It was probably her mother calling her again. She chose to ignore the messages for the moment and instead focused her attention on the refrigerator.

She was starving. Beth had skipped lunch and was feeling light headed. As usual, her fridge was bare, except for the usual necessities such as mustard, ketchup and a half bottle of green olives. She scooped a couple of olives out of the jar and popped them into her mouth as she retrieved a Chinese menu from the desk. She quickly made an order of Chinese rice, chicken balls and egg rolls as well as a few other items she had never tried. More than enough food for one person she thought.

She then checked her messages as she waited for her food delivery. Her mother had called three times in the last hour. That made sense since she was late at the office again. It even made more sense since Beth never returned the calls she made to her while she was at the office. Her tone became more stern and demanding with each message. There was also a couple of hang ups as well as a call from her grandparents. Her mother can wait, she thought, and dialed her grandparent's number.

Tom Jackson, her grandfather, was a retired detective. Audrey, her granny, was his wife and sidekick. Together they decided to open an investigation service.

Most of the people who worked for them were also retired from law enforcement and most were over sixty. Except Jack Peterson, who was also retired, but far from sixty. Beth placed him more in his early forties.

Her best childhood memories were the moments she spent with her grandparents. Her father Michael Bardos, had died when Beth was eight so that left her mother Joanna, as sole supporter and a single parent. Because of this, Beth's mother relied on her parents to take care of Beth while she worked. This arrangement allowed Beth to grow very close to her grandparents.

Beth felt that her mother resented her closeness with them. This was even more so, given the fact that Beth went into law instead of medicine like she did. But marrying a future doctor was the next best thing. Beth loved her mother, but they never quite saw eye to eye when it came to James or her life.

"Hi granny," Beth chirped.

"Beth dear, How are you?" grandma asked when she heard Beth's voice.

"A bit tired today but fine." she replied. "I had a visitor today." Beth added.

"Did you tell him to piss off?" granny asked knowing exactly who Beth was referring to.

"Now granny, you know that isn't a nice thing to say."

"And you know your grandpa and I never cared much for him. He seemed too arrogant and sure of himself for someone like you."

"He asked me again about selling the house to him. His offer sounds good. I may take him up on it."

"If you do decide to sell it to him, let me and your grandfather know. Our friend Sal has a real estate license and he can get you a good appraisal not to mention help you find another place."

Beth made a mental note to keep her suggestion in mind.

"So what's up granny?"

"Is that Beth?" grandpa yelled through the phone, not giving his wife a chance to respond to Beth.

"Yes." grandma yelled back. "Now quiet old man and wait your turn."

"Tell her about Domenic!"

"I will, I will! Just keep quiet and give me a chance." Her grandmother yelled back.

"Your grandfather is worse than a kid. He can ignore me all day but once I get on the phone he is jumping around in front of me trying to get my attention." She sighed.

Beth chuckled as she listened to her grandparent's conversation.

"If you don't sit down and wait your turn, you won't be getting any tonight." She yelled again. "And I don't care if you already did take your Viagra."

Good lord! Beth thought. Now they were talking sex again. Beth could feel her face flush. "Grandma, tell gramps that those pills will make him go blind." Beth stammered.

Beth could hear granny chuckling through the receiver. "Not to worry dear. One pill lasts him all night and by morning he is so tired that it takes him at least two months to recharge his batteries. Besides, his optometrist told him that he has perfect vision for a man his age."

Beth gave out another sigh. This was way too much information for her to handle. She loved her grandparents but their sex life wasn't something that she cared to hear about.

When Beth was ten she skipped out of school to surprise them and they ended up surprising her. She walked into their apartment and caught them in the middle of doing it on the dining room table. She never looked at that dining room table the same again. At one point Beth had visions of spending the rest of her life in therapy, after that. But lucky for Beth, she got over it after a year or two.

"What's this about my eyesight?" grandpa yelled again.

"Beth said that if you take too much Viagra, you will go blind." she yelled back at him.

"Well that makes sense. My father always told me that if you do it too much you could go blind."

They both were laughing and Beth was sitting there feeling the same embarrassment she felt when she was ten. "Grandmother!" she yelled into the phone.

"I'm sorry dear. Now where were we?"

"Who is Domenic?"

"Domenic is this hot shot divorce lawyer that just started working for us. We told him about your

Problem and he said he would represent you."

Beth moaned. It was the last thing she didn't need to think about right now.

"Well actually he is a corporate lawyer who is working on a case for us, but he used to be a hot shot divorce lawyer. He gave it up to practice corporate law. Come to think of it, the hot part is still there." she giggled.

"He probably gave it up because it was so boring." Beth said trying to ignore that last part.

"No, I don't think that was the reason, but anyway, he is going to call you in the morning and set up a meeting."

"Thanks granny but I was going to get Harold from my firm to represent me."

"Harold couldn't win a game of checkers against a chicken." she snapped. "Domenic is going to call you tomorrow and you are going to invite him over to discuss this. Have I made myself clear?"

"Yes Maam!" Beth felt herself snap to attention.

"Do you want to talk to her now?" grandma asked grandpa.

"I cant now! The Viagra just kicked in." Beth heard my grandmother chuckle.

After all these years of marriage their sex life was still going strong. Beth felt envious and embarrassed at the same time.

"I better go, your grandfather just mooned the guy in the next building." she said with slight panic in her voice. "Thomas! No one wants to see your boney ass, now stop that!" her words were followed with a click.

"I don't want to see it either." Beth whispered into phone.

The sun peeked through the California shutters of Beth's bedroom. The sky was a cloudless blue. Birds chirped outside her window, welcoming the morning sunshine and a breakfast of worms and grubs.

A New Beginning for Beth

Beth rubbed her eyes and focused on the bedside clock. "Seven thirty." She sighed. Too early to get up but once her eyes opened she knew she wouldn't be able to fall asleep again. Beth lay in bed for another five minutes then pulled herself out from under the blankets and opened her shutters.

She smiled at the beautiful Saturday morning sun. It's a good thing Beth decided to get up. It was a beautiful day and she didn't want to waste another minute of it under her blankets. She stripped down and brushed her teeth while her shower heated up.

The water ran down her body, reviving every inch of her sleepy body. Hmm she thought. It was going to be a wonderful day today. She made a silent pact with herself to not go into her home office to do work. This was going to be a day for her to putter around doing simple things like laundry and groceries. She may even try to get a little sun by her backyard pool.

Beth remembered last night's conversation she had with her grandmother. She felt agitated by the thought of having her Saturday interrupted by some divorce lawyer she had never met. But she loved her grandparents and trusted their decisions on people and their abilities. If they felt he was a good lawyer then the least she could do is meet with him. Besides, she really didn't like the idea of anyone from the firm knowing anything about her personal life. Especially when it came to her husbands infidelities.

Beth lined her green eyes with cool black powder. She brushed mascara over her lashes and applied a pink gloss to her lips. She tied her slightly damp blonde hair, back into a pony tail, pulling her bangs forward. She dressed in a white tank top and grey sweatpants and slipped her feet into a pair of white sandals.

Beth sat outside by the pool and sipped her tea while enjoy a few rays of the morning sun. It felt warm against her skin yet every so often a slightly cooler breeze would brush against her, cooling her off just as the heat was getting too warm. A perfect day for sure, she thought.

In the distance the sounds of lawnmowers filled the air. She looked around her yard and thought about doing some gardening. But only for a brief moment as she hated to get her hands dirty. During her marriage, she had tried her hand at growing vegetables. She had a small garden cordoned off for tomato plants and some cucumbers. That lasted one summer.

The following summer, she hired someone to fill it in with a fish pond which is still there today. At least she made the attempt to get back to nature even though she admitted her defeat when there were more weeds than vegetables growing in the small patch of yard.

Her day dreaming was interrupted by the sound of her phone ringing. She checked the number but it showed private name and number.

"Hello?" she answered, secretly hoping it wasn't her mother or James calling from another location.

"Hello is this Beth Singer?" the male voice asked.

"Yes, who is this?"

"You don't know me but your grandparents asked me to call you. My name's Domenic Ragonese and I were wondering if you would be free later so we can discuss your case."

Beth blew out a sigh. She wasn't in the mood to discuss anything with the law and she especially wasn't in the mood to think about her failed marriage. But she promised her grandmother she would meet with him.

"Sure, I have some time. When do you want to meet?"

"How does noon sound to you? I can be there shortly."

"Noon is good. Do you know where I live?"

Domenic laughed quietly on the phone. "Yes I know how to get to your place. Your grandparents told me everything I need to know about you and some things I didn't need to know."

Beth felt her cheeks flush. That didn't sound good, she thought.. "Maybe it's best I don't ask what they told you." She replied.

"Well, let's put it this way. I'm quite curious to meet the famous criminal defense lawyer, Beth Singer. I will see you at noon, Beth." This was followed with a click.

Too late to back out now, Beth thought. He was coming over in an hour. She thought of dressing in something more appropriate but decided against it. What the hell, it's Saturday and she was entitled to dress any which way she pleased.

The doorbell chimed as Beth ran her hands over her yellow sun dress. It was a nervous habit of hers when she was meeting someone for the first time. She never wanted to have sweaty palms to show her nervousness.

Once she met the person, she was fine from then on. It was just the initial first meeting that made her palms sweat.

She opened the door and her mouth fell open at the sight of the man standing in front of her. He was almost a foot taller than Beth and he had the most gorgeous, thick black hair she had ever seen. She felt this overwhelming urge to run her fingers through it. Domenic was carrying a bag of burgers with fries.

"Hi Beth!" he smiled, removing his sunglasses exposing brown bedroom eyes that a woman could get lost in.

Beth just stood there staring at Gods perfection. He was wearing a white tee shirt that hugged his body in all the right spots. His faded jeans revealed the perfect waist and small hips that were finished off with a butt you could bounce a quarter off. He was the kind of man that set off red lights and warning flags. He even came carrying gifts of fast food. What more could a girl ask for.

Beth put her hand to her mouth in case some drool escaped and rolled down her chin.

"Are you okay?" Domenic asked, pulling Beth back into reality.

"Oh, I'm sorry." Beth stammered. "Please come in."

"Do you always dress up on the weekends?" He asked as he followed Beth to the kitchen. "Not that I'm complaining. The dress is pretty."

"Do you always work in jeans and a tee shirt?" Beth asked with annoyance. She hadn't planned on changing but old habits die hard and she had spent the time trying to find something in between work and casual wear.

The yellow sun dress with the tiny straps was the best she could come up with.

"I only dress this way on the weekends and with pretty clients." He laughed. "It shows off my body so much better than a suit and tie."

He was right about that, Beth thought. But his remark left a sour taste in Beth's mouth. He was a cute, assumingly single lawyer, with an arrogant attitude. It was just what she needed to ruin her beautiful Saturday. At least he brought food.

Beth took two plates and two glasses from her cupboard. Domenic watched her as he opened the bag of food and took out two hamburgers and fries.

"I wasn't sure how you liked your hamburger so I put ketchup, mustard and pickles on it."

"It is exactly how I like them." She said while placing the fries on each plate. She grabbed two cold beers from the fridge and suggested they sit by the pool. Beth didn't want to waste one moment of the day sitting inside let alone discussing her separation. But if she had to talk divorces, she wanted to at least do it while soaking up the sun.

Domenic followed Beth out the back door, all the while watching her blonde ponytail sway back and forth as she gracefully moved down the steps towards the patio table.

He had read about some of her cases and her death threat against her, but he had not expected Beth to be so beautiful. When Beth's grandfather asked him for this favor, he jumped at the chance to meet her.

He had been fascinated with how Beth handled herself in court. Her professionalism and the edge she had in getting to the truth, was the talk with his past colleagues. There were never any photos of her which was understandable given her profession. He was always told that when you are representing a big client in a criminal case, it is wiser to not have your face splattered over the newspaper. It was safer to remain anonymous to the public.

Now this intelligent and beautiful woman was in need of a good divorce lawyer and he was the best. Although he gave up family law to concentrate on corporate law, he was inclined to dust off his family law books to help out a friend in need of his expertise.

"How do you know my grandparents?" Beth asked, nibbling on a few fries.

"I'm helping them on a case. Well, actually they are helping me on one."

"A divorce case?" Beth asked.

Domenic shook his head no. "It's a corporate case for a medical company."

Beth gave him a puzzled look. "I thought you were a divorce lawyer?"

"Not anymore, but I agreed to take your case as a favor to Tom and Audrey."

"So, what do you specialize in now?"

"Corporate law." He replied, wiping his mouth free of mustard and ketchup.

Beth leaned back and studied his face. Was he serious, she thought?

She had switch to family law due to her ex's and her mothers' insistence. She thought it the most boring thing to work on. If it weren't for the odd family argument, she had fears of her brain turning to oatmeal by the end of each day. She thought nothing could be less challenging or more boring than family law, with the exception of corporate law. The only way she would practice corporate law would be with a gun pointed to her head and a threat on her grandparents' life.

"I know what you're thinking." Domenic smiled.

"Is that so?" Beth said with amusement.

"You are wondering why I would switch to corporate law from family law."

"That's half right." She laughed. "The other half was wondering why anyone in their right mind want to even practice family law?"

"Hmm." Domenic narrowed his eyes at Beth.

"I didn't mean it as an insult." Beth retracted. "I switched to family law and there were times I wanted to slit my wrists."

Domenic's expression softened. "Family law is not for everyone. I just found it quite interesting and chose to follow it as a career."

Beth nodded in agreement, as she mulled over his reason.

She agreed with him. Family law was definitely not for everyone, especially her. But with every aspect of law, there were people who loved you and people who hated you. Unfortunately being a criminal lawyer and representing some nasty people, it was the good people who ended up hating you. All the nasty people loved you to death. But she had a gift of choosing the right clients. Not everyone she represented was guilty of the crimes they were accused of. She had to believe in her clients' innocence and that made her more passionate to getting them off.

"Why did you switch to family law if you hated it so much?" Domenic asked.

Beth was waiting for that question. The question was embarrassing and unavoidable. But her answer was even more embarrassing.

"I had a death threat against me. I represented a man accused of molesting his daughter. In the end he was found not guilty. His wife had concocted the story in order to get back at her husband for leaving her for a younger woman." Beth shook her head. "It was a messy trial. But not as messy as their divorce."

"Who made the death threat against you?" Domenic already knew the answer but wanted to hear it from Beth. He loved to hear her talk. He found her quite fascinating and sexy. Her intelligence just emphasized her beauty even more.

"His ex-wife and her parents made the threat. The ex-wife was a nut case. She was arrested and sole custody was given to my client. The sad thing is that their daughter was poisoned by the mother and she ended up in therapy." Beth pulled a piece of pickle from her hamburger and popped it in her mouth. "The last I heard was that father and daughter were doing great." That brought a smile to Beth's face. Her smile made Domenic's heart skip a beat.

"Is that the reason why you switched careers?"

There was a pause of silence. Domenic wondered how such a strong independent woman would allow anyone to convince her to switch her loved career.

Beth shook her head no. Her eyes met Domenic's. He smiled at her as they looked into each others eyes. He wasn't just making conversation. He was genuinely interested in her story.

"After the death threat, my husband and mother persuaded me to switch careers. I told them that in my profession, death threats were rare but not unusual." Beth lowered her head. It was obvious to Domenic that this made Beth feel uncomfortable. He didn't want to pursue anymore information regarding her decision.

He shrugged his shoulders. "It happens. What can you do?"

Beth looked up and stared, once again, into Domenic's eyes. A smile formed on her lips. This man understood. Why wouldn't he understand? He was also a lawyer. And he switched careers as well.

"What was your reason for switching?" Beth asked.

Domenic waved her question away. "It's not important. What is important is what are we going to do for you?"

Domenic crumpled his wrapper up and gathered up the empty plates. He placed them in the sink and threw the wrappers in the garbage.

For some reason he didn't want to talk about his reasons. Did he have a death threat made against him? It could have happened. But somehow Beth doubted a death threat would have convinced him to switch to corporate law. And she even had a stronger doubt that anyone in his life could convince him of that as well. A question she would bring up at another time and in another place. But a question she wanted an answer for.

Three hours had passed by the time Domenic and Beth went over their strategy for her separation and future divorce. The last thing they needed to discuss was the matrimonial home.

"Have you thought about selling it?" Domenic asked.

"James' wants to buy it from me at an inflated price."

"How do you feel about that?"

Beth thought for a moment before answering. "I really don't want the house. It's too big and holds too many memories."

"You never answered my question." Domenic said. "How do you feel about taking James' offer of purchasing the house?"

Domenic was right. She did avoid the question, although it wasn't intentional. She knew that she wouldn't get anywhere near what James offered her but the thought of Jill living in her house made her ill. Beth felt that this woman wanted to take over her life. In a way she already did. She was now James's partner so it stood to reason she would want the whole package. The only thing left was the house. Beth knew she had to make a decision.

"If it weren't for the fact that he would be moving his tart girlfriend in, I wouldn't hesitate signing the house over. But to do so knowing that she would be living here, makes me feel as if I am defeated. She won and I lost."

"What did she win?" Domenic asked. His eyes were fixed on Beth's face. He watched for any hint of hope of winning her husband back.

Beth thought for a moment. What did Jill win?

Since James walked out on her, Beth felt as if a weight had been lifted from her shoulders. She couldn't remember one moment when she missed him. On the contrary, she went out of her way to avoid him at all costs. The overwhelming feeling of walking on egg shells was gone. A feeling she experienced with him on more than one occasion. Even the feeling of loneliness was gone.

She had been living alone in the house for several months but she never felt lonely. When James was with her, that feeling was always there.

He had never spent much time with her and when he was home, he was always busy doing one of his hobbies or sleeping till noon. She preferred her single life to her marriage much more.

Beth reached for the phone and dialed James' cell number. Domenic watched her, curious to her actions.

"If you still want to buy the house from me, I will sign it over with the price you offered me. But you will have to give me two months to move. As for the furnishings, I will get first choice of all the furniture. You can have the rest. Call me if you have any questions." Beth hung up the phone and blew out a sigh. She leaned back in her chair and smiled a Domenic. "Thanks." She said.

Domenic scratched his head, not sure of what he said to help her make up her mind. But whatever he said or did, he knew she made the right choice.

Selling him the house was a giant step for Beth. Now all she needed was a place to live.

"Any suggestions on where you are going to live?" Domenic asked.

"My grandparents have a friend who sells real estate. I will call them tomorrow to arrange a meeting with him."

"Are you referring to Sal?"

"Yes, do you know him?"

Domenic smiled. "I've met him a couple of times. A nice man but." Domenic stopped short. "Maybe its better you meet him and see for yourself."

A knot formed in Beth's stomach. She didn't like that sound of that. But it was too late to back out now. She already committed herself on James's voice mail.

They sat for a moment, enjoying the quietness of the garden. She glanced at Domenic who sat beside her. His eyes were closed and there was a smile fixed on his lips. He was probably thinking about Sal. Her thoughts had left Sal and were focused on him. She studied his face. He definitely was handsome. His lashes seemed to go on forever and she had this overwhelming urge to run her fingers through his thick black hair. His face was flawless and he had a models high cheekbone and chiseled chin. He was definitely eye candy. Someone with that face and body had to have women knocking down his door. He probably had a belt that he put notches in with each conquest. She had no intentions on becoming another notch in his belt.

"You look deep in thought." Domenic said, catching Beth staring at him.

She felt her cheeks flush and the beginnings of sweat appeared on her forehead.

"I was just thinking about belts and eye candy." She stammered. She made a mental head slap as she realize what she had said.

Domenic tilted his head at her. His smile turned into a toothy grin.

Damn, she thought. He had perfectly straight white teeth. She was a sucker for a perfect smile and this man definitely had the best smile she had ever seen.

She turned away and tried to stand but Domenic reached out and took her hand, pulling her closer to him.

"Whoa, what's up with this?" she asked, startled at his move.

He leaned in to her face and gently kissed her on the lips. Beth closed her eyes as his lips delicately brushed against hers. It was a short kiss but the most erotic kiss she had experienced in a long time, maybe ever.

Domenic pulled away. He looked at Beth as she sat there with her eyes closed.

Beth slowly opened her eyes and stared at Domenic who was inches from her face, still wearing the same open smile.

"I felt you needed to be kissed." He said in a husky voice.

"Was that a pity kiss?" she asked just above a whisper.

"I don't give out pity kisses." He grinned. "Nothing I do for a woman or to a woman is out of pity."

Beth mulled over his words.

"You think too much Beth Singer." He laughed. "You need to stop thinking so much and start doing."

"How do you know I think too much and who invited you inside my head?"

Domenic brushed the back of his fingers over her flushed cheek. He felt a need to sweep her in his arms and carry her to the nearest bed and make mad passionate love to her. But Beth seemed like a woman that wasn't easily seduced. She was guarded. This may have been due to her failed marriage or maybe due to previous relationships. Whatever her reasons, she was a fragile flower that had to be picked gently. Domenic had to move slowly with Beth.

Beth closed her eyes as Domenic's fingers gently moved across her cheeks. She liked his touch but loved his kiss. They spent a few hours together and she never thought of him in a sexual way. Well maybe when she first saw him at her door, but that was the only time. Now she was having thoughts of his naked body on hers. Thoughts of his fingers touching more than just her cheek filled her senses. The thought of his lips exploring every part of her body and her lips taking in his body heated up her southern region.

It had been months since she had sex and the last time she had sex it was with James. Their sex life had never been that exciting. It became less exciting in the last year of their marriage. Beth was lucky if they would make love once a month and when they did she never felt satisfied.

There was no orgasm or no cuddling afterwards. James would just roll over and fall asleep while Beth lay there wondering if this is what she had to look forward to for the rest of her life. She had thought of taking on a lover, but she didn't need anymore complications in her life.

When she found out about her husbands affair, she understood why her sex life was so dull and almost nonexistent. Now she was a single woman and she still had not found someone. Could Domenic be the person to fill that void in her life or at least in her bed? She dismissed the thought. He was going to represent her in her divorce.

As a lawyer herself, she knew that it was wrong to mix business with pleasure. She had never had any type of relationship with a past client and she had no intentions on having a relationship with someone representing her.

"Thank you for the kiss, Domenic, but I think from this moment on we should just stick to the business at hand." Beth pulled herself off the patio chair and stood, facing Domenic.

He sat there puzzled by her change. It was obvious that she enjoyed his kiss so why the change? He thought it best not to question her. "If that is how you feel Beth, I will respect your decision. At least for now while I am representing you in your divorce, we will keep it strictly professional. But I should warn you, that it will be very difficult for me to stay in that mode for long." He stood to face her. "I find you a very attractive and sexually pleasing woman, and I have all intentions on getting you know you on a personal level."

Beth felt her stomach flutter. She had never been spoken to in such a way. He was being totally honest with her and not only did she appreciate his honestly but she was more than flattered by his words. "That is very flattering Domenic, but I'm not the type of woman who is looking for a one night stand. Nor am I looking for a relationship. I want to see what it's like to be single for awhile."

Domenic nodded in agreement. "Well I can hold out until you get tired of being single, but while you are pursuing this we could be lovers. After all you are a desirable woman with needs. And I'm a single and somewhat attractive man who could fulfill those needs."

Beth put her hands on her hips and narrowed her eyes at Domenic. Did he just offer his stud services to her? She could feel her annoyance turn into anger. "I thought you said you don't do anything for a woman out of pity?" her voice rose with every word. "Do I look like I need pity sex?"

"That's not what I meant." Domenic raised his hands in surrender.

Not that I would even welcome the idea of having sex with you, but I don't even know your last name." Beth said angrily.

"Ragonese." Domenic replied.

"What?" Beth blinked.

"My last name is Ragonese." He repeated. "I do recall mentioning my name to you when I phoned."

Beth rolled her eyes. "I think I should pay you for your legal services. That way there won't be any misunderstandings and I won't have to repay the favor."

"That wont be necessary, Beth. There is a reason why I wanted to represent you."

A light went off in Beth's head. She knew there was something he wanted. No one in the right mind would do a total stranger this kind of favor unless they had ulterior motives. Why would Domenic Ragonese be any different?

"Okay, let's have it." She said with a sigh.

"I need your help with a case I'm working on with your grandparents." Domenic sat back down on the sofa and waited for Beth to sit before he continued. Beth moved to the leather chair next to the sofa and sat in silence waiting to hear what Domenic had to say.

Domenic felt slighted when she chose not to sit next to him, but he didn't want to show this to Beth, so he continued without batting an eye. "Your grandfather's investigation service was hired by a client of mine to find out information on some thefts that have been taking place in their company."

Beth listened intently and motioned for Domenic to continue. "I have been working with your grandfather by providing information to him about all of the employees."

"Which type of company is this?" Beth asked.

"The client in question is a pharmaceutical company. They not only produce drugs but they have a whole research lab that is funded by the government as well as private funding through nonprofit organizations."

"Like the heart and stroke foundations and A.I.DS foundations? Those type of organizations?" Beth asked.

Domenic nodded in agreement. "The thing is this company has had thefts in their laboratories and apparently they are severe enough to warrant hiring an investigation service."

"What do you mean *apparently*? What type of things are they missing?" Beth's interest peaked.

Domenic shook his head. "I have no idea. No one will tell me anything. When it was first brought to my attention, I assumed they were missing large items, such ask computers and major lab supplies."

"Do you think it is something else?"

"You see Beth; I always deal with the head office. My job is to make sure that all their corporate affairs are in place. With this type of company there are always lawsuits and investigations into complaints about inadequate drug products. I have never had a reason to visit their labs. As a matter of fact, the only person I deal with is the C.E.O. and on occasion I do sit in on a board meeting, but that is only if my presence is required. And that doesn't happen too often."

Beth watched Domenic's face. It was obvious to her that this case has disturbed him.

"If they have a lab then they must be doing some type of research." Beth said.

"Yes but strictly research. I really don't have my hands on anything there. They really don't need my expertise when it comes to the lab. They have accountants who take care of the funding aspect. But if they require my assistance, I am always available."

Domenic cupped his hands together and stared at the floor. "Beth, I only found out about the lab when I was told about the thefts. This company is very tight lipped about what they have their hands in. I also believe they have their hands in other things as well but I have no proof."

Beth's curiosity got the better of her. Regardless of what role Domenic wanted her to play, she was ready to help. "When do I start?"

Domenic met Beth's gaze. A smile formed on his lips and Beth responded by smiling along with him.

"Thank you Beth. You have no idea how relieved I am to hear you say that."

"Well, I always love a great mystery, especially if there is a challenge in it. And based on what you have told me so far, this is going to be one challenging case."

Domenic looked at his watch. "We start tonight."

"Tonight? On Saturday night?"

"I'm sorry; I should have asked you if you had plans."

Beth never had plans, especially on a Saturday night. She usually spent it eating pizza and watching a chick movie that left her with red, swollen eyes, from crying.

"No, I have no plans." She replied. "What time should I be ready?"

"It's three now so how about I swing by and pick you up around eight?"

Beth nodded in agreement and walked Domenic to the door.

"I really appreciate you agreeing to help me out on this." Domenic hugged her and left Beth standing at the door.

"Wait!" she yelled to him as he started his car. "What exactly are we doing tonight?"

"A stake out." He yelled back. "Dress comfy." He was gone before she could change her mind.

"A stake out?" she mouthed the words. What the hell did she get herself into?

She had been on stake outs when she was young although at the time she wasn't even aware of it. She always assumed that her grandparents enjoyed taking her out to restaurants. No one would ever have suspected being followed by a young girl and her elderly grandparents. They never told her until years later that most of the time they were on working. At one point she felt used and betrayed by her grandparents. But then she kind of liked the thought of sitting and watching someone, even though she didn't know that at the time. But now she was grown and the last thing she wanted was to sit in a car or restaurant watching someone. But then again, the thought of working as an investigator excited Beth. It was as if she were going to be a crime fighter.

She had always wanted to be a crime fighter since she was little. Before that, Beth wanted to be a Dalmatian dog. Beth would wear everything spotted black and white and her bedroom growing up looked like the back of a black and white jersey cow. She knew that being a Dalmatian wasn't in the cards for her so Beth decided that being a crime fighter was the next best thing. She also felt that it would be a profession that would allow her to spend more time with her grandparents.

Her change from Dalmatian to crime fighter happened when she watched an episode of the old batman series that showed Lee Merewether portraying Cat Woman. Although Cat Woman wasn't a crime fighter, she seemed to ride the fence when it came to being an evil villain. Besides, batman seemed to have a thing for her and they would secretly flirt in front of the cameras. Cat woman would always try to seduce batman in each episode she was in. and batman would fall victim to her seduction. Beth liked that about her. She could be intelligent, commanding and sexy all at the same time. Beth definitely wanted to be cat woman.

Beth also loved the way the suit made her look sexy. She used to dress in her black ballet outfit and wear oversized black nylons that she would borrow from her mother's lingerie drawer. She would have her grandmother take the stocking and stuff it with newspaper to resemble a lumpy over stuffed-tail. It was temporarily pinned to the back of her ballet suit, only to be removed during ballet lessons.

She also liked the idea that Cat woman, never had need of a gun. She used her womanly charm to get what she wanted and to trap batman. This was a good thing for Beth because guns had always scared the hell out of her.

Beth's daydreaming was interrupted by the sound of her phone ringing

"Domenic told me you are going to help with the case we are working on." The voice said on the other end.

"That would all depend on what is needed of me gramps." Beth replied.

"It is so wonderful to have you back in the group. We missed being able to work with you my baby granddaughter."

Beth was thirty three yet her grandfather always called her his baby granddaughter. The phrase made her feel warm and comforted. She smiled.

"Don't get too excited gramps; I am just going to add my expertise as a criminal lawyer."

"Well I did lay down the rules with Domenic when he picks you up tonight. And you let me know if he doesn't keep his hands to himself."

Say what? What did he mean by that? Beth thought she made it clear to Domenic that she was a woman to be reckoned with.

She assured her grandfather that Domenic didn't stand a chance and for a moment she thought she heard him breathe a sigh of relief.

Beth then spoke briefly with her granny, made a promise to come for supper the next day then hung up the phone.

If Domenic thought that he was going to get anywhere with her he had another thing coming. Beth was one up on him and she was going to watch him very closely. The only problem was how was she going to convince herself of that? The gentle kiss still lingered on her lips and her body responded every time she thought of it. This Domenic fellow was going to be a challenge and Beth made a silent promise to keep herself up for the challenge. Her confidence in winning was overwhelming. Now all she had to do was convince her body of that.

Beth and Domenic drove down the highway in silence. She had wanted to ask where they were going but chose to make as little conversation as possible. She didn't want to say something that he may mistake for a come on. Not that she had a clue on how to seduce a man anyway.

Beth had traded in her yellow sundress for a white tank top and grey sweat pants. It was an outfit that had no sex appeal. At least it didn't until she climbed into his silver B.M.W. and was hit with a blast of cold air. The air conditioning made her nipples hard and they poked at her top. She crossed her arms to hide them but it was too late. She had seen Domenic peek at her out of the corner of his eye.

"Do you think you could turn down the air a tad?" Beth asked. "Another minute of that air blowing on me and I will have icicles hanging from my nose."

"Of course I can." He replied reaching for the controls and turning the air to a minimum. "You should have said something before."

"I think the fact that my teeth are chattering and my lips are blue would have been an automatic giveaway." She sighed as she rubbed some warmth back into her bare arms.

"I'm a man. I'm not supposed to notice subtle things like that." He laughed. "But I did notice your nipples."

Beth looked at him sideways. "And you still thought the air was fine?"

"You bet. I thought the erect nipples meant you were happy to see me."

Beth covered her eyes with her hand and shook her head. "You are right."

"You mean about you being happy to see me?" Domenic asked with enthusiasm.

"No. I meant about you being a man."

"Ouch." Domenic said grabbing his chest as if he had just been administered a hard blow to the heart.

"So where are we going?" Beth asked changing the subject.

"You will see. We will be there in a few minutes." Domenic said as he took the Burlington street exit.

They traveled down Burlington Street through the industrial part of the city. The smell of the steel city lay thick in the heat of the early evening air. They traveled along Burlington Street then made a left on James Street. Domenic then turned right on Barton Street and followed it until Barton ran into Locke Street. They made a left on Locke and traveled a few blocks until they came to a city park. Domenic pulled over into an empty space in front of the children's play ground. Across the street sat narrow brown row houses. Most had been bought by young couple with small children. The park across the street was a great substitute for the lack of green yard these houses were deprived of.

A New Beginning for Beth

Domenic reached into the back seat and retrieved a folder from his brief case. "Here, I want you to look this over and give me your professional opinion." He said handing Beth the folder.

She read each page carefully, saving the photos for the end. Most of the information was about a man named Peter Bucar. Based on the information that was compiled, Peter lived in one of the row houses. He used to live in Toronto near his work. He moved back home about a year ago to look after his mother who had become ill. There was no mention to what his mother was sick from. He has remained with his mother since.

Peter was only twenty seven, single and no girlfriend to anyone's knowledge. He was considered a genius amongst his colleagues. So much so that at his young age he became head of his department in the medical research field. He was also a prime suspect in the so called thefts.

A photo of Peter accompanied the profile. He looked much younger than his age. His hair was thin and rail straight. His frame was on the petite size. He had the look of someone who was more than likely bullied all through school. Beth imagined him belonging to the chess club and science club. He just had that look about him.

She recalled boys like him when she was going to school. They usually stuck to themselves. They always avoided passing the popular kids for fear of being singled out for name calling or worse. Although she was popular throughout university, she was what you would call an ugly duckling throughout high school. She was tormented and teased by some girls that left a bitter taste in her mouth. Because of this, her heart went out for boys like Peter.

"What are you thinking about?" Domenic asked as he watched Beth study the photo.

Beth sighed. "I was thinking why he would be considered a suspect. He just doesn't fit the profile of someone who would steal expensive things."

"Maybe it's the ones we least likely suspect." Domenic added.

"Maybe you're right but the only thing I could see this guy stealing is the odd pen or pencil." Beth replied. "Maybe they are wrong in their assumptions."

"I agree with you Beth, but we were told to look at him first."

Beth moved around in the seat, preventing her shoulders from sticking to the moist leather. Domenic smiled at her as he watched her brush her long blonde curls away from her face. She fanned herself with the manila envelop.

"What?" she asked as she caught Domenic smiling at her.

"You see why I wanted your help? You know there is something wrong with this case."

"It doesn't take a genius to figure out that Peter just doesn't fit the profile." Beth added.

"Do you want to get out of the car and go sit on a park bench?" he asked.

"The best idea you've had all day." Beth smiled.

They walked to a bench that was conveniently placed under a large oak tree. The humidity hung thick in the air. As the sun set, the children were called into their houses. Beth and Domenic sat in silence, watching the lights comes on in the small row houses. Each house lit up as dark enveloped the city. All the houses lit up except the one that Peter and his mother lived in. there were no cars parked in the small driveway. No signs of anyone being home.

"So what are we watching for?" Beth whispered.

"I just want to see Peter and his mother in person." Domenic said with a yawn while stretching out his arms. He found this as boring as Beth did. At least when she went on stake outs with her grandparents, they were in a nice restaurant enjoying a nice meal. Not sitting on a park bench in the dark, sweating to death from the humidity that lingered in the inner city limits. The faint smell of the nearby factories crept in on a sudden breeze.

"I just hope that these Bucars' get home before I die of heat exhaustion." Beth complained. Domenic was feeling the heat as well but they dare not take the chance of starting the car and attracting attention to the neighbors.

In this neighborhood, an idling car was a sign of a drug exchange or something even worse. At least in the park, under the tree, they were hidden from prying eyes.

"So, do you want to make out while we are waiting?" Domenic asked catching Beth off guard with his question.

"You are joking right?" Beth wasn't expecting him to say that.

"I have come to one conclusion about you Beth. And that is to never joke when it came to romance."

"There you go again. Always assuming things and coming to conclusions when it comes to me." Beth huffed.

Domenic studied her face in the light from a nearby lamp. She looked even more amazing if that were even possible.

His heart jumped slightly as she licked her lips and pretended to not notice him staring at her. He had an overwhelming urge to again kiss her lips but this time with more passion and force than earlier that day.

"Get it out of your head Ragonese." Beth remarked.

"Get what out of my head?"

"You know exactly what I'm talking about. If you even try to kiss me you'll be sorry."

"Now who is in whose head?" he laughed.

Just then a small red car made its way slowly up the street. It pulled past peters house and stopped. Then the driver put it in reverse and it slowly backed up into the driveway. The driver cut the engine and a small woman got out of the passenger side. Peter got out of the drivers side and moved towards the back of the car and opened the trunk. He handed the woman what appeared to be keys and she moved to the front door, unlocked it and went inside.

The outside light flickered on making it easier for Beth and Domenic to see Peter. He retrieved some grocery bags from the trunk and brought them inside the house. He came back a moment later and retrieved another three bags. Closing the trunk he stopped and stared over to where Domenic and Beth were sitting.

His gaze was fixed on the two people sitting on the park bench. Domenic grabbed Beth and kissed her deeply and longingly. Instinctively, Beth wrapped her arms around Domenic's neck and pulled him closer, all the while keeping her eyes on Peter.

Upon seeing their display of affection Peter shook his head and disappeared inside the small row house.

"You can stop now Domenic. He's gone." Beth mumbled while trying to pull herself away from Domenic's lips.

Domenic ignored her and kissed her even deeper. Beth moved her hands up to his chest and pushed him away. Her whole body was trembling with delight and she knew that if they didn't stop she was going to end up in a very compromising position with him. A position that she was not ready for even though the thought of it sent shivers through her.

"Well our work is done." Domenic stood and pulled Beth to her feet. His arms draped around her tiny waist and her breasts brushed against his chest. He held her for a moment hoping she would reach for him but she pushed him away.

They walked back to Domenic's car and he blinked the locks open. He held the door for Beth as she climbed into the passenger side. This impressed Beth as no one has held the door for her in a very long time. Domenic slid in next to her and started the engine. He rolled the windows down and pulled away from the curb.

"How about some supper?" he said as they drove back towards Burlington Street.

They scanned over the menu as the waitress placed two glasses of water on the table.

"Anything you recommend?" Beth asked Domenic. She had never been to Angelo's but heard the food was good. Domenic suggested a pizza with green olives, pepperoni and pineapples. Beth cringed at his selection but decided to run with scissors and try the topping combination. She agreed with the order and added a couple of beers to go with the pizza.

Beth sipped on her beer. "Did you find anything strange about what we saw tonight?"

"Not really." Domenic replied.

Beth shook her head. "Did you read the information you gave me?"

Domenic's eyes met Beth's. It was obvious that she had noticed something and was testing him.

"You want to clue me in or am I going to have to guess at what you are talking about?"

Beth smiled and pulled out the information on Peter. She read aloud the information pertaining to his mother. "Did she look sick to you?"

"She looked pretty healthy from what I could see." He answered.

"Who gave you the information about his mother?" she asked.

Domenic shook his head. "Apparently Peter told his landlord that he was moving back home to look after his mother."

"Did he tell the landlord what was wrong with his mother?"

Domenic shrugged his shoulders. "I'm not sure. I don't think it was ever mentioned."

Beth pulled a writing pad and pen from her purse. She jotted down a reminder note to find out the type of illness Peter's mother had. Seeing his mother tonight didn't sit well with Beth. She has a sixth sense when it came to cases and her gut instincts were telling her to start the investigation by focusing in on the mother.

"I'm going to call my grandpa tomorrow and ask him to get some information on Mrs. Bucar. I know she has nothing to do with the theft but if Peter is doing something illegal, she would have first hand knowledge on it.

It was past midnight by the time Domenic pulled into Beth's driveway. All the surrounding houses were lit up. Beth's house lay dark amongst them.

Beth lived in a family oriented neighborhood consisting of over sized and over priced homes. When she and James bought the house, it was with the intentions of starting a family. But family never happened. Now all she was left with was a huge empty house.

Some of the neighbors had grown kids who had moved on to their own places. But they visited often with the grandchildren. The neighbors to the right of her were great. Their daughter was divorced and she moved in shortly after Beth and James did. She brought her two children along with her and they have been there ever since.

They were of Italian decent and the scent of Italian cooking was always coming from their open windows. Lillian was always sending one of her grandchildren over with a care package of fresh sauce or dried meat that they made themselves. Beth knew that she would miss them when she moved.

The neighbors on the other side were also Italian decent but they were the complete opposite of Lillian and her husband Marco. They had teenagers who were latch key kids for as long as Beth lived next door to them. Sometimes when Beth worked from home she would see their two children sitting outside alone, waiting for one of the parents to arrive home from their jobs. The older of the two was a girl who took on the personality of her mother.

Beth had an encounter with the mother shortly after she moved in. It was early Saturday morning and James was at the hospital. She was awoken by the sounds of a loud banging. She thought someone was shooting off a gun in her house. It was shortly after the death threat so this left Beth a bit jittery to say the least.

Upon entering her kitchen she saw a ball appear at her window, bounce off the window and back into the hands of the boy next door. The child was using her kitchen window to bounce his ball off of. When Beth came along the side she saw bicycles and toys all piled up along the side of her house.

She yelled to him to stop what he was doing and to remove all his toys off her property. The mother flew out the door when she heard Beth and asked what was going on. "Your son is bouncing his ball off my kitchen window." Beth snapped at her.

"You don't have to yell." She snapped back at Beth.

Beth was in no mood to deal with her or her spoilt child. She was awoken from a deep sleep by this rude kid and now the mother was telling her she had no reason to yell? "If you were out here watching your kid I wouldn't be out here yelling at him." Beth yelled.

"I don't like your attitude." The woman sniped.

"Oh bite me." Beth yelled and turned on her heels to go back into her house.

Ever since that day they had a love hate relationship. Actually it was a hate, hate relationship. Since then Beth has had nothing but trouble from the boy. Most of the time the trouble happens between the time he comes home from school and just before the parents arrives home. She definitely wouldn't miss them.

"What are thinking about?" Domenic asked. His voice was gentle and soft.

"Nothing in particular." Beth looked up at her house and sighed.

"Do you want me to come in with you?"

Beth shook her head. "I'll be alright. I'm used to being in the house alone. Besides, it's late and I'm sure you want to get home."

Domenic leaned close to Beth and kissed her on the cheek. "I could stay the night with you if you want company."

There was nothing Beth wanted more than to have someone next to her in the morning especially if that someone was Domenic. But she had just met him and she had never slept with a man on first meetings and didn't plan on starting. But her body was telling her brain to shut up. Her body wanted to feel Domenic next to her. As usual her brain won out.

"Thanks for the offer but I just don't think that would be such a good idea at this time."

"So does that mean I have a chance of spending the night with you?" he smiled at her.

Their gaze met and Beth couldn't help but feel warm all over when she looked into his eyes.

"I refuse to answer that question on the grounds that it may incriminate me."

Domenic laughed. "Always the lawyer, never the woman. At least let me walk you to the door."

It was past ten in the morning when Domenic showed up at Beth's door unexpectedly. She ran down the stairs still in her night gown, her hair messed up from tossing around all night.

She swung the door open. "What? Why are you here so early?"

"Good morning to you too." He kissed Beth on the cheek and slipped by her with two coffees and a bag of Danishes. Beth followed him into the kitchen.

"What time is it?" she asked, brushing her hair out of her eyes. His banging had awakened her from a deep sleep and this left her senses off balance.

"It's just past ten and I thought you would be up and dressed by now. But I do love the way you look when you are fresh out of bed." Domenic grinned at her. His eyes scanned down her white satin night gown. "And I love the outfit. Promise me you will wear that when I sleep over?"

"If you sleep over." Beth corrected him.

Domenic dismissed her remark. "I bought you coffee, black. I didn't know how you took it. And I have a bag of cinnamon Danishes. They were just baked.

"I don't drink coffee." Beth reached for a cup and plopped a tea bag in it. She filled a small kettle with water and placed it on the stove.

Domenic looked at her as if he had just witnessed a mass killing. "A lawyer who doesn't drink coffee. I never heard of such a thing."

"Yes, we are a rarity." Beth said sarcastically. "We are in the same category as big foot and smart blondes. I have the market on the tea and blonde thing."

Domenic took two small plates from the cupboard and placed a Danish on each plate. Beth poured some hot water from the kettle, into her cup and sat beside Domenic sipping her tea. She didn't utter a word or make eye contact with him.

Domenic watched her intently." Are you always this grumpy when you wake up?"

"Only when someone wakes me up by banging on my front door on Sunday morning." She muttered.

"If I had a key I could have just let myself in." he smiled.

"Not in this lifetime." Beth mumbled.

"No really, I am sorry I woke you up. I really thought you would be awake by now." He added.

Beth waved him off. "It's okay. I will be fine after my tea."

Beth poured more hot water into her cup and added another teabag. "So what brings you here so early?"

"I called Sal this morning. I asked him if he had any houses for sale." Domenic smiled. "You only have two months to move. I thought I would help you get a head start on finding a place. Besides, today is Sunday and I'm sure there are quite a few open houses we can view."

Beth looked sideways at Domenic. Was he for real? The last thing she had thought about was finding a new place before she became homeless. She could always move in with her mother but then they would probably end up killing each other. Maybe not at first but Beth wouldn't have pushed it past three days. "I hadn't thought about it." Beth sighed.

"I know, Beth. That's why I'm here. Sal is coming over at eleven with some listings. We weren't sure what you had in mind so he is bringing a list of potentials."

"I know I should be grateful, Domenic, but I really am not in the mood to house hunt today."

"That's nonsense." Domenic pulled Beth to her feet. "Go upstairs and get ready. It will be fun."

Beth showered, put on some light blush and lip gloss and stroked her lashes with brown mascara. She dried her hair and wore it down, allowing the long blond curls to fall freely around her shoulders. She pulled on a jean skirt that sat above her knees and matched it with a pink tank top. She pulled out a pair of white wedge sandals to finish off the outfit.

Upon entering her family room, Domenic was in deep conversation with an elderly gentleman.

The older man stood when Beth entered the room, extending his hand to her.

"Beth this is Sal. He is a good friend of your grandparents." Domenic said making introductions.

"So you are little Bethany." Sal smiled. "I have heard so much about you from your grandfather. I help him out occasionally in his agency."

Beth took Sal's hand. "I thought you sold real estate?"

"I do that too, but being a retired detective, you can't stray too far from getting your hands into investigation."

Sal was slightly shorter than Beth, with thinning grey hair and brown eyes. He had a broad smile that had a calming affect.

"Let's get down to business." Sal said "I have a few houses and condos for you to view. Domenic wasn't sure what you had in mind so I picked a variety of places for you to view." He pulled out several listings for Beth to look over.

She scanned each one, reading all the details, and then handed them to Domenic to look over.

Beth wasn't really sure what she wanted, but she did know that a condo or apartment was out of the question. She also wasn't too keen on going back into a family subdivision. Then a listing caught her eye.

It was a farm house on twenty five acres of land. It was stuck in between Winona and Grimsby and it was beautiful. The house was white clapboard and the listing stated that it had a heated barn that was converted into a two bedroom apartment on the main floor and an entertainment room on the upper level. That would be a great place to have a home office. It also had four bedrooms two full baths and a single bath. There was a full basement that was completely finished and it also had a huge eat in kitchen. It sounded perfect to Beth. So did the price. It was low enough for her to pay for it out right and she would still have money left over in case there were some repairs. With all that land she could even sever it and sell it off as individual lots.

"What about this one?" she asked Sal.

Sal frowned. "I think this would be too much work for one person."

"I could hire people." She replied. "Besides, it won't hurt to look at it." She turned to Domenic for his opinion.

"We can at least look at it." Domenic smiled at Beth and gave her a wink.

"The price is right and it's away from neighbors. It has a lot of acres too so I can have a vegetable garden."

Domenic stared sideways at Beth.

"I know, I know. My last attempt at growing vegetables was a slight disaster. But this is different. This is a farm. The ground is perfect for vegetables.

"I wasn't thinking about you failing at growing them. My concern is that you have twenty five acres to cover."

"I'm not going to use the whole twenty five acres." Beth rolled her eyes at Domenic.

Once they settled on which houses they were going to view, Domenic suggested he drive.

"That's good." Sal added. "I haven't got my license back yet. But I hope to go for a road test next week." He beamed.

"Yet?" Beth asked. "What happened to your license?"

"Damn government took it away from me." Sal snarled. "Now I have to cab it every time I want to go somewhere."

"He had it revoked when he mistook the gas for the brake and drove his car right into a doctor's office." Domenic said trying to keep his composure. Beth glanced over at Domenic who was doing his best not to break into laughter.

Beth turned and looked at Sal in amazement. This was a story worth hearing.

"Did you really do that?" she asked.

"Yup, sure did. It wasn't my fault though."

Domenic smiled and walked down the hall. "Sure Sal." He laughed as he walked towards the front door.

"You're a mart ass!" Sal yelled back.

Beth's eyes darted down the hall at Domenic and back at Sal. "Now this story sounds interesting. Is anyone going to clue me in?"

"Well, there was this dip in the parking lot of the building and it scared the hell out of me. I panicked and hit the gas."

A New Beginning for Beth

"It wasn't a dip in the parking lot, Sal. It was the sewer drain. It has to dip a bit to drain the water." Domenic yelled from the entrance.

Sal ignored Domenic. "The next thing I knew I was staring at the receptionist desk and the door to the docs examining room."

Beth stared at Sal, taking in all this information. It left her speechless.

"Tell Beth what happened after that." Domenic yelled.

"I'm getting to that." He yelled back.

"Anyway, I drove my car right through the plate glass windows and the brick wall. I never even scratched the door to the office."

"Holy shit!" Beth blurted out. She cupped her hands over her mouth.

"Was anyone hurt?"

"Nope, except for the woman who was trying on glasses next door. It seems that one of the display cases in the optical store next door came loose from the wall and crashed down behind her. She was hit by flying frames. It scared the hell out of her and the opticians."

"It would have scared the hell out of me too." Beth shuddered.

"So what happened after that? Were you hurt? How did they get you out of the car?"

"The office was closed that day. It was a Saturday and lucky for me the doctor works every other Saturday. That happened to be the Saturday he wasn't there."

Sal continued. "And I didn't have a scratch on me but it took the cops and fire department over an hour to get me out."

Beth was puzzled. "Why did it take so long? You didn't touch the door to the office so why didn't they just call the doctor to come and open the door?"

"They couldn't find the doctor and the front of my car was pinned up against the examining room door so they couldn't get in that way either. They had to get me out through the passenger door because my driver's door was against the wall." Sal continued.

Beth was picturing this and although it was a serious thing, she had to laugh.

"It wasn't funny at the time." Sal said with a frown. "And just because I have one little accident, they pull my license. Now I have to cab it or bum a ride from everyone in order to get anywhere."

"Maybe it's a good thing you aren't driving Sal." Beth said with as much concern as she could muster without breaking out laughing again.

"You just wait and see." He replied shaking his finger. "I'm going to take another drivers test and I will get my license back."

Beth made the sign of the cross and silently prayed that god would not allow this man to pass his driving exam.

"God won't hear you." Sal said. "I got the inside track on him and he said he will help me pass my license exam."

Beth made another sign of the cross just to be sure.

As Domenic drove down the highway, Beth was asking question after question about the farmhouse.

"Have you seen the house yourself?"

"Sure have and it's a beauty. About two years ago they put a new roof on the house as well as the barn. And the windows are all triple glazed." Sal beamed. "Did I tell you about the swimming pool out back?"

Beth scanned the listing but there was no mention of a pool. She has a pool in her backyard but rarely uses it. At this point she could take it or leave it. But she guessed it wasn't a bad idea to have one just in case she wanted to entertain during the summer.

"It's a new pool. There's no mention of it in the listing but wait till you see it. They made it look like a beach. They even have sand at one end to give that beach effect."

Sal continued to tell Beth and Domenic about all the new things in the house. The barn was converted into a studio upstairs and a two bedroom apartment on the main floor. They used it for their son shortly after he got married. He moved out and the owners were left with a huge house and barn. They decided it was too much for them to handle and none of their kids wanted it so they put it on the market. They plan on downsizing to a bungalow that they purchased, so they are desperate to sell before the closing date.

"I never told you the best part." Sal said. "It has its own cemetery."

Domenic veered towards the shoulder and managed to gain control of the car again.

Beth looked at Domenic and his expression was as stunned as hers. Then they both looked back at Sal.

"Can you run that by us again?" Domenic wasn't sure if he had heard Sal right.

"Yes sir. It has a really old cemetery a few yards from the house. It belonged to the owner's ancestors. Apparently they had plans of passing the house down from generation to generation so they made a family cemetery on the property."

Beth gulped hard.

"That explains why the price is so low." Beth said.

"But you can hardly see the tombstones from the window. There is a stone fence around it with a gate you can lock up." he assured her.

"Well that's comforting. No chance anyone breaking in or out of the graveyard." Sarcasm flowed with her words.

"Don't be scared off by a little cemetery. There is only about a dozen or so graves. And you can even make a spot for you and your loved ones. It's zoned for that."

The thought of staring out the window everyday and looking at her future resting spot gave Beth the chills. But the house did seem to have everything she could ever ask for.

Beth shrugged her shoulders. "It wont hurt to look at is so why not?"

They arrived within ten minutes. It was far enough away from Beth's neighborhood so there was little chance she would run into James and Jill but close enough for her to get to her office. They pulled into a gated driveway which was paved. That's a good sign Beth thought. At least she wouldn't have to worry about gravel.

The driveway was long and curved slightly past an orchard of cherry trees. To the left was the infamous cemetery. Just as Sal mentioned, there was an old stone fence surrounding the cemetery and on the other side of the fence she could see simple tomb stones. It was actually quite quaint and it would definitely be a conversation piece for visitors.

They moved a little further down the driveway and stopped in front of the white clapboard house. It had a large wrap around porch with a swing near the front door. Beth felt the excitement build inside. She fell in love with it from that moment.

"Don't show too much enthusiasm." Sal leaned over to Beth. "I wanted to try and negotiate a lower price for you."

Beth nodded in agreement even though she was willing to pay the already low price for it.

They walked around the house, inspecting the foundation. Sal talked about all the things the house had to offer besides the cemetery.

It has all new plumbing and electrical. It's in move in condition and there are two full baths and a half bath. The owners gutted the whole house and they even raised the house to put in a full finished basement.

There's a three car garage next to the barn and the barn was converted into a two bedroom apartment on the main floor so whoever bought it could us it as a rental property. There is also a second floor that they used for family gatherings but can easily be converted into another apartment or office.

Beth nodded in agreement and pretended to scrutinize everything Sal told her but she had already pictured herself sitting in the porch swing drinking cold lemonade and watching the sunset. If the inside was a nice as the outside then Beth definitely found paradise.

They climbed the stairs to the front porch and Beth made a move towards the swing. She sat there swinging back and forth closing her eyes while listening to the faint sound of birds chirping in the distance.

"I think we lost her." Domenic smiled as he joined her on the swing.

"I think I lost you both." Sal sighed. It was going to be an easy sale but he really wanted to help Beth out with the price.

"I like this house." Domenic said.

Beth looked at him and her expression was in agreement.

"Me too." She whispered.

"There are two gas fireplaces. " Sal continued. "One is in the basement and one in the master bedroom. There is also a wood burning fireplace in the family room. And did you notice that the exterior isn't wood? Its vinyl siding." He added. "No maintenance."

"How big is this house Sal?" Domenic asked. "It seems pretty large for one person."

Sal scanned the listing for the exact size. Thirty five hundred square feet and the basement is another fifteen hundred."

It was as big as Beth's current house and more.

"All this area is new." Sal pointed to the back of the house.

A New Beginning for Beth

Beth walked to the end of the porch and leaned over to see the back of the property. "What about the barn?"

"I don't have the size on here but we can ask the owners."

They walked over to the garage and took a look around. Beth noticed a riding lawn mower outside the garage and asked if that would be included. Sal assured her that all the farm machinery is included. The owners were moving to a small ranch type house closer to the city and have bought a condo in Florida for the winter. They have no need for any of the equipment.

There's farm equipment? Those words finally hit Beth in the head. She wasn't just buying a house. She was buying a farm. A moment of panic flowed through her.

"This is a working farm. Or at least it is listed as one." Sal smiled.

"Just how much of a working farm is this?" Domenic asked

"I assume from all the fruit trees and the crops growing in the distance that it is a full working farm."

Beth kept silent. She didn't want the fact that she was getting in way over her head to deter her from buying the property. So it was a working farm. She did have that tomato garden one year. It would have produced more tomatoes if she had pulled the weeds. It's not as if she was a total moron when it came to growing vegetables. And there is farm equipment to do all that. No chance of her encountering a worm or snake up close sitting on a tractor.

As for the trees, she could have a fruit stand and sell all the fruit. Whichever type of fruit these trees produced. But she knew in her heart that it would be way too much work for someone who was raised in the city.

Living in suburbia was as close to the country she had ever come. She never even went camping, except for that one time her grandparents thought it would be cool to take her camping in a tent. But as she got older her idea of roughing it was going to a resort without room service. Come on Beth, she thought. You are starting a new life. Why not take the chance and completely transform your life and become a country girl? Although her brain was convincing, her body was beginning to ache at all the work she would have if she purchased the house. Damn that body of hers.

They walked further past the garage to take a look at the barn. The converted barn was what caught Beth's eye to begin with. It looked small from the road but as they walked closer, they were all overwhelmed by the size of it. It had to be at least two thousand square feet.

"This is a two story barn." Sal said as they moved towards the door. "You could use it as an in-law suite." Sal slapped his hand over his mouth after he realized what he had said. "Or you could make it into a guest house and office." Good comeback Sal thought.

The barn was covered in the same vinyl siding as the house. There were new windows on both stories of the barn.

"It looks like a house." Beth said as they stood there studying the outside.

Domenic agreed.

There were glass French doors on the side of the barn that faced the driveway. Window boxes full of flowers were placed on the windows that were on either side of the French doors.

This has to be the nicest barn they had ever seen.

They entered through the French doors and were immediately shocked at the appearance of the inside. Upon entering through the French doors you immediately found yourself in a small foyer into where there were stairs going up to the second story. There was a closet on one side and another set of French doors that opened onto a cozy living room. It was very rustic looking with high ceilings and oak beams that crisscrossed the ceiling.

There was a stone fireplace with a gas insert and the furniture was oversized yet comfortable looking. There was a small half wall that separated the living area from the dining area. And beyond that there was an open concept kitchen. The kitchen was small but it had enough counter space to work on. All the appliances were built in, including the fridge and they were also included in the price.

They walked back through the living room where there was a hallway past the fireplace. This led to the main bathroom and two bedrooms.

"There's only one bathroom in the apartment and a powder room upstairs." Sal seemed disappointed.

"I can live with that." Beth assured Sal. "To have this incredible barn is like a dream come true. "

A New Beginning for Beth

They checked out the bathroom and it was more then adequate with a separate shower and a huge Jacuzzi tub and bidet. There were two sinks with a long counter and makeup area. Next to the shower there were cupboards and drawers to store towels and toiletries. Beth was awe struck by the size of each room.

They continued on by checking out the master bedroom which was enormous in size. The spare bedroom was slightly smaller but still large enough for a king size bed or two queen size beds.

Beth fell in love with it immediately. For a moment she forgot about the main house and wanted to move into the barn.

"If the main house is as nice as this then I am sold!" She said with excitement in her voice.

Domenic put his arm around Beth's shoulder. "Don't you find it a bit strange that they are asking so little for a property like this?"

Beth thought for a moment. He was right. The price just didn't seem right for what she had seen so far.

"Sal, are you sure the price is right?"

"I checked it personally." He replied. "But seeing all this, I am wondering that myself."

They went back through the first set of doors and headed up the stairs to check out the second floor. The ceilings weren't as high and it wasn't as large as the first floor. The entire second floor was open and it was obvious that they used it as some sort of games room or party room. Tables and chairs were stacked up along the far wall. There was a small powder room to one side and a kitchen was partially closed off to the other side.

"I see why they used this for family gatherings. It is one huge room!" Beth said.

They all agreed.

"Let's go take a look at the main house." Sal said ushering Domenic and Beth down the stairs.

They walked back to the front porch and were greeted by an elderly couple. Standing there on their front porch, they looked as if they could have been on the cover of some better homes and gardens magazine.

He was dressed in casual slacks and a button down shirt. She was dressed in a bright pink flowered sun dress. Their skin was aged and tanned from years of working outside. They introduced themselves as Ivan and Natalie as they extended their hands to greet them. They welcomed the trio of visitors into the front door and Ivan began to tell them all about the history of the farm.

The house was over one hundred years old and had originally been his grandfathers. It was handed down to him from his father and he wanted to hand it down to his kids but their children had other ideas of living in the city. They all moved to the states except for their daughter who is a doctor in Toronto. No one had any desire to live on the farm.

"Who could blame them?" Natalie said. "They saw how difficult it was to run the farm."

Ivan gave Natalie an icy stare. It was obvious that Ivan wasn't pleased with having to part with the farm. But Natalie just rolled her eyes at her husband. She couldn't be happier to finally retire to the south.

"I noticed you are situated far from the road. Is the sewer and water on the city line or do you have a well and system tank?"

"We had it converted to the city a few years ago when our well started to dry up. It cost a pretty penny but it was worth it." Ivan replied.

The décor of the house was done in neutral tones. It was move in condition. The kitchen was large and bright and the floor was covered in terra cotta tile which Beth loved. It made it seem more country. As in the converted barn, the kitchen has all built in appliances which Natalie assured Beth was included.

A window overlooked the backyard as well as a set of French doors that led to the back part of the wrap around porch. An open family room was situated off of the kitchen. A fireplace with marble surround graced the far wall of the family room so it could be viewed from the kitchen.

Even if Beth didn't see the main house, she was already sold. She fell in love with the converted barn. The owners allowed Domenic, Sal and Beth to venture upstairs where there were four bedrooms, a main bathroom and a master suite. All the rooms were large and airy and sheers delicately covered each window. This allowed light to flow through the entire upstairs. There was hardwood throughout except for the bathrooms which were neutral slate tiles. It was obvious that the house had a professional decorators touch.

"What kind of closing date are you hoping for?" Beth asked the couple.

"Whatever in convenient for you, will be fine for us." Ivan replied.

A New Beginning for Beth

"I've seen enough." Beth said to Sal.

They thanked the owners for allowing them to view the house and they left through the back patio doors.

"Aren't you going to inquire about the cemetery?" Natalie asked as they walked back out onto the porch. They all stared over at the cemetery.

"Not really." Beth replied. "I think it's kind of cute and I certainly wouldn't have to worry about my neighbors." They looked relieved that the cemetery wasn't an issue for Beth.

Ivan turned to Domenic. "You must be the silent type seeing that your wife asked all the questions."

"You think he is my husband?" Beth looked at Ivan then at Natalie.

"Well you are married aren't you?" Natalie asked with some concern.

"Not yet, but we plan on getting married soon." Domenic said, wrapping his arm around Beth's shoulder. All Beth could do was nod and smile. He stopped her from saying anything more. "That's why we are looking for a house."

"That's good." Natalie sighed with relief. "We don't want anyone living in sin in our family house. And we certainly don't want someone buying it with the hopes of selling off the land to build smaller houses."

Beth knew where this was going and decided not to argue. She didn't want to take the chance on losing her dream home.

They thanked them again and they all climbed into Domenic's car and disappeared down the driveway.

"I want the house." Beth said looking back at Sal.

"I figured that the moment I saw the look on your face when we went into the barn." He laughed.

"What are you going to do with all that space? Domenic asked.

"I'll think of something. Maybe I will rent out the main house and live in the barn."

"Who would want to rent a house right next to a cemetery except maybe some devil worshippers or weirdoes? And would you want to have them as neighbors?"

"I never thought about all of that." Beth thought for a moment.

Beth looked over at Domenic. "You know Domenic; did anyone ever tell you that you were a dream squasher?"

"A what, squasher?"

"You're a dream squasher. Here I am all excited about this beautiful place and all you can do is bring me down by forcing reality on me. I love the house and I want to buy it. I have enough money to do just that and be mortgage free." Beth lay back in the leather seat.

"I'm not a dream squasher. I'm just being practical here. It's a lot of house and land for one person. Why do you think their kids didn't want it?"

"I can always sever the land and then there won't be so much work."

"I hate to interrupt and be a dream squasher too but the land can't be severed."

Beth glanced at Sal.

"What? What do you mean the land can't be severed?"

"Because of the cemetery the city won't allow the land to be severed. At least not at this time it isn't possible. Maybe in a few years but right now as it stands there is no way they will allow it."

Beth crossed her arms and let out a sigh. She didn't have any words to express how she was feeling right then. She was feeling another let down added to her already long list of let downs. Could she really keep up with the house and all the acres? She didn't want to lose the house but she knew in her heart that Domenic was right. It would be nearly impossible for her to maintain it alone.

Think Beth, think. There has to be a way to keep it up. I had all the equipment to maintain the farm but she just didn't have the time or knowledge to do it all herself. Then a thought came to her.

"What if I rent out the land? Beth asked. "I can do that, cant I Sal?"

Sal shrugged his shoulders.

"There are dozens of fruit trees and a lot of flat land that was obviously cultivated for vegetables. What if I made separate plots and rented each area to people who wanted to have a garden but because of their living situation didn't have the space. I could charge a flat fee for the summer and that would give me some income and the land would be looked after. As for the fruit trees, I could include a price for them to come and pick their own fruit." The idea sounded far fetched but it was a possibility.

A New Beginning for Beth

Sal thought over Beth's suggestion.

"It sounds crazy but I think it would be a great idea." Domenic said.

"This would be great for seniors who are living in apartments. We could have them bussed in once a week to work on the gardens." Beth added.

"And when I get my license back I could drive the bus." Sal added.

"No!" Beth and Domenic shouted in unison. The last thing Beth needed was a bus load of seniors smashing into the front of her house.

"I could set up the main house as a gathering place for them to come and spend the day. They could prepare all the vegetables and fruits in the kitchen while working on the gardens." Beth was getting more excited with every possibility.

"Maybe you could even arrange for inner city families to participate in growing their own produce?" Domenic added. "It would be a great way for the kids to spend their summer holidays. They could volunteer to help the seniors with their gardens and they could get compensated with free fruit and vegetables for their families."

The idea was perfect. Beth had met a few councilors working in family law. She could make a few phone calls to get the ball rolling. This could turn into a major project and she would be helping a lot of people and the community. She felt a sense of pride knowing that by buying this house she could do so much good.

"Let's go back to my place and put in an offer." Beth smiled.

By the end of the day, Beth was the new owner of a farm, converted barn and twenty five acres of land. She asked for a month closing date so she could have her decorator in to see if anything needed to be changed.

For the first time in a long time she felt happy and that her life was worth more than just being a lawyer. This would also make people see that although she was a criminal defense lawyer, she was still a woman with a big heart. Beth felt it important to have the public see her in a different level, especially now, since she was going back into her first loved practice of criminal law.

"It's getting late and I should be going." Sal said after the three of them celebrated with pizza, wings and beer. Domenic offered to drive him home which Sal accepted.

"Do you want to come for the ride?" he asked Beth. "You could stop in and say hello to your grandparents."

"Thanks but I think I will stay here. Besides, I doubt if my grandparents are up at this time."

If they were up they were probably doing something she would rather not see. She has made it a habit to always call them before she came over ever since the dining room table incident.

"Will you be up for a bit?" Domenic asked. "I was thinking we could watch a movie and pop some popcorn."

It was obvious to Beth that Domenic didn't want to call it a night. She was tired and although she would normally enjoy the company, she just felt that Domenic was hoping for more than what he suggested.

But Domenic did indeed have other ideas. He was fascinated with Beth. Smitten would probably be the right word for it. But he was moving as slowly as he could with her. She was going through a divorce and although Beth never made her feelings or emotions known, he was sure that it was a painful one. After all, her husband left her for another woman and has plans of moving her into their matrimonial home.

Beth was definitely a hard nut to crack when it came to her emotions. The most he ever saw of her showing any sign of excitement was when she saw the farm house. He had watched her intently as she moved from room to room. Her eyes would get wider as they looked at each room of the barn and the farmhouse. And they would sparkle like sunlight when she smiled and that smile tugged at his heart. Domenic secretly hoped that one day her eyes would glisten like that for him.

Beth could see the disappointment in Domenic's eyes. For a moment she wanted to reach out to him and hug him but she chose not to. Her logical side told her that it was best to keep her relationship with Domenic strictly platonic. But her emotional side wanted to feel his lips again.

She caught him staring at her during their visit to the farmhouse. He was deep in thought as he watched her. She wondered what he could be thinking about. As they wandered through the barn and the house, she had thought what a perfect place to raise a family. Maybe have some animals like a cat and dog. Maybe even a milking cow. She also thought about Domenic and possibly making him a permanent fixture at the farm. But that damn logical side kept kicking in.

A New Beginning for Beth

Since she met him she found her logical side and emotional side wresting with her brain and heart. She was in no condition to get involved with anyone especially a good looking lawyer who was representing her with her separation and divorce. But her heart was telling her that she should take a chance.

When it came to her work, Beth always took chances. She would win the impossible cases and she would go where no lawyer dare tread. But when it came to her love life, she played it safe. She married James who was a safe bet for her mother's approval. They bought into a safe neighborhood. Everything about her marriage was safe except for James's love for her. She never felt safe about that. He always told her he loved her but throughout their marriage she could never shake that little doubt she had. Since he left her, she realized that she never truly loved him either.

Her mother was a doctor and so was James. She felt that she married him to please her mother. But now here she was looking at Domenic with wanting eyes but there was nothing safe about him. He was gorgeous with his dark hair and blue eyes. When he flashed his perfect smile at her she would feel all warm and fuzzy inside. She never felt fuzzy with James.

"I think I'll pass tonight. But can I have a rain check on that?" Beth yawned.

Domenic nodded. He was disappointed but he knew not to insist. "I will call you tomorrow." He kissed her on the forehead. She waved bye to both the men, locked her front door and dragged her tired body upstairs to her bedroom. She laid in her king size bed, tucked snuggly under her white comforter, reminiscing about the day. It was a good day and she found her dream home.

Life was looking up for sure. Now if she could just figure out why her thighs quivered each time Domenic smiled at her then she would have things sorted out. But her heart was telling her why. "Shut up heart!" She whispered. "I have no intentions on getting involved with another man. Once bitten twice shy, they say." She spoke as if she were talking to a friend. Yes. Once bitten twice shy, she thought as the dark enveloped her and took her away to dream land. Tomorrow she will make it clear to Domenic that their relationship will be nothing more than a working one.

Chapter Two

Beth awoke to the sound of rain against her window. It had been quite humid the past few days which made the rain a welcoming sound. Beth closed her eyes and curled up into a ball. She didn't want to leave the comfort of her bed.

Her phone broke the sound of the rain and she sighed, pulling the comforter over her head. Not now, she thought. I don't want any phone calls this morning. I just want to stay in bed and sleep all day. Beth groaned as she reached for the phone.

"Are you still in bed?" the voice asked. Immediately upon hearing Domenic's voice, Beth's southern region heated up.

"Damn." She muttered with embarrassment.

"Are you okay?"

"What time is it?" Beth searched for her watch.

"It's almost nine. I thought you would be at the office by now."

"Damn it!" Beth leaped from the bed still holding the phone in her hand. "I'm due in court in an hour!" she shouted.

"Beth, maybe we should talk later?" Domenic suggested. "How about I pick you up at your office around one and we can have lunch together?"

A New Beginning for Beth

"Sure, sure, that sounds fine with me. One o'clock. See you then." She hung up not really sure what she had agreed to.

Beth showered and dressed in record time. Why didn't her alarm go off? She realized she forgot to set it again. Maybe she should start setting it in the morning. She grabbed her brief case, poured a tea in a travel mug and headed out the door. She stopped in her tracks, somewhere between her garage door and her car. Wait a minute Singer. Did you just agree to have lunch with Domenic? Beth thought for a moment. Yep. You agreed. She shook it off to a work lunch and took her place behind the wheel of her car. "I will worry about it later." She said as she pulled out her garage. She also decided to lay things on the line with Domenic about spending less time socially. After all, he is her lawyer and her emotions are very fragile right now.

This all sounded good in theory but Domenic didn't seem like the type who did anything that sounded good in theory. She also found herself missing him last night when she laid in bed. But she wasn't going to let her need for sex with Domenic allow herself to be hoodwinked into getting naked with him. Beth made a mental note to check out a sex shop for something that came with double "A" batteries but didn't come with baggage and laundry. And she would do that right after lunch with Domenic.

Mary stuck her head inside Beth's office. She was grinning ear to ear. Beth looked up at her and immediately thought of the cat that swallowed the canary.

"What now?" she asked.

Mary moved her whole body inside the office and sashayed over to Beth's desk. "There is a good looking man waiting to see you. He says he has a lunch date with you?" Mary was salivating with every word.

"Don't get too excited. That's my divorce lawyer." Beth brushed off the imaginary drool that was dripping from Mary's mouth. She had rape and pillage written all over her face.

"He's a divorce lawyer? Remind me to get him when I need a divorce." She smiled ear to ear.

Beth rolled her eyes at Mary. "Don't you think you should get married first before you start planning your divorce?"

"Details, details." Mary waved her hand in the air. "I thought you were getting Howard to take care of your divorce?" she looked around the room in fear of anyone in earshot of their conversation.

"I was but my grandfather suggested Domenic."

"Oh, Domenic. Even his name is sexy."

"Oh please. Just go tell him I will be out in a minute." Beth said dismissing any notion of the lunch date being more than platonic.

Mary closed the door behind her and Beth retreated to her washroom to freshen up. She ran her fingers through her blonde hair, applied some light face powder to dull the shine on her face and stroked on some pink lip gloss. She puckered her lips in the mirror and made kissing sounds. She stopped short.

What the hell are you doing Singer? You made a mental promise not allow your body to do the talking for you when it came to Domenic. She thought to herself. Here she was blowing pink shiny kisses at herself in the mirror. "Okay no perfume." She mumbled as she placed the bottle of channel back on the counter. "It's just a friendly platonic lunch and nothing more."

So what if he happens to be the best looking guy she had laid eyes on in a long time. Maybe ever. So what that he kisses as if he could do it for a living. So what if you could balance a tea cup on his firm round butt. It was strictly platonic and nothing more. Beth got a grip of her emotions gathered her purse and opened her office door.

Her jaw dropped as Domenic turned around. His blue eyes, sparkled like oceans as his perfect smiled grew at the sight of her. His black wavy hair was slicked back except for one lone strand that dangles down his forehead and swayed as he moved towards her.

He was dressed in a lightweight, navy Armani suit. His tie was red with tiny white dots and he topped his suit off with a white crisp shirt.

Beth? You're a goner. She thought he could not get better looking in his jeans and tee-shirt. Now he was even a better package wrapped in Armani. He leaned towards her and kissed her on the cheek. At that moment she thought she heard Mary groan with delight.

"You smell wonderful." Domenic took a deep breath taking in the scent of channel perfume.

All Beth could do was smile. "So where are you taking me for lunch?"

"I know a great little bistro that serves dozens of appetizers."

Beth gave Domenic a puzzled look. "Have you been talking to my grandparents again?"

"Yes and they told me how you love appetizers." Domenic laughed.

Domenic was beginning to grow on Beth. Any man who would take her to a restaurant just for the appetizers was okay in her book. Maybe she could let her body do some talking after all? It's not like she's showed it much action lately. Maybe that trip to the sex shop can wait a couple of days.

By the time they arrived at the restaurant, the lunch crowd had dispersed to a few men in suits sitting at the bar and a couple of tables where casual meetings were taking place. Beth and Domenic were shown to a quiet booth away from prying eyes and Beth slid herself onto bench, carefully holding her black skirt so it wouldn't ride up and expose more of her leg then were necessary.

They looked over the menu and ordered several appetizers from potato skins to slush puppy's. They topped it off with French onion soup as their main meal.

Beth sat silently sipping on her coke as Domenic studied her. "So tell me Domenic, is this a social lunch or a work lunch?" she said feeling a tad uncomfortable with him staring at her.

"It can be any kind of lunch that you would want it to be." He smiled. "But to be honest, it is a little bit of both."

"Is this anything to do with my separation?"

Domenic shook his head. "Nope. Actually I need your help. Well your grandparents and I both need your help."

Beth's curiosity was aroused. "What is the problem?"

Domenic wrung his hands together. "It's this case I'm working on. It has me stumped."

"Tell me what's going on that have you stumped?" Beth asked as the first of their appetizers arrived.

"As you know I represent a huge pharmaceutical company. You also know that they asked me to hire some outside people to investigate a series of thefts in one of the medical buildings."

Beth nibbled on some fried cauliflower as she listened intently to Domenic.

"I had worked with Jack a few times on some cases so I hired your grandparent's service to help out on the case. Their investigation service is the best, yet we are all confused by this case."

Beth stopped eating and examined Domenic's face. His face wore a worried expression and the tone of his voice turned serious.

"What seems to be the problem that you have run into?" Beth asked putting on her best lawyer face.

"All the employees and visitors have to go through security. They've tightened security because of the thefts yet there have been no signs of anything being stolen. And anything of value couldn't be removed without being noticed." Domenic ran his fingers through his hair, ignoring the stray strand that still dangled free. Beth could tell that this case was really bothering Domenic. Based on what he told her so far, it didn't make much sense to her either.

"Why would a company want you to hire investigators to probe into thefts if they have security?" Beth asked.

"That's just it. They have metal detectors and security guards everywhere. There is no way anyone can walk out of there with a pencil without it being noticed. Yet they believe someone is stealing from them."

Beth and Domenic sat in silence trying to figure out a logical explanation.

"There is something else too." he added. "Do you remember the other night when we were watching Peter Bucar?"

Beth nodded.

"I told them about what I had seen and that I still didn't feel he was involved in the thefts."

"Do they still want you to investigate him?"

Domenic shook his head yes. "I don't know why. What we have so far is that there is nothing unusual in his pattern. Based on what we have seen from him is that you could set your watch by his routine."

"That makes him easier to follow." Beth added.

"Exactly. But he has been watched for a month now and he hasn't altered his pattern once. If he was stealing, we would have seen something by now."

"Maybe he knows about the investigation so he has been keeping himself clean?" Beth offered her suggestion.

A New Beginning for Beth

Domenic disagreed. "No one other than the suits at head office knows about his investigation. Unless Bucar has a friend on the board he wouldn't have a clue."

Domenic picked up a potato skin dipped it in the sour cream and took a bite.

Beth leaned back in her seat. She scanned the table that was covered with an array of appetizers. Her mind was going a mile a minute, thinking of reasons for what was happening on this case, none of which made sense to her.

"I want to see this case through to the end." Beth said.

Domenic's face expressed relief. He had wanted to ask her for her continued help but he didn't want to bog her down with more work than she already had. But she was the best criminal lawyer. She had a knack for getting inside of criminals heads. And if this Peter Bucar was really guilty of stealing then who better suited to figure him out then Beth Singer?

Domenic's heart melting smile reappeared. "We need someone to get close to this guy. Someone like yourself, who is attractive and smart. Someone he wouldn't suspect was hired to watch him."

"You aren't seriously thinking about having me meet up with this guy?" Beth crossed her arms waiting for a reaction.

"Can you think of a better way to study this guy? It's right down your alley." Domenic munched on some bruchetta bread. Some of the tomatoes fell to his plate and he scooped them up with a spoon and popped them in his mouth.

"You do have a point." She replied. "We can't very well arrest him and then appoint me to represent him. I would need to get close enough without him suspecting anything."

Beth watched Domenic's face. His eyes twinkled. A sure sign that he had a plan already set up.

"I bet you have a plan on how I am going to get close to him." Her eyes narrowed as she realized that she was set up by this gorgeous man. She also knew that her grandparents had a hand in this as well. How else would Domenic know the right words to use to peak her interest in this case?

Domenic leaned back in the bench and smiled.

"You have an outstanding reputation in the legal world. It was a shame and a shock to many people when you gave up criminal law for family law. But because of your background, you would be the only person capable of pulling this plan off." Domenic was buttering Beth up for the big bang and Beth knew it.

"Flattery won't get you everywhere." She huffed.

"Everywhere or anywhere?" A small smile formed on the edges of Domenic's lips.

"So why don't you get to the point?" Beth rolled her eyes at him.

"I didn't even know of the connection between you and the agency until your grandfather asked me to represent you." His face went back to being serious but kept the everywhere comment in the back of his mind for later.

Domenic was trying hard to make it impossible for Beth to back out of helping him. What Domenic didn't realize was that Beth had already decided to help out. She was just as stumped by what she knew so far as Domenic was. This was going to be a tough case yet she would be given the opportunity to be right in the front lines of the mystery. It was a place where she loved to be when it came to unusual cases.

"So Domenic, what exactly is it that you and my grandparents want me to do?"

"We need you to meet Peter and strike up a friendship." He blurted out without hesitation.

"And how do you suppose I do this?"

"It's all arranged." He replied.

"I thought so." Beth said wryly. "I bet this was planned for a while."

Domenic shook his head. "Nope. Tom only brought it up with me very recently."

"So tell me this plan." Beth asked.

"As you know, Peter is a creature of habit. He always eats lunch at the same restaurant across the street from the building he works in."

"Don't they have a cafeteria?"

"Yes but for some reason he prefers to sit alone at the same table in the same restaurant, five days a week."

"He even orders the same thing for each day. Today is Monday so he always orders a chicken western sandwich."

Beth thought back to all the meals she had in restaurants with her grandparents. This is why they always knew so much about the people they were following. She remembered going to one restaurant everyday at the same time for a whole week.

"Your grandparents are pretty thorough. They know every little thing about this guy's behavior."

"You'd be surprised." Beth laughed as she mentally recalled her childhood with her grandparents. "So when do I make contact with him?"

"In a couple of days. We have everything arranged for Wednesday so clear your day for then." Domenic said munching on one of the appetizers.

"As it turns out, I don't have any court dates because I'm in transition." Beth said.

Domenic cocked his head at her. "What do you mean by transition?"

"I'm slowly handing over my family clients to one of my colleagues. I'm returning to criminal law."

a smile formed on Domenic's face. He liked the sound of that. "There will be a lot of people happy to hear that."

"I'm sure there will be. But there will also be a lot of prosecutors who won't be too thrilled. I'm a tough cookie when I'm in court defending my client's innocence." She added.

Domenic nodded in agreement. He remembers reading about her in the newspaper and how she would literally rip apart the prosecutor's case against her clients. She was more than a tough cookie. She was a tiger. In her case a tigress that was hungry for blood. The district attorneys office was more than happy to see her leave criminal law.

"So is the business aspect of our lunch complete?" Beth asked, her voice lowered with a sexy undertone to it.

Domenic's eyes widened. "What did you have in mind?" his voice became husky and deep.

Beth leaned in and gently kissed Domenic on the mouth. Her body had been thinking about his kiss all night and day and she could no longer take sitting there across from him without feeling his lips on hers. Beth opened her eyes and moved back into her seat. She waited for a response from Domenic but he sat there, dumbfounded and confused by her sudden boldness. He looked at the food on the table, picked up a potato skin and sniffed it.

"What are you doing?" Beth asked a bit annoyed that he didn't follow suit by advancing towards her for another kiss.

"Is there alcohol in these things?" he asked with slight sarcasm in his voice.

Beth crossed her arms, annoyed at his comment. She was finally giving in to her urges and making the moves on this man who has made her thighs quiver for a couple of days, and he thinks she's drunk. The feeling of rejection was filling her body and her annoyance was turning to hurt.

"That's the last time I make advances towards you." She cried.

Domenic leaned over put his hand in her hair and pulled her close to him. He kissed her hard and long before she had a chance to rebel. His lips parted and Beth could feel his tongue probing her lips for an opening. She instinctively opened her mouth and their tongues intertwined together.

Her body was heating up with passion that was long forgotten. She hadn't felt this passion and heat for someone in a long time. All she could think about was her need to feel his naked body on hers.

"Your place or mine?" Beth whispered.

Domenic kissed her neck gently then sighed. "Neither."

Beth pulled away and stared him down. Was he rejecting her? He was so hot and heavy for her a day ago and now when she was offering herself to him on a platter, he was turning her down. "What do you mean by that?" her voice filled with anger.

Domenic reached for Beth's hand but she pulled away. She was sitting on the edge of her seat, ready to bolt from the restaurant at any given moment. "Beth, ordinarily I would jump at the chance to make love with you. Believe me when I tell you that this is more difficult than you think to have to pass on it today. The problem is that I have another commitment in an hour and I don't want our first time to be a quickie."

Beth wasn't buying into it. She was feeling rejected and unattractive. First her husband leaves her for another woman and now the first man she shows any interest in since her husband left, is turning her down. Tears stung the back of her eyes as she tried to blink them away.

"You have another commitment." She repeated his words. "Just great. I don't even get to know what this commitment is." Domenic opened his mouth to speak but Beth waved his attempt to respond, away.

"I better go." Beth said standing and tucking her purse under her arm.

"What about Wednesday?" Domenic asked.

"Wednesday is still on. Just leave a message with my secretary with the time and place." Beth disappeared out the door without looking back.

Domenic sat alone staring at the remaining food. "Do you want me to wrap that up for you?" the waitress asked.

"No thanks. Just the check." He replied pulling out his wallet. He felt terrible and knew he had to make it up to Beth. He had thought about her from the moment he met her. He wanted to get to know this beautiful, intelligent woman.

He wanted to make the sadness in her eyes, disappear. But all he managed to do was humiliating her and push her away. Ragonese how are you going to fix this one? He thought.

Beth washed her makeup off and slipped into her bathing suit. She tied her hair up, grabbed a towel and headed for her backyard pool. The sky had cleared of dark clouds and the air hung heavy with humidity.

The water was warm but refreshing as she swam the length of the pool and back again. She tried not to think about her humiliation at the restaurant but the memory kept flooding her brain. Each thought made her angry then sad. She was feeling sorry for herself and the swimming was not helping her.

The last time she felt this frustrated was the day James walked out on her. But she never felt as hurt as she did today. Even after being married to James for seven years, his leaving never hurt her as much as Domenic's rejection had.

Beth's concentration was broken by the sound of her phone ringing. She blew out a sigh as she reached for her towel. Her answering machine picked it up just as she reached for the receiver. Beth pushed and button to shut off the machine. "Hello?"

A familiar voice replied. "Hey stranger, how are you?"

A smile formed on Beth's mouth. "Nancy! You're back! How was your trip?"

"It was great girlfriend. How have you been while I was gone?"

Beth felt a sense of warmth come over her with the sound of her best friend's voice. Nancy Ruben and Beth had been friends ever since their parents put them together in the same playpen. They lived together their first four years of university. Beth went on to law school and Nancy went on to marry Harry Ruben. Her life continued with the arrival of a daughter, followed a year later by twin boys.

In spite of their lives taking different directions, they remained best friends. She was godmother to her daughter Emily and spoiled all her children. They shared so much throughout their friendship. And Nancy was there to offer a shoulder for Beth to cry on when James walked out.

"How was your holiday with Harry? Did you and Harry have a great time in Greece?"

"It was fantastic!" Nancy laughed. "We didn't want to come home."

"I bet you didn't. I also bet the kids missed you terribly."

Nancy sighed. "I missed them too. By the way, Harry and I want to do something special for you in appreciation for the wonderful holiday you surprised us with."

"No need to do anything, Nancy. It was my pleasure. You both deserved to get away and I am glad I was able to give that to you."

"Well regardless, it is something we want to do."

Beth smiled knowing that Nancy wouldn't be happy until she repaid her for buying the cruise trip of Greece for her best friend and her husband. But she knew how stressed out Nancy was with having three babies to take care of.

Even when Beth was going through her separation, Nancy always had time to listen to her. And Harry always understood. He never once showed annoyance towards Beth for taking up so much of his wife's time. They were true friends to Beth and she never forgot it.

"I want to hear all about your trip and I also have some news for you."

"Is this good news? Or are you and James getting back together?" Nancy asked.

"There is no way on God's green earth that I will take James back." Beth laughed.

Nancy blew out a sigh of relief. "That in itself is good news."

"I bought a house. Well actually I bought a farm and a converted barn."

"That is great news!" Nancy screamed. Beth had to pull the phone away from her ear before she went deaf from the excitement in Nancy's voice. "What's it like? When are you moving? Did you sell your house?"

"Hold on girl. Let me answer one question at a time." Beth laughed.

"Never mind answering right now. I'm coming over so put the kettle on."

"Harry, I'm going over to Beth's for a bit. Can you watch the kids?" Beth heard Nancy say as she hung up the phone.

An hour later, the friends were enjoying a cup of tea next to the pool. Beth had showered the chlorine out of her hair and changed into jean shorts and a white tee-shirt and tied her wet hair back. Nancy had stopped at the donut shop and bought a dozen of Beth's favorite donuts and they were happily devouring them while washing them down with their tea.

"So tell me about this farm." Nancy asked.

Beth's voice was full of excitement. "It's beautiful. It has a barn that has been converted into a two bedroom apartment as well as a studio on the second floor. I am thinking of using that as my living quarters. Beth told Nancy of her plans for inner city families and senior citizens. Nancy thought it was a great idea and offered to help. She knew Nancy would want to help. She always volunteered her time with the kindergarten class that her daughter was in.

"There is something else about the farm that I didn't tell you." Beth's voice lowered just above a whisper.

"Sounds serious." Nancy said moving in closer to Beth to hear what she had to say.

"The land comes with its own graveyard."

Nancy looked at her. She wasn't sure if Beth was joking or dead serious.

"I'm not joking, Nancy. I actually own a cemetery now."

Nancy bit her bottom lip and narrowed her eyes just like she always did when she was deciding on something. "Well that's just great! Think of the fun you can have with it. And you won't have to worry about a burial plot when you pass on to the great law office in the sky."

"Fun? I never thought of a graveyard as being fun." Beth said.

"Sure it's fun. Halloween would be a great time to decorate it." Nancy had it all figured out. "You will see when Halloween rolls around." Nancy patted Beth's hand.

"Now what are you going to do about the house you have now?" Nancy asked.

"I sold it." Beth said avoiding eye contact with Nancy.

Nancy shook her head. "Don't tell me you are letting James have it."

"Okay, I won't tell you." Beth took another donut and broke a small piece off and popped it in her mouth.

"Why would you let James have the house, Beth? You know he will move the tart in as soon as you move out."

"He gave me a great offer and I need to start with a clean slate."

Nancy knew she was right. Beth needed to rid herself of the memories of James. And what better way to start that than to sell the house they shared.

"If James wants to live here with Jill then so be it. It won't be easy for him to get rid of the memories that we had in the house."

Beth was right. James and Jill would always know that this house held memories of her and James. Maybe it didn't bother them but it bothered Beth. She needed to start a new life with a new house. Maybe even a new man. Her last thought saddened her. The rejection she felt earlier came flooding back.

Nancy sensed the change in Beth's demeanor. "What's wrong, Beth."

Beth hesitated. "I met a man the other day." She finally confessed.

"Well that's great! What's he like?"

"He's gorgeous and single. At least I think he's single. My grandparents sent him over to help me with my divorce."

"Okay. So did he help you with more than your divorce?"

Beth nodded. "He's a great kisser."

Nancy smiled. "That's a start. So did he do anything more then kiss you?"

"That's just it. He had been hinting to me that he found me attractive and then today during lunch I decided to make the move."

"I gather he didn't respond positively." Nancy said.

"How could you tell?" Beth asked.

"Well for one thing, you're hair is wet and smells like chlorine which means you have been swimming. And second, you are sitting here with me and as far as I am aware of, there is no gorgeous guy waiting for you in your bed."

"You're right on both counts." Beth said. "Not to worry. It's not as if I haven't been rejected before." She laughed slightly, trying to brush off her sadness. "Besides, he is helping me with my divorce and I'm helping him with an investigation. I'm going to keep it strictly a working relationship."

"Sure you are, Beth." Nancy didn't sound convinced.

Beth wasn't convinced either. She hardly knew Domenic and she felt the pangs of jealousy when he turned her invitation down for plans he had made earlier. What could have been more important? He never even asked for a rain check on her invitation. But then again she never gave him the opportunity to ask for one. She ran from the restaurant without as much as a good bye. Maybe it was for the best. Mixing business with pleasure never worked. And this working relationship she had with Domenic was no exception.

Beth and Nancy hugged goodbye and made a promise to do lunch soon. Once Nancy disappeared down the street, Beth dragged herself upstairs, and changed into her pajamas. She climbed into bed, covered herself with her blankets and closed her eyes. It's going to be strictly a working relationship from now on. She thought as she drifted off to sleep.

She drove to her grandparent's apartment to be briefed on their plan for her meeting with Peter Bucar. Domenic had left Beth a message with her secretary on meeting at her grandparents for ten in the morning on Wednesday. The sun was out in full force but the humidity from the past few days, had disappeared. It was hot and dry. Another beautiful day, Beth thought. But Beth didn't feel beautiful.

She had refused Domenic's phone calls and wasn't looking forward to seeing him today. She didn't act very mature when she ran from the restaurant two days ago. But it was either that or he would see her crying.

She could never handle having Domenic see her cry or anyone for that matter.

Her grandparents lived in an area of the city that consisted mostly of apartment buildings that catered to seniors. Most buildings were three, four and five stories. The larger buildings housed variety stores and hair salons on their main floor. Some even had optometrist's offices and dental clinics.

Beth pulled into the visitor parking lot just beyond the building and noticed Domenic's car off to the left. Beth sighed as her stomach fluttered with nervousness. She pulled into an empty space next to his car. Must be my lucky day, Beth thought. Not only does she have to see Domenic today but she has to park next to him in the parking lot.

The building was a small three-storey apartment with a back entrance that also housed an intercom and a resident directory. Beth buzzed apartment three C then heard the click of the main door unlock. Beth walked to the elevators that were on the other side of the lobby. As the doors opened onto the third floor hallway, a familiar smell of chocolate chip cookies filled Beth's senses. Audrey had left the apartment door open just like she always did when she knew someone was coming. Beth entered the doorway and stood inside their small entranceway. There was a kitchen on the left side and a coat closet on the right. Further down the short hallway was a living-room, dining room combination.

The living room doubled as a reception area. The rooms were decorated with bright colors of pink and green. A matching flowered sofa and love seat was the sitting area and they also had an array of end tables and a coffee table. Cute feminine lamps were on each end table and a crystal jar filled with candy, was placed on the coffee table. These were for visitors and relatives. Off to one side sat a small desk with a computer. In the dining room there was a large hutch and china cabinet as well as the infamous oak table. Beth shuddered as she recalled that day. Nothing had changed in all the years that they lived here.

Granny was coming out of the kitchen carrying a tray of cookies and milk. Something she always did when Beth came to visit. Even though Beth was in her early thirties, she still looked forward to nana's homemade chocolate chip cookies. Domenic appeared from down the hall and smiled at Beth. Beth attempted a weak smile and nodded in acknowledgement of Domenic. His smile faded and decided not to attempt a conversation with Beth at that time. He took the tray of cookies and milk from Audrey and placed them on the coffee table.

"It's so nice to see you dear." Granny said hugging Beth tightly.

"I missed you nana." Beth replied wrapping her arms around grandmother. "Where is gramps?"

"He'll be out in a minute. Duty calls you know." Domenic looked puzzled at that reply.

"That means he's in the bathroom." Audrey said to Domenic.

"Is that our little Bethany?" a voice called from down the hall. It was followed with the sound of a toilet flushing. Within seconds the door opened and they were joined by Tom.

"If anyone needs to use the bathroom, I would suggest waiting till the air clears." Audrey grimaced at that remark and tapped her husband lightly on the back of the head. That always indicated that he stepped out of line again and she needed to put him back in his place.

Beth's grandparents, Tom and Audrey, were in their mid seventies. They weren't the type of people you would think of when you thought private investigators. Tom stood five feet ten inches when he stood straight up. He was hunched over slightly, mostly due to osteoporosis. Although his hair was grey, his mane was full and wavy. If it weren't for the aging features, he could have dyed it darker and passed for late fifties. His smile was full of dentures, all straight and white. The kind of smile you would see on George Hamilton, except grandpa was as white as Casper the ghost. He was so white that he made Casper look like he belonged in the hood. Mary was a short grandmotherly type. Her hair was typical grey and her eyes were chocked full of love.

Gramps was dressed in his usual buttoned down shirt and tie with pleated pants. The pants, he wore slightly higher around his waist. He had more hair on his chest than Nana had on her head and because of this she opted to wearing one of those invisible nets that hugged her hair closely to her head.

"How you doing cutie?" gramps said hugging Beth closely.

"I'm good gramps." Beth replied returning his hug even tighter. "Sorry about your marriage falling apart honey. I know it can be tough given the circumstances of the breakup."

"No you aren't!" Nana snapped. "Just last night you were saying how happy you were that Beth finally dumped that sorry ass doctor."

"Well that too. But our Beth is here and she doesn't need to hear that right now."

"Yes she does. He was a scum bag and she should have kicked his ass to the curb years ago."

It had been a few months since James left her and she had hoped her grandparents would have stopped bringing it up. But once again they were trying their best to make her feel better but were failing miserably.

"Gramps don't worry about it. I'm totally over James and have moved on so let's stop talking about it and start discussing why we are here." Beth said calmly.

Domenic sat quietly at the dining room table, watching the whole episode from the side lines.

For a moment, Beth had forgotten he was there. That was until he suggested going over the plan for today. Then a feeling of embarrassment came over Beth. She still hadn't forgotten how he rejected her advances and all the feelings of that day came flooding back. She put on her best professional face and took her place on the opposite side of the table from Domenic.

He watched her intently and tried to make eye contact with Beth, but she would have none of that. She glanced down at the information on Peter Bucar and pretended to be reading each word. But she wasn't interested in the paper. The only thing on her mind was Domenic's reason for rejecting her and what was so important that day that he turned her down.

Over the past couple of days she had convinced herself that he had another woman in his life and that he was afraid to tell her. She had also convinced herself that Domenic Ragonese was a cad and womanizer and no matter how much he begged her, she wasn't about to give in to his charm. Even if it meant poking her eyes out so she wouldn't be persuaded by his smile and good looks.

Audrey glanced at her only granddaughter then at Domenic. "Is there anything wrong with the two of you?"

Domenic and Beth looked up at Audrey then at each other. Both reluctantly shook their heads no.

"Why would you think there was something wrong between us?" Domenic asked.

"Well for one thing, you can cut the tension in this room with a knife. And second, you haven't said one word to each other."

"I would rather not talk about it." Beth said. "Can you just clue me in on what I am supposed to do today?"

Audrey studied Beth's face. She had seen that face before. Beth wore the face of a hurt little girl. Did Domenic hurt her in some way? She couldn't understand how since Domenic had made it clear that he was very interested in Beth. She thought it best not to press the issue and instructed Beth of what she was to do today.

Once at the restaurant she was to be seated at Peter's favorite table. The restaurant would be filled to capacity when Peter arrived at his usual time. That is when Beth would call the waitress over and offer a seat at her table for Peter. Hopefully he would take the bait and accept her invitation and then it was up to Beth to do the rest. The rest included an exchange of phone numbers and a promise of a date.

The way Beth was feeling she wouldn't be the least bit surprised if Peter turned down her invitation and ran out of the restaurant screaming in terror.

As they finished their game plan Domenic suggested they ride together in his car. Tom and Audrey accepted the offer but Beth felt it better she drive her own car. It was one thing to sit in her grandparent's apartment with him, but it was another thing to have to endure sitting next to him in his car.

"Don't be silly Bethany. You can ride with us." Tom said.

Beth sighed and rolled her eyes. Her shoulders slumped down as if she were carrying a heavy weight. "Okay gramps, but I'm not going to be happy about this."

Tom waved her words away and they all piled into Domenic's B.M.W. with Beth sitting in the front seat.

Once they arrived at the restaurant, Beth waited in the car with Domenic as her grandparents entered the restaurant. They didn't want anyone to think they were all together so it was best they went in ahead of her.

"Beth, I owe you an explanation about the other day."

Beth looked at him. His eyes held concern for her but she ignored it. "You owe me nothing. I'm so over that day that I have blocked it out of my head."

"You don't act as if you are over it." He replied.

"Look Domenic, just forget it. I was stupid to do what I did but in all honesty, you had led me to believe you were interested. I realize now that you aren't any better than my ex-husband and you like to play games." Beth opened the car door and climbed out.

"From now on Domenic lets keep our relationship strictly professional." She added leaning in the car window. Her voice meant business but her heart was breaking. She fought back tears as she crossed the parking lot to the restaurant.

Domenic sat silently pondering over what just happened between him and Beth. He knew that nothing he said to her would convince her of his feelings for her. If she only knew that from the moment he laid eyes on her, she had taken over every part of him. She was constantly in his thoughts and his body reacted when he reminisced about the kiss in the park and the kiss in the restaurant.

He loved the way she smelled and the way her nose would crinkle when she smiled. He could hear her voice and her laughter in every sound that he heard. She had captivated him in every sense of the word yet he had managed to break her heart. And because of this he was more determined than ever to win her over. He wanted to prove to her that he wasn't like her ex-husband. He truly cared about Beth and wanted her to be happy and feel loved. His heart ached as he watched Beth disappear into the restaurant.

Beth looked around at the people seated in the restaurant. She saw her grandparents seated next to the only empty table in the place. She scanned over at all the seniors who were seated at the array of booths and tables. She glanced at Sal who was seated with a few other people who she also recognized from her grandparents agency. They definitely made sure the restaurant would be full.

She noticed Jack Peterson sitting alone in the corner. He was the youngest member of the agency. Although he was much too young to be retired, he was given that option when shot in the line of duty while working as a homicide detective. His hair was salt and pepper and his face was free of deep lines and wrinkles. His grey eyes added character to his face and his smile was broad and inviting. They glanced at each other just for a brief moment to acknowledge each other but not long enough for anyone outside the circle, to notice.

A New Beginning for Beth

"It's a full house today." The waitress said scanning the restaurant for an empty table.

"Are you always this busy?" Beth asked pointing to the small table by the window.

The waitress sighed not wanting to relinquish the only available table to Beth. "Not like this. The seniors must have got their old age pensions today."

"At least there's one table left for me." She smiled and walked ahead of the waitress.

The waitress followed carrying the lunch menu. She handed it to Beth who was seated with her back to the window, just as she was instructed. The waitress shoved her hands in her apron and scanned the door as if she were waiting for someone. Beth knew who she was waiting for and knew that any moment, Peter would be walking in the door.

Beth ordered lemonade and lazily scanned the menu to bide some time till Peter arrived. The door of the restaurant opened and Domenic stepped inside. He glanced over at Beth then turned away as the waitress welcomed him. She motioned at the full tables and Domenic looked around as if he were looking for someone. Beth watched as Jack waved to Domenic to get his attention. Domenic walked over to Jack, they shook hands and the waitress followed behind with a lunch menu. Their seats were positioned in such a way that they had full view of her table. Although no one was looking at her, she felt all eyes were focused in her direction. This made for an uncomfortable feeling.

She watched as her grandmother got up and walked to the ladies room. A minute later her cell phone rang. "Honey, don't be nervous. Just act natural." The voice said.

"How could you tell Nana?"

"Well for one thing, your face is shiny from sweat. You always get that way when you are nervous."

Beth took a paper napkin from the dispenser and gently blotted the shine from her face. "Thanks Nana. I'll be okay." Beth hung up the phone and she watched as her grandmother exited the washroom and took her seat next to her grandfather.

The door to the restaurant opened and Peter Bucar stepped inside. He was much shorter than what Beth expected. He was wearing navy slacks that looked more winter wear than summer wear. His shirt was a plain white buttoned down dress shirt with short sleeves. His shirt pocket held a variety of pens as well as a calculator. He pushed his wire framed glasses up and scanned the room in dismay. The waitress welcomed him by his first name and they both looked over at Beth who was sitting at his regular table. They exchanged a few words and she could tell that Peter was annoyed at the inconvenience of not having a table for lunch let alone his regular table.

Tom motioned for the waitresses' attention. His plan was to get her in Beth's vicinity so she could make the offer of sharing her table with Peter. The plan was well thought out which and orchestrated perfectly.

A few minutes later Peter was sitting across from Beth. It was obvious he was uncomfortable sitting at the table with a stranger. Beth put on her friendliest smile. "Hi, my name's Beth. The restaurant is quite full. I'm glad you don't mind sharing the table with me."

"Thanks for offering. I usually sit at this table when I come here for lunch." Peter mumbled without making eye contact.

"Your name is?" Beth asked.

"Peter. Peter Bucar."

"It's nice to meet you Peter. I gather you eat here often if this is your usual table." Beth wanted to keep the conversation light. She encouraged Peter to talk so that he would become more trusting of her and feel more relaxed.

"Everyday." He replied.

"Well then, what would you recommend I order?" Beth asked. She already knew what he ordered on Wednesday. It was meatloaf day for him and in spite of her not caring much for meatloaf she opted for it at Peter's suggestion.

Peter added lemonade with his order.

"The food must be good if you come here everyday." Beth had to get him talking to make him feel comfortable.

"It's not the best food but it beats eating at the cafeteria."

"I know what you mean. Cafeteria food is not my idea of a good time." A smile broke across his face and their eyes met for the first time.

His eyes were soft brown and slightly sad. It was if he was hiding something beneath the surface of his professional exterior. Because of this Beth didn't want to engage him in a personal conversation too quickly. He seemed to be under enough stress with having five minutes of his life taken over by seniors during his lunch hour. Breaking into conversation with a total stranger may be too much for him to handle in one day. They were saved by total awkwardness with the reappearance of their waitress and a tray of food.

"So you must work nearby to come here everyday?" Beth asked.

"Why do you ask?" Peter snapped. He had his guard up for some reason and Beth had to move slowly.

"I'm sorry. I was just making conversation but if you prefer to sit here in silence that is fine by me." Beth picked up her fork and poked at the brown slab of meat that was covered in dark brown sauce. She made a slight gagging sound as she cut into the meat.

Well this is going to be fun. Beth thought. She was rating this moment somewhere between having root canal or a toe nail removed. Neither of which she has had but have heard they weren't pleasant.

"I'm sorry. I shouldn't be so rude. I have been under a lot of pressure at work and this is my only source of relaxation during the day." Peter's voice was soft and apologetic.

"That's okay Peter. We all are entitled to a bad day. I know you don't know me but sometimes it's better to talk to a stranger then a loved one when you are having a bad day."

Peter looked up at Beth and studied her face. He managed a weak smile. "Thanks Beth but I will be okay."

"Anytime, Peter. You seem like a really nice guy."

Peters smile broadened. "You think so?" it was obvious he wasn't accustomed to hearing complements from women.

"Of course I think so. Why would you doubt that?"

"I don't know. I'm not what you would call a ladies man."

"I have always been curious about that." Beth finally found something to talk with Peter about. He needed his self esteem brought up a bit and Beth knew that flattery would get her foot in the door. "What do men consider good traits to make a man a ladies man?"

"Well for one thing, I'm no GQ man. And secondly I must have the most boring job in the world."

Beth sat back in her chair and studied Peter's face. "First off Peter, not all women look for perfect eye candy when it comes to men. I am recently separated and my husband was the GQ type. I never really thought of him as handsome. I find guys who are a less perfect, more attractive."

Peter's eyes widened. "Less perfect?"

"Um, well let me rephrase that. I like guys who are more off beat then magazine men." Beth could feel her cheeks blush. "Let me rephrase that again because I don't think I am explaining myself very well."

Peter laughed. "It's okay Beth. I understand what you are saying."

Beth blew out a sigh. "Well that's good Peter. I thought I was going to have an aneurism if I tried to explain myself again."

Peter's eyes softened even more and he let his guard down slightly. "If you have an aneurism, I can find a cure for it so I could save your life."

"Is that so? Are you a doctor?"

"I'm better then that. I'm a scientist and I find cures for diseases." He sat up in his chair. It was obvious that he was proud of what he did for a living and rightly so. To do what he does can be so rewarding.

Beth was awestruck. "That is so interesting. Have you found the cure to anything?"

Peter nodded. "Yes but I can't disclose any of that. We are on a strict confidentiality contract."

"Now I am very impressed. And you think you aren't attractive?"

Peter cocked his head slightly at Beth. "What do you mean?"

"Let me clue you in on a little something about women, Peter." Twenty year olds may love to have a man who is GQ but women like me find it more of a turn on when a man can hold a conversation that doesn't include beer and hockey. In other words, GQ is good for the young but IQ is where it's at. " Beth smiled broadly. Her green eyes twinkled as she leaned closer to Peter. "What you just said to me was a turn on and I would go out with you in a heart beat."

Sweat formed above peters lip as he swallowed hard. Beth held her position hoping he would either kiss her or ask her out on a date. She hoped for the latter.

Peter lowered his head as his cheeks flushed red. "Thanks." He muttered. "You don't have to flatter me."

Beth leaned back in her chair and studied Peter's face. He was cute in an off beat sort of way. He was also shy and Beth had a feeling that he wasn't all that experienced with women. She turned the conversation in another direction for fear that he may bolt for the door any second. "I'm a lawyer."

Peter looked up at her. His eyes widened." What kind of lawyer?"

Beth didn't want to tell him the truth about her going back to criminal law. "Family law. I help people with divorces. Are you in need of a good divorce attorney?" Beth smiled.

"No not me. I'm not even married." He laughed.

"Do you have a girlfriend?" Beth was prying now.

"No girlfriend. Well I mean I had one but we broke up." Peter was hesitant in giving any further information.

"That's too bad Peter. Maybe you will find another girlfriend." Beth smiled as their eyes met.

She momentarily glanced over Peter's shoulder where Domenic was sitting with Jack. His eyes were fixed on her even though he was in conversation with Jack. Every so often jack would glance over at her to see what was so interesting for Domenic.

Peter nodded in agreement. "Maybe but I'm so busy with my work that it is difficult for me to find someone."

"What about the weekends? Are there places you like to go to on the weekends?" Beth asked. She was trying to get him comfortable with her and it seemed to be working.

They went from being total strangers to talking about relationships and personal enjoyments.

"That's a bit complicated." Peter took a bite from his meatloaf. His eyes momentarily closed as he savored the meat.

"Don't tell me you work on the weekends as well?" Beth said as she studied his face.

"No I draw the line on working the weekends." He quipped. "It's just very complicated."

"Oh, I see. You have your kids on the weekend." Beth knew that wasn't true but she wasn't going to let it go. She wanted to know what was complicated about his life. From what she read about him, his life seemed the least complicated of anyone she had ever known. It was so routine that you could set your watch by it.

Peter laughed. His eyes briefly showed warmth without sadness. "I don't have any kids either."

"So what's holding you back from enjoying yourself on the weekends?"

Peter narrowed his eyes. "You ask a lot of questions."

Beth blushed. She tried to find the right response. "I'm sorry Peter. I'm just trying to get to know you. I apologize if I made you feel uncomfortable. I think it has a lot to do with me being a lawyer. I'm always asking questions."

Peter watched Beth for any sign of dishonesty. Beth knew he was studying her. There was a brief moment of silence between them.

"It's my mother." Peter said, lowering his voice as if embarrassed by his words.

"Your mother?" Beth was puzzled.

"Yes. My mother lives with me and her health isn't very good. It's one thing to leave her during the day because I have to work, but I prefer to stay with her on the weekends so I can take care of her."

Beth had observed his mother that night. She didn't seem as if her health was bad. But according to the information they had accumulated on Peter, his mother had been sick. But she looked fine when Beth saw her getting out of his car. Why would Peter use her as an excuse?

"Are you married Beth?" Peter asked.

"I am in the process of a divorce. I think I mentioned that already." Beth stuttered.

"Oh yes you did. That's a shame that your marriage didn't work out." Peter said sympathetically. But his voice seemed full of hope. It was obvious to Beth that Peter was mulling over his next move now that he knew she was single and available. But he made no move to ask her out.

It was almost time for Peter to go back to work and Beth had not gotten a date with him. She was feeling defeated and a bit unattractive. When she was in university she was never without admirers. But here she was trying to woo some guy who was much younger than her and who was not what one would consider a ladies man. She wondered if she emanated the aura of a loser. Well she wasn't going to be defeated. If this guy wasn't going to ask her for her number then she would just have to do it herself.

"I better get back to work." Peter looked at his bill then took out his wallet and retrieved twenty dollars.

Beth bit her bottom lip. "Peter, I know we just met, but if you would like to go out sometime we could exchange numbers." Peter stared at Beth. His mouth slightly open and he seemed a bit dumbfounded by her suggestion.

"I haven't really met anyone since my husband and I separated and you seem like a nice decent guy. We could just go out as friends." Now she was sounding desperate and she could feel heat slowly rise from her chest and neck as her face flushed from embarrassment.

His silence was killing Beth. Did she overstep her boundaries? She was more rejected with each ticking second of silence. "Maybe it's a bad idea Peter. Just forget what I said."

"No, please, I would like to see you again. You're really easy to talk to Beth." Peter didn't want to forget it. He was attracted to Beth but he was surprised that someone as beautiful as her would even give him the time of day.

Beth smiled and pulled out a pen and paper. She wrote down her cell number and told him he could always leave a message if she doesn't answer. He in turn wrote down his cell number and suggested the same. "Maybe Friday night we could go out to supper." Beth chirped feeling less unattractive.

Peters smile turned to a frown. "Well Friday night I take my mother out."

"What about Saturday night?" Peter asked.

"I can't do Saturday because I have to pack. I bought a new house and I don't have much time to pack up everything."

They both went silent thinking of a time when they can work in a dinner date. "Where do you usually take your mother? Maybe I can meet up with you afterwards?"

Peter was hesitant to divulge that information. He seemed a bit embarrassed by it. "Well to be honest, I take my mother to bingo every Friday night."

"Sounds like fun! I haven't been to bingo in ages." Beth said with enthusiasm. She hoped Peter would suggest she tag along and her hopes came true.

"You're more than welcome to come along. It's not really exciting and not where I would consider on taking someone on a first date but you are welcome."

Peter gave Beth the address of the bingo hall and he glanced at his watch before wishing her a good day. "I'll call you on Thursday to confirm." Beth waved to Peter as he exited the restaurant. She watched him as he crossed the street and disappeared inside the brown building where he worked.

She glanced over at her grandparents who threw her a smile and a nod of approval. She leaned back in her chair and blew out a sigh. She accomplished what she set out to do. It was even better than she expected. Not only was she going out with Peter but she was going to meet his mother. It would be the perfect opportunity for her to find out exactly how sick his mother is.

"Who was the woman you were having lunch with?" the voice asked Peter as he retrieved his lab coat from the hook behind his office door.

"I just met her and were you spying on me?" Peter asked. Amanda startled Peter and he was not pleased that she was watching him during lunch.

"I wasn't spying." Her voice raised an octave. "I was walking past the restaurant and happened to see the two of you sitting there. I just figured you moved on after we broke up."

Peter rolled his eyes then turned to face Amanda. Her red hair was pulled back in a tight bun. Her lab coat buttoned, covering her dowdy flowered dress. "Look Peter, it's difficult enough to be in love with you and have to see you everyday at work. But do you have to flaunt your other women in my face and then lie about it?"

"Amanda, I'm not lying about it and I'm not flaunting anyone in your face. It didn't work out between us and if you feel uncomfortable about working with me then I can arrange a transfer for you to another department."

Peter was trying to keep his cool but his insides were churning and boiling. He ended the relationship with Amanda after she became too possessive and almost delusional with their relationship. She hated the fact that he moved back to live with his mother. And she hated the fact that he would not commit to a long term relationship with her. He had never wanted to get involved with a coworker. Especially someone who worked so closely with him but she kept insisting they become more than just colleagues and him giving in to her advances was the worse mistake he had ever made.

"Are you going to see her again?" Amanda's voice cracked as she fought back her tears.

Peter's eyes softened as he saw the sadness in her eyes. But he knew that if he gave in to her that it would be a disaster again. He had to stand firm. "Quite frankly, Amanda, I don't see how that is any of your business. And I would appreciate that from now on, any conversation between us is strictly professional."

Amanda blinked back the tears. "If I can't promise to keep our conversations professional what would you do?" Amanda moved closer to Peter.

Peter knew this side of Amanda. He knew her temper. He backed away slightly as he sensed the change in her. "If I have to, I will have you fired."

"You know you can't do that Peter. If you do I will bury you." A smile formed on Amanda's lips. Her eyes glowed evil.

Peter felt his heart drop into his stomach. He knew Amanda wasn't quite stable emotionally but he wasn't sure how much unstable she was. Would she really try to destroy him? He thought it best to not try to find out. "Amanda, you know I care about you. I just can't give you what you want in a relationship. You deserve so much more but I just can't give it to you." His voice was calming but he wasn't so convincing.

"Cut the crap, Peter! Just don't try anything stupid or else you will regret it." Amanda turned on her heels and went to the lab, slamming the door behind her.

Peter stood there, his heart pounding and sweat pouring from his forehead. He knew then that something had to be done about Amanda. But for now he would have to just focus on work and get through the day. He will worry about her later.

Chapter Three

Beth closed a box and sealed it with tape. She marked the word "kitchen" on the top with black marker and pushed it into the family room. It was two days since she had seen Domenic and she was feeling a bit lonely. She left work early to try to get some packing done and to focus her thoughts on something else besides him. But every time her thoughts would go back to Domenic.

Was she missing him? That was ridiculous. She hardly knew him. How could she be missing him? But she couldn't shake this feeling that she had for him. A few times she had picked up the phone to call him. But each time she hung up. What excuse would she have to make contact? She couldn't use her divorce as an excuse. He had that all under control and he would contact her if there was any news. She certainly wasn't going to call him up and ask him to come over because she missed him.

The last thing she needed was to get involved with a man who had secrets. She spent seven years married to a man with secrets and when the secrets came out, they devastated her. She wasn't about to put herself in that position again.

Beth checked her watch as she put her packing supplies away. She had made a small dent in the kitchen but knew that it was far from finished. Maybe I should leave some things for James, she thought. Then she dismissed the idea.

The thought of Jill using the things that she bought with James irritated the hell out of her. It was better for her to keep everything. After all, she would need everything for her new house. After looking at the five boxes she had packed, she decided to look into a moving service that would come in and pack everything for her. At the rate she was going it would take her six months just to pack all that she wanted.

Beth checked her watch as she picked out a white cotton skirt and tank top to wear. She covered the top with a powder blue sheer blouse. Peter had phoned her the night before to confirm their date. After her call she contacted her grandfather to give him the news. He assured her that some of the staff would be at the hall to keep an eye on things.

Beth suggested not having Jack and Domenic in that hall. Seeing that bingo was usually full of elderly people she said they would stand out like sore thumbs. Tom suggested they be accompanied with a few elderly couples as not to draw attention to themselves. Beth still didn't like the idea. Not just because of them drawing attention but she really didn't want to see Domenic. Her heart tugged at her chest as she dreaded the evening.

Although she was curious about Peter's mother, she knew that it would be difficult for her to spend the evening playing bingo while Domenic sat nearby. She made a sign of the cross and prayed that Domenic would have other plans with his secret girlfriend.

It was just before eight when Beth arrived at the bingo hall. The sun was still high in the sky and painted a bright orange as clouds were began to fill the sky. Just as he promised, she spied Peter standing outside the front doors of the hall, waiting for her. "Show time." She mumbled as she pulled herself out of her car, put on her best smile and walked towards Peter. Once he spotted her he smiled back. His smile was more one of relief. Maybe he thought she would stand him up.

Beth took the initiative and greeted Peter with a kiss on the cheek. This caught him off guard but made him feel more secure with Beth. She wanted him to feel comfortable with her and let him know that she was happy about this date. The kiss did exactly what she had hoped for. He put his arm around her waist and walked her inside the building.

The building used to house a family owned grocery store but went bankrupt when larger chains of grocery stores moved into the area. It was too difficult for them to compete so they closed the store and sold the building. It sat vacant for a couple of years until it once again changed hands and the new owners decided to turn it into a bingo hall. Seeing that most of the population in that area was seniors, they figured on making a killing.

They were right. Bingo had turned a big profit for them with having daily bingo game. But they made the big money on the weekends. This was also obvious with the amount of people who attended their Friday night games.

Upon entering the main hall Beth was amazed at the size of the room. Although it was a no smoking building, the smell of stale cigarettes hung low in the air obvious to those who were non smokers. The room was full to the brim with an array of characters.

There were the typical seniors who seemed to have reserved tables grouped together. There were the inner city people who would use every break to feed their nicotine habit. Then there were the few people like her who came with a friend or family member because they had nothing better to do on a Friday night.

In spite of the variety of people they all had one thing in common. They all hoped tonight would be their night to win the big jackpot. The odds were always in favor of the house as the jackpot would only go if a bingo was called within a certain amount of numbers. So most would go home disappointed and wonder how they were going to feed their three kids with what little they had left.

Beth always felt sorry for welfare kids. Spending time in family law, she was exposed to these types of people. There were some parents who had no choice but to go on welfare, but then there were the others who used the money for their own satisfaction and the kids were left with nothing. It's a shame that the system never monitored how the money was spent when it was given to these people.

"Are you okay?" Beth asked Peter as they walked into the room.

"Of course, why would you ask?" he replied.

"You seem a bit agitated or upset." Beth said.

"Oh, it's nothing. I just don't think this is the best place to take a date on a Friday night." He was a bit embarrassed by the show that he was exposing Beth to on their first date.

"I don't mind. I haven't been to bingo in ages so this is a nice change of pace." Beth reassured him.

A New Beginning for Beth

He felt a little more at ease after Beth assured him that it would be a fun evening and she was looking forward to it.

"Where is your mother?" Beth asked looking around the room.

"I hope you informed her that I was joining both of you." Beth said.

"Not exactly." Peter hesitated. "I told here that someone was joining us but I didn't mention it being a woman."

"Why is that?" Beth was curious to why he wouldn't divulge that information. It's not as if it were important.

Peter didn't answer right away, but Beth had already guessed it.

They walked towards the snack bar and moved closer to a small table which housed four chairs. Most of the tables were long and attached to each other giving the impression of a school cafeteria style set up. This table was small and it seemed out of place. There was a small elderly woman sitting alone at the table. She seemed much more petite than Beth remembered from the night she saw her getting out of the car.

She was busy checking her rows of bingo cards, trying to memorize all the numbers for fast dabbing with her red dabber. She looked up and smiled as Peter and Beth approached.

"Mother, I would like you to meet Beth." Peter said.

"Beth, this is my mother, Alice."

Beth extended her hand in friendship and Alice immediately cupped it in both her small frail hands. "This is a nice surprise." Alice said gleaming. "Peter never told me he was meeting a lady here, especially someone as beautiful as you."

"It is so nice to meet you Alice." Beth said with a smile. "Thank you for the compliment. Anymore of those and my head will swell."

"I took the liberty of buying you a few bingo cards and a dabber." peter said, pulling a chair out for Beth.

"Thank you Peter. That is very thoughtful of you." Beth said as she sat next to his mother.

"So Alice, I understand that you and Peter are regulars here." Beth asked.

"Every Friday night." She beamed. It was obvious to Beth that Alice loved her outing with her son.

"Peter takes you every Friday night or do you sometimes come with friends?" Beth asked trying to stir up conversation.

"Peter takes me but I don't think this is a place for a young man like him. He really should do something else on a Friday night." She frowned looking over at Peter.

Beth's glanced sideways at Peter as he rolled his eyes. "Mom, you know it's not a problem for me to take you."

"I know dear but my friends are more than happy to have me come along with them. Besides, you could have taken this pretty young lady out to dinner and a movie instead of to a stuffy old bingo hall."

Alice was embarrassing Peter. Something Beth was all too familiar with since her mother did the same thing to her on occasion.

"I don't mind really, Alice. I haven't been to bingo in a long time so I may need your help with all these cards." Beth tried to avert the attention away from Peter who was feeling slightly uncomfortable and out numbered by the two women.

"You know I don't want you taking the chance getting in a car with those people." Peter said. "Half of them shouldn't even be on the road."

I knew exactly what Peter was talking about. Especially after hearing the mishap that Sal had with his car and the optometrist office.

"Half of them can't even see, and it's just a matter of time before they wrap their cars around a telephone pole and they get their licenses pulled. I just don't want my mother in the car with them when they do." Peter told Beth.

"He is such a worry wart." Alice sighed.

"You're his mother and he loves you. He doesn't want anything to happen to you." Beth said feeling slightly caught in the middle of their disagreement.

Alice patted Beth on the hand and smiled at her. She could tell that Alice was beginning to warm up to her.

"So what's the first game tonight?" Peter asked trying to change the subject.

"By the look of the board it looks like a straight line or four corners." Alice replied.

Peter explained that each game had a different method of winning. There was a board that housed all the numbers called and next to that was a board that indicated the way to win.

"Sometimes you have to get a Z or an N or some other letter." Alice added. "And sometimes you have to get outside the free or around the free. Then comes the big jackpot at the end where you have to get a full board in thirty numbers or less."

"The odds aren't very good for that given that you have twenty four numbers to fill a card." Beth said.

"Twenty five if you count the free." Alice added.

"How much do you win if you get it in thirty numbers or less?" Beth was curious about this jackpot game.

Alice looked up at a lit board that indicated the jackpot prize. "If you get it within the thirty numbers you can win five thousand dollars. If it doesn't go tonight then the next prize down is three hundred."

"Sounds like a good prize to bring home if you are lucky." Beth said. "Has anyone ever managed to win the big one?"

"Agnes Rosebaum was the last one to win the big one." Alice said.

"She's a friend of my mothers." Peter said.

Alice grunted as if disgusted with the word friend. "She won it six months ago and spent it on sexy lingerie. Then she went out and got herself a new boyfriend."

Peter blushed and Beth's eyes widened.

"A new boyfriend? What did she do with the old one?" Beth asked trying to lighten the mood.

Peter and Alice laughed in unison.

"There she is over there." Alice pointed to a pink haired woman who was slightly overweight for her height. Her lipstick looked like it had been applied with a crayon in the dark and it was as pink as her hair.

"That woman has the pink hair." Beth blinked twice to make sure she wasn't seeing things.

"Doesn't she look ridiculous? She looks like a two dollar hooker." Alice replied. "And see the man sitting next to her?"

"The man that's sitting beside her with a miserable look on his face?" Beth asked.

That brought another laugh from Peter and his mother. Their laugh was exactly the same, Beth thought.

"He sure is miserable and it's his own fault." Alice said. "When Agnes won the money Charlie started to show interest in her. Everyone knows he was only in it for the money."

Alice leaned in closer to Beth and lowered her voice. "Once she and Charlie started dating, Agnes spent some of that money on sexy things at satin and lace. Everyone at the senior centre knows she is a bit of a floozy and from what I have been told; she is always demanding sex from poor Charlie."

"Okay mom!" Peter sighed. "I don't think Beth is interested in someone's sex life especially when that someone is over seventy."

As hard as she tried not to, Beth couldn't help getting a mental picture of Charlie and Agnes doing the bedroom tango and it wasn't a pretty sight. All those wrinkles intertwined made for sad viewing.

"Oh stop being an old stick in the mud." Alice huffed. "Don't you have some hotdogs to buy?"

Beth let out an uncontrollable giggle and flashed Peter a smile. "Sorry Peter, I think your mother has spoken. Besides, I'm only human and I love to hear some good gossip on occasion."

Peter blew out a sigh. "Beth, excuse me while I get some hotdogs and fries. Bottled water okay?"

Beth nodded to Peter and urged Alice to continue.

Alice turned her attention back to Beth. "You know, Peter doesn't like it when I talk about sex. What is wrong with this boy?"

Beth felt her cheeks redden slightly. "I don't think it's the sex conversation that has him upset. I think the fact that *YOU* are talking about it is what bothers him."

Beth knew exactly how Peter was feeling. Everyone always knew their parents thought about sex and actually did it from time to time, but there was always something taboo about them discussing their sex life with their children.

In spite of this, Beth was beginning to like Alice more and more. She didn't seem like someone who was not well. She was alert and witty and young at heart. Peter on the other hand was very uptight about anything his mother said or did. But Beth knew too well what the elderly can be like. She had her own two demons to deal with. And she spotted them three tables over sitting with Sal and Domenic.

What the hell was Domenic doing here? Beth thought. Well if Domenic was here to spy on her she was going to give him something to talk about. Well, at least to think about.

"I gather you and Agnes aren't friends?" Beth asked.

"On the contrary, we are best friends. But since she hooked up with Charlie we hardly see much of each other."

"Maybe when the money runs out Charlie will dump Agnes and she will come back to being with you."

"The money is gone but Charlie doesn't know that. Agnes won't tell him because she knows he will leave." Alice's mood became somber. "I feel sorry for Agnes. She never married or has any family. At least I have Peter and his older sister. Everyone at the senior center treat her like family. Even in spite of her rough exterior."

"Or her pink hair." Beth mumbled.

Alice chuckled. "And her pink hair. But it hasn't always been pink. She dyes her hair with the seasons. Come the autumn she will dye her hair orange."

"You're joking?" Beth wasn't sure if her leg was being pulled by Alice.

Alice shook her head. "It's the damnedest thing you ever saw. You think the pink is bad, wait till you see her orange hair. And on Halloween she sticks felt triangles in her hair and secures them with tape. She looks like a pumpkin."

Beth watched Agnes as she put a wet kiss on Charlie's' cheek and Charlie crunched up his face in disgust. That's what you get for being a gigolo Beth thought.

"I dare ask what she does for winter and spring." Beth shuddered.

"Spring time she chooses between yellow, blue or green. Depends on her mood I suppose. And in the winter she goes red for Christmas. I'm talking fire engine red."

"Please don't tell me she puts Christmas lights in her hair." Beth sighed.

"Not anymore. She tried it one year but she used those big glass bulbs. She didn't have any small lights. She burnt her scalp pretty bad. Since then she has had this fear of Christmas lights." Alice tried to hold back her laughter as she recalled Agnes running around trying to get the lights out of her hair. Smoke was billowing off her head as her hair started to singe and the smell of burnt hair filled the air.

Beth had to meet this woman. Not only did she sound kooky in her own right but she sounded fascinating as well.

"Tell me about this senior center." Beth wanted to find out more about Alice while they were alone. "Do you go there often?" Beth asked.

"Not as often as I would like to." she replied. "Peter likes to keep me a prisoner since he moved back home."

She leaned closer to Beth again. "But I do sneak out during the day when he's at work." she whispered.

"I heard that!" Peter said as he approached carrying a tray full of hotdogs, fries and three bottles of water. "And I know that you sneak out during the day."

"What's wrong with her going to the seniors club?" Beth asked.

"Nothing is wrong except that these people put ideas in her head. Look at the way she is acting tonight." Peter rationed out the food for everyone and stuck the tray at the end of the table.

It was obvious that he was quite annoyed with his mother.

"I see nothing wrong with her." Beth jumped to Alice's defense. "She is just a spry woman for her age and she wants to enjoy the life she has left."

"Exactly!" Alice said crossing her arms. "That's what I have been trying to tell him. Just because you don't have a social life Peter, doesn't mean I can't have one either."

Peter glared at his mother. Beth could feel the tension fill the air.

This was getting too uncomfortable for Beth and she glanced over at the exit. For a brief moment she thought of bolting for the doors but she needed to get to know Peter and bingo was about to start.

"Peter, would you mind getting me some jube jubes?" Beth smiled. She wanted to get Peter away for a moment while he calmed down.

"No problem." He snapped to attention and left the table to stand in line along with the last minute bingo players scrambling for snacks before the first call of numbers.

"Is he always like this?" Beth asked. She was concerned about the tension between Alice and her son.

Alice nodded dabbing all the free spaces on her bingo cards. "Ever since I got out of the nursing home he has kept me so close to him that I can hardly breathe."

Beth pulled peters cards closer to hers so she could keep an eye on them as the caller yelled out the game of one line or four corners. The room went quiet as the first number was called. Peter looked over at us and Beth gave him thumbs up to let him know that his cards are being checked. The people at the snack bar ran around feverishly trying to fill the orders as the

A New Beginning for Beth

customers were getting impatient at missing the numbers. Peter just stood back calmly, knowing that his cards were fine.

Peter didn't' care if he missed the entire game. He was just relieved that he was away from his mother for a moment.

Beth and Alice kept their eyes on the cards as they spoke. Every so often they would glance up at Peter who was still standing in line and glancing over at them.

"You were in a nursing home? I thought that was for the elderly who couldn't look after themselves? You don't seem like the type." Beth said making conversation in between the calling of numbers.

"I'm not that type." Alice stayed fixed on her cards. "But there was a time about a year ago that I wasn't able to take care of myself."

Beth glanced up at Alice who was busy dabbing away at her cards. "What happened?"

"I don't really remember much of it. But according to my son I had made a spectacle of myself and I had to be put in a home."

"Well I'm glad to see that you got better. But I still don't see how you making a spectacle of yourself would warrant being put in a nursing home. Unless he did it to punish you and I don't think Peter is that cruel." This was puzzling to Beth and she wanted to know more but she thought it best to not push the subject in case Alice got suspicious and mentioned it to Peter.

"How are we doing ladies?" Peter asked as he sat down across from Beth and handed her the candy.

"I think you need one more for a bingo." Beth pushed peters cards over to him.

"Well you did the work, you finish the game. Maybe we'll get it." Peter pushed the cards back to Beth.

"BINGO!" Alice screamed as she reached over and dabbed the number that Peter needed. Beth hadn't heard the number being called. It was a good thing Alice was watching.

A sound of disappointment filled the air as one of the helpers called out the numbers on Peters winning ticket. It paid thirty dollars which Peter split with Beth.

"I could use some of that luck." Alice said leaning towards Beth and rubbing her on the shoulder.

"Maybe you will be next. Beth replied

Alice shrugged her shoulders and glanced over at her friend Agnes. Her eyes lost the twinkle they had when Beth yelled bingo. "With my luck I would win and there would be at least half dozen others who would win at the same time."

"You want to rub my shoulder too?" Beth smiled at Peter. She leaned across the table to him exposing her cleavage. Peter felt heat rush from his toes that settled in his lower half at the sight of Beth's perfect cleavage. Peter's hand gently moved over her shoulder rubbing it for luck but more just for the opportunity to touch her soft skin.

Beth glanced over to wear Domenic was sitting and his eyes were fixed on their table. His mouth was moving as he conversed with her grandparents, but his eyes never wandered from her table.

Beth felt sorry for Alice. She seemed to have a negative attitude about herself. She also felt sorry for her being alone all the time. It was obvious that she missed Agnes's friendship now that she had a boyfriend. Maybe Alice wanted a boyfriend too? Maybe that's why she was always looking over at Agnes.

"Tell you what Peter. If it is okay with you, I wouldn't mind taking your mother to the senior's center once or twice a week."

Alice's eyes widened and she looked over at Peter. She had the expression of a child silently hoping her father would buy her the puppy she saw in the window.

Peter looked over at his mother. "What about your work?"

"I do a lot of my work at home so I can always drop her off and pick her up afterwards. Besides, I don't think it is healthy for her to be alone all the time." Beth winked at Alice who in turn flashed Beth a smile.

"I think me taking her would ease your mind." Beth added. "that way she wont be risking her life by riding with one of her friends."

"And it beats taking the bus." Alice jumped in.

"Well I can see that I'm out numbered as always." Peter smiled. "As long as it isn't a problem for you Beth, it won't be a problem for me. At least I will know she is in good hands."

Alice shook with excitement as she wrote down her phone number and handed it to Beth. Beth in turn did the same thing. Alice kissed the paper with Beth's number and tucked it safely away in her wallet.

"You're a very kind person Beth. I'm really glad I met you." Peter leaned over and kissed Beth on the cheek, catching her off guard. His kiss was gentle and warm.

Beth smiled. "Thank you Peter. That is very sweet." Beth reciprocated with a kiss on Peters cheek. Alice's mouth smiled brightly and her eyes twinkled with delight as she watched her son enjoy being with this new woman in his life. She liked Beth and was excited to know there was someone who cared enough about her to want to spend time with her.

Beth was right about her being lonely. Alice was tired of sitting in her small house day after day. But she hated sneaking behind her sons back even more. Ever since he cured her and took her out of that terrible nursing home. She hated upsetting him. Now he brought this angel named Beth into their lives and for the first time Alice felt as if her days were going to be better.

Beth glanced over at Domenic who was fixated on their table. His eyes widened when Beth and Peter exchanged their kisses. She saw his face turn a pale pink as he turned his head away for fear of witnessing anymore personal displays between them.

Good! Beth thought. She wanted to make Domenic jealous. Just as she felt jealous when he turned her down that day and wouldn't tell her what plans he had that were more important. But this game upset Beth. She had never been one to play childish games with men. But she found that Domenic brought out all these emotions that she never had with James.

She made a promise to herself to try and get over him. Once her divorce was finalized there was no reason why she would have to see Domenic again. In the meantime she would keep a distance between them by only seeing him when it was absolutely necessary.

The air was hot and sticky as everyone exited the bingo hall. Clouds were slowly moving in, covering the night sky.

"They call for rain tomorrow." Alice said as she watches the clouds move past the full moon. "I can feel it in my bones."

Beth observed Alice rubbing her arm.

"I had a great time tonight Peter." Beth said as they walked towards the exit. Alice grabbed Beth's arm when they reached the stairs and Beth instinctively held onto her as they descended the stairs towards the parking lot. Cars were jammed at all the exits as everyone fought to be the first out of the lot.

"I'm glad you enjoyed yourself. I promise next time I will take you someplace much less noisy and bright." He smiled as he watched Beth and his mother walk arm and arm towards the parking lot. It was obvious that his mother took an immediate liking to Beth. This made things easier for him. Unlike Amanda, Beth was kind and gentle. She didn't mind spending time with his mother. And also unlike Amanda, his mother liked Beth just as much. But he still didn't know her that well. He had to tread lightly until he got to know her better.

Peter didn't want to divulge too much about himself or his mother until he was sure of her intentions. At first he didn't think her driving his mother around was a wise idea. But he conditioned his mother on what is appropriate to talk about and what isn't. So far she was good at keeping quiet about their secrets so any qualms he had about this arrangement disappeared quickly.

"Maybe you should take Beth out for something to eat." Alice urged her son.

Peter looked at Beth for agreement. "Do you want to go out? We could drop my mother off and go for a bite to eat."

"After those two hotdogs and french-fries and candy, are you kidding? I won't be eating all weekend." Beth laughed.

Peters hope faded. "I guess I went overboard a bit on the food."

"You think so?" Beth laughed. "You bought me enough food to last me for the whole day."

"I guess I should take that as a no." Peter's voice lowered.

Beth saw the disappointment on his face. "In all honesty Peter, I would love to. But it has been a long day for me and I am a bit tired. Maybe we can plan something for tomorrow night?"

His face brightened at her suggestion of a second date. Then it faded again. "I can't. I made plans for tomorrow night. But I'm free on Sunday. Maybe we could do something then."

"Okay. How about if we plan for a picnic by the lake? Call me Sunday morning and we can decide then." Beth suggested.

Peter thought it was a great idea and agreed to phone Beth first thing Sunday morning.

They walked over to Peter's car and Beth opened the door for Alice and helped her in. Peter started the car and turned the air conditioning on full blast for his mother. He then walked Beth to her car. Beth beeped her car on and it started up without the use of the keys in the ignition.

"Remote starter, I'm impressed." Peter said as they stopped next to the driver's door.

Beth was feeling as awkward as Peter was. In all reality this was Beth's first date since her marriage ended and she realized that things never changed. That moment of uncertainty was still there when it came to saying good night on the first date. Should you kiss on the first date or shouldn't you. But Beth was a woman of the world. She was a successful lawyer and should just take the initiative and kiss him.

"I had a really great time tonight." Peter said taking Beth's hand.

"Me too, Peter. It was a fun date and your mother is so sweet. Thanks for introducing me to her."

"Thank you for putting up with her. And I also want to thank you for offering to take her to the senior's center. That is a load off my shoulders. Now I can go to work and not worry about getting a call from the police to identify her body." He laughed even though he was serious about what he had said.

"My pleasure Peter." Beth smiled as their eyes met.

This date started out as her finding out more about Peter but by the end of the evening she actually liked him. He was cute and intelligent and he loved his mother. His shyness made him even more attractive and Beth hoped that he was innocent in what he was being accused of.

She really wanted to see him again but she knew that if it turned out that he was involved in something, any hope of a relationship with him would be destined for destruction. She decided to worry about that bridge when she crossed it. For the moment she wanted to kiss him and plan for their next date.

They stood in silence as they watched the last of the cars take their place in line for the exit. There was no reason to rush out because they would have to wait in line anyway. Peter reached out and took Beth's hand. He suddenly pulled her close and kissed her on mouth.

His kiss was firm and wanting. She leaned against the car as Peter pressed his body against hers. Beth could feel how the kiss made Peter feel. It was obvious to Beth that if given the chance Peter would drag her into the backseat of her car and make love to her.

Peter had the same thoughts but it was their first date and he didn't want to come on too strong. He liked Beth and didn't want to scare her off. He would wait till Sunday before he pushed a little further.

After a few minutes of probing each others mouths they separated. They stared into each others eyes. Peter had Beth's face cupped in his hands. His fingers stroked her cheeks as he kissed her forehead. She liked his touch but she was a bit hesitant. So much for being a woman of the world, she thought.

"I better get my mother home." Peter said as their foreheads touched. His voice was deep and Beth felt a rush of passion through her body.

She nodded in agreement and gently kissed Peter on the mouth before they parted ways. She got in her car and watched as Peter walked across the lot. He looked back at her to make sure she was safely in her car and then climbed in next to his mother who was busy listening to the news on the radio.

"They expect rain tomorrow." She said as Peter put the car in drive and made his way to the line for the exit. "I told you it would rain."

"Yes you did mom. You definitely knew that." Peter replied not taking his eyes off the car in front of him.

"That Beth is such a sweet girl. What plans do you have tomorrow night that you can't see her?"

"I have to see Amanda tomorrow night." Peter said reluctantly.

The mood in the car changed. "I thought you broke it off with her. You know she is evil."

"I know mom, but I have to get things out with her. She is bugging me at work and is threatening me."

"Why don't you fire her? You hired her so you can fire her."

"It's more complicated then that mom. Let's not talk about it okay?"

Alice made a zipping motion on her lips and promised not another word.

Beth watched as Peter and his mother drove down the street. She had seen Domenic, Sal and her grandparents leave right after. Beth waited for an opening and pulled out of the exit and headed home.

She felt the evening was a great success. Peter and his mother both felt comfortable with her. She knew that Peter would never give her the information she needed. That was obvious. The answers lied with Alice. If anyone would know anything, she would.

She made a mental note to arrange a get together with Alice early in the week. Tuesday would be the perfect opportunity to see Alice. As for Peter, she knew that the date on Sunday wouldn't result in any information but she didn't care. She was excited to see him just the same. She made plans in her head on what to bring with her and what to wear.

She was still deep in thought as she pulled into her driveway and didn't notice the car parked in front of her house. As she exited her car, Domenic appeared from inside the parked car. He approached Beth as she was fumbling with her keys to find the right key for her front door.

"That was some kiss he gave you." Domenic said.

Beth dropped her keys as she realized he was standing next to her. "You scared the hell out of me!" Beth screamed as Domenic reached for the keys and handed them to Beth. She snapped the keys away from Domenic and he followed her to her front door. "I didn't think you were watching."

"I was watching everything." He replied. "How much money did you win?" He knew she was annoyed with him and he made an attempt to change her mood.

But Beth wasn't that easily swayed. She was still feeling the hurt of his rejection. "I won one hundred dollars including the money that Peter split with me. I split the money with his mother because she didn't have a bingo all night." She didn't make eye contact with him once for fear she would break into tears.

"That was nice of you." Domenic's voice was soft and mellow. He watched at Beth locked her front door, flipped on the hall lights and kicked off her shoes. He followed her into the kitchen and flipped the hall light off for her as she turned the kitchen lights on.

"Why are you here?" Beth asked turning to Domenic but still refusing to look him in the eyes.

"I wanted to make sure you got home okay. And I also wanted to apologize for the other day."

"You don't owe me an apology. You had other plans. End of discussion." Beth knew it wasn't the end and she also knew that he did owe her an apology. But she didn't want him to know how much his rejection hurt and embarrassed her.

"I believe I do owe you an apology and an explanation." He insisted.

"Look Domenic, you don't owe me anything, okay? You are my lawyer and you're representing me in my divorce. What you do in your private time is your business." Beth made the first eye contact with Domenic.

Domenic suddenly reached out for Beth, grabbed her and pushed her against the kitchen island as he wrapped his arms around her and kissed her with so much passion it caught Beth off guard. She at first resisted but her body quickly heated up and she welcomed the kiss and his touch. He held her close as they lingered against the kitchen island. She felt his body get hard as he pushed himself closer to her.

Her body tingled as he ran his hands under the back of her shirt and stroked her bare skin ever so gently and pulled her closer. Her arms instinctively wrapped around him and she held him as they kissed. After what seemed like an eternity, Domenic picked Beth up and carried her up to her bedroom.

His strength was over whelming for Beth as she wrapped her arms around his neck and kissed his ear and cheek. Her breath was heavy with desire as Domenic gently placed her on top of her bed. He watched her in admiration as she laid there, her eyes longing for him, her body quivering for his touch. He removed his t-shirt and Beth gasped at the beauty of his body.

His chest had just the right amount of hair and his stomach was firm and buffed. She reached for him and he instinctively came to her, covering her with kisses. He straddled her and sat up pulling her shirt and tank top off at the same time, exposing her breasts.

Domenic cupped her breasts. "Beautiful." He whispered. His voice husky and low with desire.

Beth pulled him close to her and he leaned down and kissed her breasts. His tongue played with her erect nipples and Beth moaned with delight as he gently took her nipple between his teeth and ever so gently tugged on it. He then moved down her body, kissing her stomach. His hands reached for her skirt and pulled it off exposing her white lace thong.

Domenic sat back to admire the woman before him. She was beautiful. He had thought of this moment from the first day he met her. His first thoughts were of her when he woke up in the morning and dreamed of her throughout the night. She had infiltrated his every sense and now she lay before him, wanting him. He couldn't resist any longer. He gently pulled her panties off and sighed with passion at her nakedness. His hands explored every part of her body. Her body moved with his touch.

A New Beginning for Beth

Beth put her hands in Domenic's hair. She ran her fingers through his silky black hair urging his face towards her. He knew what she wanted but he fought the desire. He wanted to explore her with his hands. He wanted to touch every part of her with his hands before he took her body with his mouth.

He lay on top of Beth, kissing her mouth. His tongue moved in and out of her mouth, feeling ever inch of her tongue and mouth. His mouth moved to her ear. His breathing was heavy and unsteady as he moved from her ear to her breasts. He lingered for awhile, flicking her nipples with the end of his tongue. This sent Beth in a frenzy of wild desire.

He moved down to her stomach, only staying for a brief moment before finding his way to her hot spot. She steamed with the longing desire to be kissed and licked. He obliged her by moving his tongue slowly and quickly as she moved her body up towards his mouth. Within minutes she exploded with the ultimate orgasm. Her body quivered and shook as Domenic held firm, his tongue still moving over her clitoris. She couldn't take anymore. She needed him inside her.

Beth wiggled away from him. She had never felt so much pleasure but her body wanted more. She begged him to go inside her as she reached for his pants and opened the belt. He removed his pants to expose the hardness she had felt. He removed a condom from his pants and Beth held his member as Domenic put on the protection.

Tears formed in her eyes as she felt his slowly push his way inside her.

Domenic saw the tears roll down her cheeks as he moved up and down her body. "Are you okay?" he asked. He was worried he hurt her.

"Don't stop." Beth begged. "Please don't stop." Beth held him tight against her pulling her legs up to allow him deeper access to her body.

Sweat poured off their bodies as Domenic moved faster, his breath getting heavier with each movement.

Beth felt herself orgasm again and she shivered under the weight of his body. Domenic was lost in his own passion as he pushed deeper inside her thrusting harder until his body exploded. He moaned loudly as his thrusts became slower. He whispered Beth's name as his body fell against Beth's, shaking and dripping with sweat. Beth held him close, lost in her own orgasm but enjoying his just as much.

If this was what making love was really like, she had been deprived all her life. Beth had never even come close to having an orgasm like the one she had just experienced, let alone have two. At that moment she forgot her anger and embarrassment. She forgot about her failed marriage or all her packing that needed to be done. Beth forgot about Peter and Alice and pink haired Agnes. Her whole world as she knew it didn't exist for that moment.

The only thing that existed was the man who held her in his arms. For that moment life was good and perfect. Just the way she had always wanted it to be. Beth lay awake, listening to the night birds as Domenic fell asleep. His arms still wrapped around Beth. Their legs intertwined. She moved a stray curl from his face and watched him sleep.

His eyes twitched as he went deeper into a R.E.M. sleep. She gently kissed his forehead and leaned back closing her eyes. As the night took her to dreamland, she smiled as she recalled the past two hours of love making. Domenic managed to make her come two more times and he came a second time as well. They tried every position possible. Even some she had never heard of. They continued until they fell into each others arms with exhaustion. Tonight her dreams will be filled with happy thoughts. Thoughts of her and Domenic making love every night just as they did tonight.

"Yes, life is good." Beth whispered.

Chapter Four

*B*eth *checked the time on* her alarm clock. Eleven thirty. She couldn't believe she slept through the whole morning. The sound of rain rattled against her bedroom window. She could hear Domenic in the kitchen and the smell of bacon cooking as she lay in her bed. She thought to join him but she would have much rather had him join her. Her wish came true as Domenic opened the door with one hand, while carrying a tray with the other.

A smile formed on his lips as he saw that Beth was awake. "Good morning sleepy head. I thought I would serve you breakfast in bed." He placed the tray of food at the foot of the bed. a white rose from her front garden was placed in a small crystal vase and added to the plates of toast, eggs and bacon. Domenic removed to rose and gently ran it from the top of Beth's head to the bottom of her chin. he stopped at her nose and lips so she could smell the perfume of the freshly picked flower and feel the velvetiness of the petals. He placed the rose in her bed hair, just behind her right ear then leaned over and kissed her on her left cheek.

He seemed too good to be true for Beth. She had never met anyone so handsome and romantic all wrapped up in one person. She had read about men like this. Mostly in Cosmo, but to actually meet someone like that, for Beth, was like finding the pot of gold at the end of the rainbow.

Domenic took a bite of toast and sipped his coffee as he watched Beth take a bite out of her eggs. "What are your plans for today?" he asked making conversation.

Beth sighed. "I need to find a company that will pack all my things up for me."

"I noticed in the family room that you attempted to make a dent in your packing."

Beth nodded. "Hardly a dent. I cleaned out two cupboards from the kitchen."

"I know a good moving company that can do that for you." Domenic said.

They ate the rest of their food in silence. Beth reached for a robe and made her way to the bathroom as Domenic gathered the empty plates and cups and placed them back on the tray.

"I'm going to take a shower. Care to join me?" Beth asked. Her voice low and inviting.

Domenic groaned. "I will with one condition."

"And what would that be?" Beth asked in her most seductive voice.

"We just shower. After last night I don't think I could get it up with a crane." Domenic removed his shirt and pants and stood there in his boxers.

Beth blew out a sigh and dropped her robe, exposing her naked body. "Suit yourself. Whatever you want Domenic." She wiggled her butt at him and went into the bathroom.

Domenic watched her from the side of the bed as she leaned over to turn on the shower. She was driving him crazy and he knew that he would need to be put in traction if he went into that bathroom.

"To hell with traction." He muttered. Domenic dropped his boxers and joined Beth in the shower.

Beth sat at the kitchen island as she watched Domenic load the dishwasher with the breakfast dishes. It was almost three and she was still tired. She also found it difficult to sit on the hard stools that lined the kitchen island, thanks to Domenic. The rain had stopped and the sun was peeking through the left over clouds.

A New Beginning for Beth

Domenic placed the dish towel over the small towel rack in the cupboard. "We never got a chance to talk about last night."

"I know." Beth smiled. "There is a lot we need to go through."

They walked into the family room and curled up on the leather sofa. "I didn't learn much about Alice except that if this woman was ever ill she is fine now. Also, did you know that she was in a nursing home? It was around the time that Peter moved home." Beth said.

Domenic listened intently. "Did Alice ever say why Peter put her in a nursing home?"

Beth shook her head. "From what Alice told me, she had done something that was quite embarrassing and this prompted Peter and his sister to arrange for her admission into a home."

"Are you planning on seeing him again?" Domenic asked. His voice and demeanor changed.

Beth wasn't sure if he was asking on a personal or professional level. "We arranged a picnic for tomorrow by the lake. But I gave Alice my phone number."

Domenic tilted his head at Beth. "Why did you do that?"

"It seems that Peter doesn't like the idea of his mother driving around with her friends. Apparently they went to the same driving school as Sal." Beth smiled. "So I offered to play taxi for her when she wanted to go to the senior's center."

"Good idea." Domenic commended Beth on her quick thinking.

They both agreed that if Peter was doing anything illegal then Alice would have some knowledge of it. This would also give Beth a chance to get inside their house without Peter there.

"Now that we have last night out of the way, what shall we do with the rest of the day?" Beth lowered her voice and moved in close to Domenic.

He instinctively pulled her close to him and kissed her on the forehead. They sat together, enjoying the quietness of the house and the comfort of each others company.

"Tom called me this morning while you were sleeping." Domenic said.

Beth sat up and looked at Domenic. "What did he want?"

"He is working on this case and asked me if the two of us were busy tonight."

"What did you tell him?"

"I told him that as far as I knew we had no plans. So I asked him what was up."

Beth knew immediately what her grandfather was hinting around to. "Let me guess. He needs help on the case."

Domenic nodded. "It seems that this man hired the agency to follow his wife. The wife has been going out every Friday and Saturday night for the past two months and she won't tell him where she is going."

"So he wants us to follow her?" Beth already knew the answer.

She had been on a few of these stake outs and sometimes they were fun. But she didn't feel like being on a stake out tonight. She only wanted to lay in bed with Domenic and spend a quiet night sipping champagne and eating strawberries. Tonight was a champagne kind of night.

Domenic could sense Beth's disappointment. "I'm sorry Beth. He really sounded desperate. How could I say no to your grandfather?"

Beth sighed and crossed her arms. "Easy, just say NO!"

"Maybe it's easy for you but your grandfather has a way of making me feel guilty. I don't know how he does it but he does."

"He used to be a detective and was considered the best interrogator in his division. He had a way of bringing suspects to tears. He could even make the innocent ones feel guilty. I know first hand because he used to try it on me."

"It won't be so bad Beth. We don't have to be there till nine." Domenic wrapped his arm around Beth. "Until then we can do whatever you want."

"What I want and what my body is capable of doing right now are two entirely different things." Beth laughed.

Domenic pulled her close and kissed her gently on the lips. "I know exactly what you are saying. As much as I would want a repeat from last night, I probably would have to ice my private zone for a week after that."

That brought a smile to Beth's lips. Not that she didn't have a smile before; she had been smiling since he showed up at her doorstep last night. It was the best night she had in a long time and she never wanted that moment to end.

"Oh, I forgot to tell you something." Domenic sat straight up and looked Beth square in the face. "I called around for a moving company. I found one that will come in and pack everything for you and once moved they will even unpack everything too."

Beth blinked twice. Was he too good to be true? James would have complained about spending the money and insist they do it themselves. Then he would find excuses to why he couldn't help and Beth would be stuck doing the whole thing. But Domenic was only thinking about Beth. "You did that for me?"

"Of course silly." Domenic pinched Beth's nose gently. "He is coming over first thing Monday to give you an estimate. I left his number above the stove if Monday isn't good."

Beth sat there in silence, staring at Domenic. This was all too new for her. All the attention he was giving to her. And the incredible sex she experienced. It was all too surreal for her. There had to be something wrong with him besides his love for family and corporate law.

"Are you okay Beth?" Domenic asked. "You don't mind that I did that for you, do you?"

"I really appreciate that Domenic. That was very sweet of you. And yes, Monday is perfect for me to see the guy."

"You seem deep in thought. I was a bit concerned that I overstepped my boundaries with making the appointment."

"It's not that. It's just that no one has ever done something like that for me before. Its going to take some getting used to." Beth smiled to reassure Domenic that she was very pleased.

"Is there anything else I can do for you?" Domenic asked. "Maybe give you a massage or run a bubble bath."

Beth knew he was kidding around with her but she felt that if she were to ask for those things, Domenic would do them for her without hesitation. She thought for a moment at what she would like. Then a thought came to her. "You know what I would like?"

"Tell me and I will do it for you." Domenic said.

"Now that I am going to be living on a farm, I would like a pet."

Domenic tilted his head. This was a strange request but he has learned so far that Beth was full of surprises. "What kind of pet are you think of?"

"Not a cow or horse but something small such as a cat or dog or maybe both."

Domenic jumped to his feet and pulled Beth up. "Get your shoes on girl. I know the place to go."

Thirty minutes later they were at pet land looking at the kittens and puppies.

"Are you sure that these dogs don't shed?" Beth asked the sales girl.

"I sure am. They are a cross breed. This chocolate brown one is a cross between a poodle and a shitzu. They call them a shipoo."

Beth held the brown puppy in her arms. He was so cute and quiet. His big brown eyes stared up at her as he nuzzled closer to her chest. "What do you think Domenic? Do you think he likes me?"

"How could he not?" Domenic smiled.

"I'll take him." Beth giggled as the puppy licked her face. "I would like to get a kitten too."

"We have some Siamese kittens on the other side if you are interested in one of those." The girl said as she took the puppy from Beth.

Domenic and Beth went over to the area of the store that housed the kittens. She peered in at three Siamese kittens sleeping in a cage. Two were curled up together and one was asleep with a furry stuffed rabbit. She was so cute that Beth fell in love immediately and asked if she could have the kitten's toy rabbit as well.

Fifteen minutes later they exited the pet store with everything needed to look after both pets as well as a hundred dollars worth of toys. Domenic put everything in the trunk and Beth placed both cages in the back seat. The puppy whined a little as the kitten slept threw the whole thing.

"Are you sure that kittens alive?" Domenic asked. "She hasn't opened her eyes the entire time we were buying her."

"The girl did say that she just had her needles and that she is a bit groggy from that. She said the effect will wear off by tonight and she will be up and playing in no time." Beth said peering in on the sleeping kitten.

"I just had a thought." Beth said. "If we are working tonight who will look after my pets while we are out? I certainly don't want to leave them alone the first night away from the pet store."

Domenic thought for a moment then pulled out his cell phone and made a quick call to Sal. After an exchange of words Domenic hung up the phone. "It's all set. Sal said he would be more than happy to animal sit for us. He loves animals."

Beth sighed in relief. Domenic came through once again. She was beginning to really like Domenic. But she dare not say the L word, even to herself.

Domenic turned the car around and headed for Sal's apartment. He lived on the third floor of the same building as her grandparents. It was a little known fact that her grandparents actually owned the entire building.

All the people living there were seniors and they worked for the agency. Their pensions didn't allow them the privilege of luxuries so her grandparents charged them very little rent in return for their expertise in law enforcement. All the seniors who live in the building are grateful to them for allowing them the dignity of having a nice place to live. But most of all, to be given the opportunity to do something constructive with their lives. Getting old doesn't mean you have to wait to die.

Domenic parked close to the entrance and helped Beth retrieve the cages from the back seat. They also took the food and kitty litter as well as a few toys for the animals. "This should tie them over until we get back." Beth said as they carried everything into the lobby of the building. Domenic rang Sal's apartment and he buzzed them in.

Sal lived on the top floor of the building. His apartment was similar to Beth's grandparents except that it had only one bedroom. All the seniors in the apartment shared in keeping the common areas clean. Like usual, Mrs. Woolworth was busy vacuuming the hallway.

She smiled when she saw Beth walking down the hall. "Beth dear it's been a long time." She said as she clicked her vacuum off and greeted Beth with a hug.

"Yes it has been Mrs. Woolworth. I see you are busy cleaning as always." Beth replied hugging her back.

"Oh yes one has to keep busy." She looked at the cages that she and Domenic were carrying. "What do we have here?" she asked peering in at the sleeping puppy.

"I bought a kitten and puppy today. Sal's going to look after them for me while I do a job for gramps."

Mrs. Woolworth backed away from the puppy cage. "Is it a male puppy?" her tone changed.

"Yes it is. Why?" Beth asked.

"I don't like male dogs." She frowned. "Ever since I was a little girl."

"My grandmother used to have a big male German Shepard and one day I was playing in her yard on a blanket and that damn dog came up behind me and mounted my back. It started humping wildly on me and I started screaming. My mother and grandmother heard my screams and granny grabbed a broom and whacked the dog across the backyard. It went flying in the air and gave out a large yelp when it hit the ground. My mother grabbed me and my grandmother chased that dog half way down the street." She gave out an involuntary shiver as she recalled that day.

"I asked my mother why the dog was trying to kill me. She told me that it wasn't trying to kill me, it was trying to give me a hug."

"Hug my ass. That dog was trying to screw my backside." She again looked down at the cage that Beth was carrying.

Beth and Domenic tried not to laugh. Although it was funny they could see how frightening it would be for a child to have a big dog do something like that to them.

"My dog won't grow as big as a German Shepard. And I plan on having him fixed before that ever happens." Beth assured her.

"Good plan." Mrs. Woolworth replied. "Get his nuts cut off before he knows what they're for and starts humping anything that moves."

Domenic stood there with a big smile on his face. He didn't dare jump in on the conversation for fear that Mrs. Woolworth would suggest the same for him.

"We better go Mrs. Woolworth. It was really great seeing you again." Beth hugged her and made a promise to not be a stranger.

"Oh before I forget. Tell Sal that he needs to get that hearing of his checked. Either that or turn off the price is right and put on the soaps. I'm tired of hearing come on down while I'm out here cleaning. I keep thinking that it's my time and it isn't god calling me."

"I'll let him know." Beth said with a laugh.

Domenic shook his head as he followed Beth down the hall. "She's quite the character that Mrs. Woolworth is."

"She's tame compared to a few of the people living in this building." Beth replied.

"I can hardly wait to meet everyone." He chuckled.

They arrived at Sal's door and knocked loud. As predicted, Sal was home watching television. He greeted them with a big smile.

He had new dentures but they seemed too big for his mouth. This made his smile seem more like the Cheshire cat in Alice in wonderland.

Domenic and Beth put the cages down and Sal peeked in at the sleeping animals.

Beth poured a litter in the kitty box and Domenic filled their dishes with their food and one dish for water.

"Now make sure when the kitten wakes up that you bring her to the kitty litter." Beth said. "You don't want her to have an accident in one of your plants."

Sal nodded. "No problem. I have had cats and dogs in my lifetime so I know how to look after them." He opened one of the cages and gently took the sleepy puppy into his arms. "Have you named him yet?" he asked as the puppy blinked his eyes open at Sal.

"Haven't thought about that. You think about a good name for them." Beth suggested.

"I always believe that the name should suit their personality. I'll come up with a few suggestions." He put the puppy on the sofa and retrieved the kitten. She was still sleeping. "What's wrong with the kitten?"

"She had a needle today so she is still a bit groggy. She should wake up soon." Beth said as she looked over at the kitten.

"She's a cutie. A Siamese cat?" Sal asked.

Beth nodded. "She's supposed to have blue eyes even as she gets older. It's hard to tell what color her eyes are. She hasn't opened them since I bought her."

"Thanks for babysitting while we do this job for Tom." Domenic said.

"It's the least I can do seeing that I made a good commission on that farm you bought. I'm going to buy a new television. Maybe one of those big screen plasma's." he smiled.

"Let me know when you get it and we can watch the hockey game together." Domenic said.

"You got it." Sal winked.

"Oh speaking of television, Mrs. Woolworth suggested you turn the TV down when you are watching the price is right. She is having delusions of ghosts and the devil." Beth suggested.

"That old bat is hearing things again. I wouldn't waste my TV time on the price is right. Maybe the devil is calling her down." Sal blew out a puff of air in disgust.

"I'm just the messenger. Not the complainer." Beth put up her hands and headed to the door.

She gave Sal a hug and promised to be back around eleven to pick up the animals.

"So tell me about this case we are on tonight?" Beth asked as they drove through the city.

Domenic reached into the back seat to retrieve the file on Dorothy McDonald that Tom had faxed over and handed it to Beth. Beth scanned through it, reading each page and memorizing Dorothy's photo.

"According to her husband, she took up bowling every Friday and Saturday night yet she doesn't own a bowling ball." Domenic said. "She leaves the house around seven every Friday night and doesn't come back until past one in the morning."

"How long as this been going on?" Beth asked.

"She had started this about a month ago. We would have gone last night but you were with Peter so this will be our first chance tonight. Domenic turned into the bowling alley parking lot and found an empty parking space in the front of the building. "If we play it right we might be able to solve this mystery in one shot."

Beth climbed out of the car and stretched her back. "I know this is a far fetched question but why doesn't her husband just follow her? Why hire an investigation service to do something he could do himself?"

"He can't. He's in a wheelchair and he relies on Dorothy for his transportation."

Beth scanned the information again." Is this age right?"

Domenic looked at it. "Yup, that's the right age."

"Says here that she is eighty six. What's up with that?"

Beth looked at her photo again. She had bleached blonde hair, teased and hair sprayed so high that it added six inches onto her height. Her face was lined from too much sun tanning and her makeup was colorful and there was plenty of it. Bright red lipstick was caked onto her weathered lips and her smile was similar in size to Sal's. They must go to the same dentist, Beth thought.

The photo was given to them by her husband and was professionally done. Burt sat next to Dorothy and had the same weathered skin. He was balding with strays of grey and wore large black framed glasses that covered most of his small face. He too had the same dentist as Dorothy and Sal. They looked like the typical couple that spent their summers up here and their winters in Florida soaking up the sun in some senior complex.

We were to act like a couple out on a date. We would make sure that we get a lane nearest to Dorothy just in case she really was there to bowl.

"I don't feel so good about this situation." Beth turned to Domenic.

"What do you mean? It seems like an easy case Are you afraid she might be packing?" Domenic smiled.

"I mean, what would a woman like Dorothy be doing having an affair? It just doesn't make sense."

"Don't you think senior citizens have sex?"

Beth was all too familiar with that question. And she knew the answer to it as well. "You know what I mean."

"It's like this." Beth continued. "There are a lot of seniors that join bowling leagues. Maybe she joined a league just to get out of the house. Based on what I read in the file, this Bert seems to be a bit demanding of her. She never goes anywhere and whenever she does go out it is mostly with her husband. A person can suffocate when they are with the same person day in and day out. Maybe she really is bowling and her husband is just sour because she wants a night out without him."

"You have a point." he said. "Whatever the reason we will find out tonight, or at least find out if she really is bowling."

Jack was watching for her to leave and phoned them as soon as she was on the road. He followed her to the bowling alley to make sure she was going there and waited until she parked her car. Beth and Domenic had positioned themselves inside.

They sat at a table that had a view of the entrance as well as the main shoe and alley rental desk. If she was meeting someone to go bowling with, they would surely see them renting shoes and getting their score sheet for a game.

Dorothy entered the bowling alley and they spotted her right away. They watched her as she walked up to the shoe counter and disappeared in the back room. Beth and Domenic looked at each other unsure on what to do then.

Domenic phoned Jack who was parked outside the building. "She disappeared."

"What do you mean she disappeared? I just saw her walk in the bowling alley." Jack said.

"We saw her too but then she disappeared in the back room. Are you sure she doesn't suspect being followed?"

"There is no way she is aware of that. Just walk around and see if you can locate her. I will keep my place here and watch the door. If she comes out I will phone you."

Domenic hung up and looked for Beth. She had already walked up to the counter to look for Dorothy. She waved to Domenic to get his attention.

"What can I get you?" a voice said to Beth.

Beth turned to respond and came face to face with Dorothy. She was wearing a staff shirt with her name embroidered on the front pocket.

A young man appeared from the back room. "See you next week Dorothy."

"Have fun tonight Steve." She said back to him and waved as she watched him exit the building.

Dorothy turned her attention back to Beth. "Sorry about that. Now where were we? Oh yes, what shoe size dear?"

Dorothy wasn't having an affair. She was working part time at the bowling alley. Guilt rushed through Beth's body as Dorothy stared at her. Her cheeks felt warm as she felt embarrassed and unsure what to say.

Domenic had joined her at the counter and was just as shocked at seeing Dorothy standing there.

"I'm sorry honey but I really need to know your shoe size if I am to get you the right shoes." Her voice hinted of annoyance and she was tapping her long painted nails on the counter.

"Size ten regular." Domenic said.

Dorothy turned and selected a pair of men's tens and placed them on the counter. "Your girlfriend seems to be a bit unsure what her shoe size is. Do you have any idea?"

A New Beginning for Beth

"I'm sorry." Beth stammered. "I was admiring your um nail polish. I love the color." She had to think fast.

"Thank you. It's called summer sizzle." Dorothy held up her hand to show off her fake hot pink nails.

"It certainly is a summer sizzle color." Beth said taking a closer look at Dorothy's nails. "I'll have a size seven regular."

Dorothy smiled and retrieved a pair of shoes for Beth. She sprayed them and ripped off a score sheet. "Two dollars each for the rental and each game is three dollars."

"Have you been working here long?" Beth asked trying to stir up a conversation with Dorothy.

"Not too long. Just a few weeks." She replied. "I came in here one night and saw the part time help wanted and I thought it would be a perfect way to make some extra money and surprise my husband with that remote wheel chair he needs."

"A remote wheel chair is a lot of money. How long will it take you?" Beth asked. She shot Domenic a look of "I told you so".

He just stood in silence pulling out some money to pay for the rental of the shoes.

"Our insurance pays for most of it but on our pensions it would be hard to come up with our part. So having this job is a godsend. I will make the money in pay and tips just in time for our wedding anniversary in the fall." She gleamed. It was obvious that she loved her husband.

Beth and Domenic were feeling guilty for even suspecting Dorothy of cheating.

"I'm sure your husband will love the surprise." Beth said as she took her shoes from the counter. She pulled a twenty out of her purse and put it in the empty tip jar. "This should start you out tonight."

Dorothy had a surprise look on her face. "Well that certainly will." She chirped with excitement. "A few more tips like that and I won't have to work till my anniversary."

Beth and Domenic thanked Dorothy for their shoes and went over to lane seven.

Domenic gave Jack another call to relay the information back to him and suggested he go to the husband and assure him that Dorothy is not cheating. He also suggested to tell him what she is doing but to make sure he doesn't let her know that he knows what she is up to. It would destroy Dorothy's surprise.

Beth got up and bowled a gutter ball and then managed to knock down a couple of pins with her second ball.

"I feel awful about this." Beth said as she sat down next to Domenic.

"Me too." Domenic said, tying up his shoes. "At least it has a happy ending."

"True. But it's a shame that Bert will know the secret. I hope he can act surprised on their anniversary." Beth got up and marked her score.

"Anyway, we are here so let's bowl." Domenic picked up a bowling ball.

"It's your turn." Beth said. "You have to beat my score of 2."

They arrived just past eleven to the apartment building. Domenic parked the car in one of the visitor's parking spaces. "I wonder how Sal made out with the pets." Beth asked.

"How difficult can it be? They are just babies. He probably had a great time with them." Domenic replied.

They rode the elevator to the third floor and as they got closer to Sal's apartment door, there was a loud crash from inside his apartment and it was followed by a high pitched yelping sound from the puppy.

Domenic and Beth quickly raced to the door. Domenic pounded hard on the door all the while yelling to Sal.

Sal opened the door and greeted them with a smile. His shirt had a large rip in it and had somehow managed to come untucked from his now wrinkled trousers. His grey hair was out of control. Beyond him laid the remnants of a lamp. All the pieces were scattered on the floor. He had the new puppy in his arms and was comforting it.

"What happened?" Beth asked taking the shaken puppy from him.

"Oh we had a slight accident." Sal looked back at the broken lamp.

"I can see that." Beth and Domenic walked past Sal into the living room. "Where is the kitten?"

Sal smoothed his hair back in place and tucked his shirt in. "That there little kitten is sure a lively one. She is full of spit and vinegar if you ask me."

"Well kittens are known to be active." Beth said, surveying the room for more damage and a wandering kitten.

A New Beginning for Beth

Just then they noticed the curtains begin to move and within seconds that little kitten made its way up the curtains. It dangled midway just hanging there. There were several tears in the sheers from previous climbs.

"Not again." Sal sighed and quickly moved to pick her off of the curtains.

"This little kitty sure loves to climb curtains." he said as he grabbed the bundle of fur and gently removed her from the torn sheers. It started to meow furiously and all her claws stayed retracted. Sal held her at arms length to avoid becoming like his tattered curtains.

"Would you mind opening one of those carrying cases so I can put her in?" he asked with slight panic in his voice.

Domenic quickly grabbed the case and held the door open while Sal shoved the wild kitten inside.

"Yup, full of spit in vinegar." He chuckled as he locked the door of the case.

Beth and Domenic surveyed the room. A plant was overturned and dirt was spilt out onto the carpet. Besides the broken lamp there were a few broken dishes as well as Sal's remaining supper lying on the floor.

"This place looks like a war zone." Domenic said. "What happened in here?"

Sal sat down on the couch trying to gather his thoughts and steady his nerves before answering. Beth was beginning to get this sinking feeling in the pit of her stomach that this kitten was a bad idea. She also wondered if the kitten wasn't drugged up for a quick sale.

He rubbed his hand which had several scratches. "After you left the little kitty woke up so I went into the kitchen and poured a bowl of milk for the puppy and kitten. I had left them both on the sofa to get acquainted seeing that they were going to be spending a lot of time together. The next thing I knew pickles was on the floor crying and claws was half way up my curtains."

Beth blinked twice. "Pickles and claws?"

"Pickles is the name I came up with for the puppy and claws is the kitten's new name. That's if you want to keep those names." He said.

Domenic was dying to hear this story. "Tell us what happened Sal."

Sal looked over at Domenic and then back at Beth. "The puppy wasn't hurt. I think he was more frightened by the kitten than anything.

I put the milk down for the puppy and I plucked that little kitten from the curtain. She was crying like she was afraid so I figured that she was just as scared of the puppy as he was of her." Sal's face turned serious. "I tried to cuddle her."

He put his hand on Beth's shoulder. "Don't try cuddling that little thing. She doesn't like to be cuddled."

"This story is getting interesting." Domenic laughed.

Sal turned to Domenic. "This is no laughing matter son. That kitten can cut you in two with those razor claws of hers if you try to cuddle her."

Domenic tried to put on a serious face but couldn't get past his uncontrollable giggling.

"That little thing ripped my shirt to shreds." He said while surveying the large tear in his once neatly pressed shirt.

"You know how much these shirts cost? These shirts don't grow on trees." Sal shook his head in disbelief.

"I'll buy you a new one." Beth said trying to calm Sal down. "Would you just get to the part when we heard the lamp break?"

Sal studied her face before continuing with his story. "Anyway, I held that poor kitten next to me and I guess she thought I was a curtain and started digging her claws into my shirt. Unfortunately her claws were also grabbing my skin and left some nasty marks on me."

He opened the tear in his shirt to reveal a big bandage that he placed on his stomach and chest. It was difficult for Beth to tell how bad the scratches were but from the size of the bandages, they seemed pretty big. Beth suggested he let her rewrap it and put some antiseptic on it.

Sal went into the kitchen and retrieved his first aid kit that he kept above the stove, and gave it to Beth.

She helped him remove his shirt and gently pulled at the strips of white tape. "Continue with the story while I fix you up."

Beth surveyed the damage of the scratches and came to the conclusion that buying the kitten may have been a bad idea.

Sal continued. "I put her on the floor beside the puppy. I thought once she saw the milk she would calm down a bit." He shook his head in disbelief. "She took one look at the milk and then at the puppy who was already drinking from the bowl and she hissed at that poor dog. He wasn't doing anything. He was just having himself a drink. He started to cry and I had to scoop him up off the floor to protect him from that fireball."

Domenic and Beth made eye contact. It was obvious that they were thinking the same thing. Sal caught wind of their facial expressions. "Oh don't get rid of her. She is a sweet thing really. She's just a bit territorial. Once I gave the puppy his own bowl she was fine with him. They both drank their milk side by side."

"That's a relief." Beth said. "These are pretty deep scratches so I will need to put a lot of antiseptic on them. It might sting a bit."

"I've been shot before so this is kids stuff." Sal said as he looked at the scratches. "I'll tell you about it sometime."

Beth soaked a cotton ball with antiseptic and gently dabbed it on the scratches. Sal winced as the antiseptic stung but then calmed down. Beth took out some gauze and folded it into long thick strips. She squeezed some ointment onto the gauze and placed it over the wounds. Then she cut a few small strips of first aid tape and put them over the gauze making a grid design so the bandage wouldn't open up.

Sal looked down at Beth's handiwork. "Looks pretty good but aren't you going to kiss it better?" He gave Beth a wink.

"No, that's Domenic's job." Beth smiled and glanced over at Domenic.

Domenic had his hands up. "I draw the line on kissing a man's chest.

Sal wrinkled his nose at Domenic. "After they were finished their milk I wanted to give them something to play with so I took a few of the toys out that you had left me. The puppy loved them. He was rolling around chasing the soft ball. The kitten only wanted to climb the curtains again. I think she just likes to be in high places." Sal glanced over at the curtains then back at Beth and Domenic. "I had to take her down seven times. "

"So how did the lamp get broken?" Beth asked.

"Well, nature made a call and I figured I would be just a moment. I left the bathroom door opened just so I could keep an eye on them."

"That's when the lamp fell over?" Domenic asked.

"The best I could figure out is that the kitten must have tried to climb on it and knocked it over. It must have scared that little puppy because he was just yapping in fear. That's what you both heard when you came to my door."

"Seems normal to me." Domenic said, scooping up the puppy. Pickles immediately started to lick his face.

"I'm glad that no one was hurt." Beth said, trying to find some sanity in this evening of bedlam.

Except for the curtains and lamp the only other injury was to poor Sal.

Sal and Domenic packed up all the animals' belongings and Beth placed the puppy in the other carrying case. "Sal let me know the cost of the new lamp and curtains as well as the shirt. I will be more than happy to pay for any damages. Besides, it's the least I can do after what you went through tonight." She hugged Sal gently and thanked him again for helping her out.

Domenic started up the car as Beth placed the animal cases in the back seat. The air was thick with humidity and the heat in the car was unbearable.

Summers in southern Ontario were unpredictable. The temperature during the day can range from twenty Celsius to thirty five Celsius. The evenings can dip as low as ten Celsius or be as hot and humid as it was now. The opened the windows and waited for the air conditioning to kick in before they drove out of the parking lot and headed back to Beth's house

They rode in silence as Domenic maneuvered the car down the deserted streets, occasionally passing another car on their way to some dance club.

"Can you get your money back on the cat? Domenic asked.

"Don't think so." Beth replied.

There was silence except for the gentle meow of the kitten.

"You don't think so or don't want to?" Domenic asked.

"I can get her declawed so that will help with the climbing problem." Beth said.

Domenic nodded in agreement. "But they don't do that until they are six months." he added.

More silence again.

"Tomorrow I'll get one of those climbing things I saw at the pet store." Beth added.

Domenic nodded again still staring out the front window as he pulled onto Beth's street and then into her driveway.

"You don't seem too worried about your curtains." Domenic took the bags from the trunk of the car and grabbed the kitten cage from the back seat.

"I don't plan on taking the curtains with me." Beth smiled as she took the puppy cage and unlocked her front door.

Domenic nodded. "Makes sense to me." He smiled.

Beth took the litter into the laundry room and filled the cat tray up. She sprinkled some litter deodorizer on top of the litter and pulled the sleepy kitten out of the case and placed her in the litter. Claws sniffed around the litter then scratch a little hole and did her duty. She then covered it with some more litter and sat down in the litter.

Domenic had taken the puppy outside in the backyard and he did his little duty in a small patch of grass. Beth had filled their dishes with fresh food and filled two bowls with water. Domenic showed the pickles his food while claws munched away at hers.

Beth and Domenic watched the two animals as if they were parents watching their children walk for the first time. "So this is motherhood." Beth said. "I guess it's not just me anymore."

"How do you suppose Sal came up with the name pickles?" Domenic asked. "I can see how he came up with claws for the cat. But pickles?"

Beth thought about it for a moment then came to the conclusion that there were some things best left unknown. She didn't care to know but did like the name. "It doesn't matter. I'm keeping the names. I think they are perfect."

Domenic nodded and kissed her. "I better get going so you and your children can get some rest."

Beth actually expected Domenic to stay but she was glad that he was going to leave her alone with her new babies so they could get acquainted. "Thanks Domenic. Besides I have a date tomorrow with Peter." Then a thought came to her. What was she going to do about her pets?"

Domenic promised to come by and look after them while she was out with Peter. "Aren't you going to make sure Peter doesn't try anything with me?" Beth asked pulling him close to her. She kissed him on the neck which got a reaction from Domenic.

"I think you will be safe with half the seniors arranging a big picnic right next to the two of you." Domenic replied in between kisses. His hands moved from Beth's waist to her behind. Domenic squeezed it as he pulled her close to him. Then he stopped and noticed four eyes staring at them.

Beth turned around as she saw her kitten and puppy staring at them. "Maybe we shouldn't do this in front of the children."

"Maybe you're right." Domenic laughed kissing her on the nose. "I'll say my goodnight now."

Chapter Five

*B*eth *was sitting in here* kitchen reading the Sunday paper. She sipped on her tea as she watched claws climb the family room sheers. Once she reached the top she would cry for Beth to help her down. Being a good mother, Beth would pick her from the curtains, pulling each paw out of the torn sheers and place claws on the carpet next to one of her toys.

"Stay there and behave." Beth would scold claws. But as soon as she went back to her paper, the kitten would make her way back up the curtains only to cry to be rescued again.

The puppy was running around chasing a sponge ball. He would yap at the ball then nudge it with his nose to make it move and then chase after it only to catch it, roll around on the floor with it and then start the whole process over again. If only humans could find interest in little things, Beth sighed as she watched her new pets play to their hearts content.

Domenic arrived around eleven and let himself in the unlocked front door. "Good morning!" He yelled from the entrance as not to startle Beth. Pickles ran down the hall barking at the top of his lungs. He went from playing with a ball to being protector of Beth. As soon as he reached Domenic his tail wagged wildly and whined until Domenic picked him up in his arms.

Domenic walked into the kitchen where Beth was sitting and kissed her on the cheek. "Are you ready for you big date?"

"As ready as I'll ever be." She replied. "I'm going to pick up some KFC for our picnic and I have a bottle of white wine in the refrigerator."

"Sounds like a romantic picnic." He said as he made himself a coffee.

Beth narrowed her eyes at him "are you jealous?"

"Me jealous? Very unlikely. I just don't want you to get yourself in a situation that you can't get out of." He was lying and they both knew it. Domenic had developed deep feelings for Beth but he knew that a woman like Beth doesn't like to be rushed. She needed to be handled delicately and that took time. She was burned badly when her husband left her and the last thing she needed right now was more complications.

Domenic put his cup of coffee next to Beth walked into the family room and pulled the kitten from the sheers. "She's quite the climber."

"She sure is." Beth said watching the whole display.

"She did quite the number on these sheers." Domenic examined the damage claws did to the white sheers.

"She sure did." Beth beamed.

"If I didn't know any better I would think you were proud of that." Domenic remarked, putting the kitten back on the floor and giving her a small toy mouse to play with.

"Have you ever seen a cat climb faster? Of course I'm proud."

Domenic studied Beth's face. He wasn't sure if she was joking or serious. He thought it best not to ask anymore questions. "So what are you planning on wearing to this picnic?"

"I haven't decided. What do you think I should wear?" Beth was curious to know why Domenic was so interested in her fashion but deep down she knew the answer.

"How about jeans and a t-shirt." He suggested.

"How about a pair of hot pants and a bathing suit top?" Beth laughed.

"Don't even joke about that. If you show up in something like that he will be all over you like white on rice. And I won't be able to help you pull him off."

"I know that. You will be here babysitting the babies." Beth smiled.

A New Beginning for Beth

Domenic's face went stone cold. He wasn't hiding his jealousy very well and Beth picked up on it right away.

"Don't worry Domenic. I am planning on wearing sweatpants and a tank top. Nothing too sexy but nothing too drab either." Beth leaned over and kissed him. "I don't have to meet him for a couple of hours." She whispered in his ear.

Domenic felt his body heat up. She had a way of making him hot like no other woman could. But he resisted. "What kind of man do you take me for?"

Beth pulled back and looked at him. She was confused. "What do you mean by that?"

"Oh sure Beth, you make love to me and then go off on a picnic with another man, leaving me behind to care for our children." He crossed his arms and acted insulted.

Beth sat there in silence just staring at him. She wasn't sure how to take that. "I didn't mean it that way. You know very well that this picnic is strictly business." Beth stood up and wrapped her arms around him. "Tell you what. When I get back why don't we do something together?"

"Like what?" Domenic asked. He was playing the wounded soldier now.

"Anything you'd like. I will leave it up to you." She smiled, hugging him closer.

Domenic put his hands are her arms and stroked them gently. He loved the way she felt next to him. He loved the way she made him laugh and how she tried to comfort him. Domenic, you're falling too fast, he thought to himself. But he liked where he was falling and he didn't want to stop.

"Okay Beth. I will come up with something nice for us tonight." He took her hand and kissed it gently on the palm.

Beth felt a rush of passion go through her body. No one had ever kissed her palm before and she thought it was the most romantic and loving display of affection she had ever experienced. She held that hand up to her mouth as if to transfer the kiss to her lips. She stroked his hair with her other hand.

"Are you sure you don't want to take advantage of this free time?" she asked again.

Domenic looked at her. "In all honesty I would in a heart beat. But I want tonight to be special so I would rather save my energy for then."

Beth's heart jumped. The dormant butterflies that lay sleeping in her stomach woke up and fluttered wildly. She had never met anyone like Domenic. He was every woman's dream all wrapped up in gorgeous paper. And he wanted her. She felt so loved at that moment that she was feeling guilty about going out with Peter. But she knew she had to do it. And Domenic knew it as well.

"I better go get ready." Beth said.

"I think you should too." His voice was husky with desire.

Beth had picked up the food for the picnic and grabbed some ice from the corner store. She took the time to pour the ice in a small cooler that she put in the trunk of her car and put the bottle of wine in the ice as well as a variety of soda's and the salads. Peter was bringing a blanket and radio and a Frisbee.

She arrived at the park thirty minutes before Peter, to scope out the right place. She saw the first few seniors arriving at the park. She knew most of them from the agency. She watched as Sal struggled to carry a cooler to their designated picnic area and place it on one of the tables that they pulled together.

"I won't be without backup." Beth mumbled to herself as she watched her grandparents get out of their car just across from hers.

They looked over at her and gave a subtle wave in her direction. She raised her fingers off the steering wheel to acknowledge them. She didn't want to make too much out of it in case Peter had already arrived and was watching for her.

Then she spotted Peter's car pull up. She checked her watch and sure enough he was on time. One o'clock to be exact. He sure is punctual, she thought.

He opened his trunk and pulled out a blanket and radio. He slipped a yellow Frisbee under his arm and slammed the trunk. Turning, he scanned the parking lot for Beth. She had already got out of her car and was waving to him. A smile formed on his face as he spotted her across the lot and he walked over to greet her. She took the initiative and welcomed him with a kiss. This caught him off guard and his face flushed under the bright sun.

"So what did you bring for food?" he asked as he peered inside the opened trunk of her car.

"Nothing fancy, just KFC." She replied as she took the blanket and radio from him.

Peter pulled the cooler from the trunk and Beth slammed it shut. He motioned for her to put some of the things on top of the cooler so she wouldn't have to carry everything. She obliged his suggestion and they walked over to a nearby table which was conveniently unoccupied under a huge maple tree.

The seniors were gathering about one hundred feet away and Peter wrinkled his nose as the lack of privacy. "Maybe we should find a more secluded spot."

Beth glanced over at the elderly people who were laughing and talking amongst themselves. "This spot is fine with me. The park is pretty crowded and if I had to be stuck next to anyone during our picnic, it might as well be seniors. There's no chance that their football would accidentally smash into our food."

"You have a point there." Peter replied.

"Besides, they are too busy with each other to notice us." Beth said as she unpacked the food and placed it on the table.

Peter laid out the blanket near the table, removing any branches or rocks that were in the way.

Beth watched him as he smoothed out each corner and stood back to survey his work.

He was definitely a perfectionist. Beth would have just thrown the blanket down and worried about anything in the way, afterwards. He reminded her lot of her ex-husband in that department.

Peter came over to join Beth at the table.

"Are you hungry?" Beth asked as she opened the tub of chicken.

"Starving." Peter replied peeking in at the pieces of chicken and pulling out a leg.

Beth placed some fries on his plate as well as her own and then handed him one of the salads. Peter scooped up some macaroni salad and filled the empty space next to his fries, being careful not to allow the hot food to touch the cold food.

Beth watched him out of the corner of her eye. Definitely her ex-husband, she thought as the hairs on the back of her neck stood up. Peter was beginning to look a lot less attractive to her as the day progressed. This was a bad thing for Peter but a good thing for Domenic, Beth thought.

They ate quietly only to comment on the food or the weather. Beth realized that her and Peter had nothing in common and he would not be someone she would want to see again. But she was there with him for one reason only. And that was to get him comfortable with her so he would let his guard down and maybe confide in her. But what was he going to confide in her about?

If he was doing anything illegal she would be the last person he would tell. Maybe her being a lawyer may make it easier for him to tell her things he would not normally say to anyone. Either way she knew she had to convince him of her interest.

"Are you enjoying yourself?" Peter asked.

"Of course, why do you ask?"

"You seem deep in thought. I got the impression you would rather be somewhere else."

"I'm sorry about that. I have a lot on my mind with my work, my upcoming divorce and my moving to a new place in a month." Beth apologized.

Just then, Peter's face went white. Beth looked over her shoulder to see what made his expression change. She noticed a red haired woman walking up from the parking lot and coming towards them. "Are you okay? You look like you had just seen a ghost."

"Not a ghost. Just someone I know." He answered, getting to his feet. "Excuse me a moment, Beth. I'll be right back."

She watched as Peter met the red haired woman half way between their table and the parking lot. Beth looked over at her grandparents and casually signaled to them to check it out, but they were already ahead of her. Two people were walking towards them looking as if they were walking towards their car. They had seen her arrive shortly after Peter and decided to jot down her license plate number so they could check it out later.

As they passed they could over hear them arguing. Peter was accusing her of stalking him and she was accusing him of lying to her about the woman he was with.

Peter looked over at them as the passed by but the woman didn't take her eyes off of him. She was angry and Beth could see her anger even from her distance.

Suddenly the woman slapped Peter across the face, knocking his glasses off. He quickly retrieved them from the grass and grabbed her hand before she could slap him again.

"I will phone you tonight and we will talk about it then." He said trying to calm the hysterical woman.

"There is nothing to talk about. I have had it with your lies. I'm going to destroy you!" she screamed. Beth watched her as she turned and walked back to her car.

The woman noticed the two elderly people loitering around her car and told them to get away from her car. She then climbed in, revved the engine and squealed out of the parking lot, throwing stones in her path.

Peter stood there watching her disappear through the gates. He looked back at Beth who had seen the whole episode. He wasn't sure if he should go after the woman or just forget the whole thing and try to enjoy the rest of the day with Beth.

Beth walked over to Peter. "Who was that woman?"

"She's my ex girlfriend." Peter said lowering his head in embarrassment.

"She didn't act like an ex girlfriend. She acted more like a woman who caught her boyfriend cheating." Beth remarked.

"She's an ex, trust me on that. She just won't accept the fact that I don't want to date her anymore."

"You know you can press charges against her for assault. I was a witness to this and so were half the people in the park." Beth suggested.

Beth took hold of peters hand in a sign of support. "She has enough problems. I would never add to it by having her charged."

"Suit yourself Peter. But let's forget about her and just enjoy the rest of the day." Beth pulled Peter back to the table.

Peter resisted for a moment, staring at the lot to make sure the woman didn't return. Then he gave in to Beth and returned to the table to finish off his food.

"Maybe you won't see her anymore, now that she has seen that you have moved on." Beth said as she took some fries and dipped them in the gravy.

"I wish that were true." Peter said not looking up at Beth.

"Why wouldn't it be? Do you think she is stalking you?"

"It's worse than that." Peter said. "She works with me. She's my assistant."

Beth sat there in silence, staring at Peter. "You mean to say you went out with your assistant? Are you nuts?"

Peter's eyes met Beth's. "I'm beginning to think I am."

It was obvious to Beth that Peter was in a bad situation. Although she didn't hear the extent of the conversation, she did manage to hear the last part, thanks to the woman losing all sense of reality and screaming at the top of her lungs. She thought about keeping it to herself but was curious as to know why she threatened to destroy Peter.

"What did she mean when she said she was going to destroy you?" Beth asked.

The color rushed to peters cheeks. "You heard that?"

"Who couldn't hear it? She screamed it loud enough." Beth said assuring Peter she wasn't eavesdropping.

"I have no idea, but she probably will complain about me to my superiors and try to have me fired." Peter didn't seem too worried about it.

"Can she do that?" Beth asked.

Peter shrugged his shoulders. "I'm not sure. Probably, but they won't take her seriously."

"If she does, let me know. I can help you with any legality concerning your rights." Beth suggested.

Peter didn't seem too concerned with the woman's threats. This made Beth curious but she chose to drop the subject. Knowing her grandparents connections, she would have all the information on the woman, by the end of the day. In the meantime she would just focus on Peter.

It was past six by the time Beth arrived home. Peter wanted to see her tonight, but she used the excuse of packing her things, as a way to get out of it. She did promise to meet for lunch once she knew her schedule for work. He promised to call her later on Monday.

"How was your date with Peter?" Domenic asked as he greeted Beth at the door.

"It was interesting to say the least." Beth said as she placed the cooler in the foyer.

Domenic picked up the cooler, emptied it of any left over food, and placed it in the garage.

Beth took the leftovers into the kitchen placed some chicken on a plate for Domenic and put the rest in the refrigerator for later.

Domenic joined Beth in the kitchen took a piece of chicken from the plate and bit into it. "What did you learn today?"

Beth made herself a tea. "Peter had an office romance that went sour."

Domenic stared at Beth. "Is that so? And he told you this?"

Beth shook her head. "He didn't have to. She showed up to confront him."

"That must have been a sight."

"It sure was. If Peter hadn't intercepted her halfway between the parking lot and me, she probably would have torn my hair out."

Domenic smiled. "I doubt if she would have got a punch in. I'm sure you could have taken her."

Beth laughed. "She was pretty hysterical. She made a scene in front of everyone at the park."

Beth's voice softened. "I felt bad for Peter. He was so embarrassed."

"Did he talk to you about it?" Domenic asked.

"No and I didn't push the subject. But there was one thing that puzzled me about the conversation they had." Beth's face turned serious.

Domenic's curiosity peaked. "What was that?"

"Before she left, she threatened to destroy him. I asked Peter about it but he didn't seem too concerned about her threat." Beth sipped her tea.

It was obvious to Domenic that this bothered Beth. "What were your feelings about it?"

"I think that this woman is worth watching. And I think she has something on Peter."

"If that were true, why wouldn't Peter be concerned?" Domenic asked.

"That's just it. He didn't seem concerned but the rest of the day he kept looking at his watch and at the parking lot. I think he was worried." Beth replied.

"Is that your professional opinion or is it one of those women intuition things?"

Beth narrowed her eyes at Domenic. "If you must know, my gut is telling me this. And my gut is usually right."

Domenic moved closer to Beth. He leaned in and kissed her on the neck. Beth closed her eyes and let out a soft whisper of a sigh. At that moment she realized that she missed Domenic's touch all day. It was nice opening her door and finding him standing there to greet her. It felt comfortable and not at all an intrusion.

"What does your gut tell you about me?" he whispered between kisses.

Her gut told her a lot of things about Domenic. But it wasn't her gut that was speaking right then. It was another part of her anatomy and it was screaming feelings to her. This worried Beth. She didn't want her friendship with Domenic to be ruined over her passion for him. And she wasn't sure Domenic was the kind of guy who could have friendship with the woman he was sleeping with. Everything was moving too fast between the two of them.

Domenic stopped kissing Beth and looked into her eyes. "You're thinking too much." He said, slightly annoyed.

"How can you tell?" she sounded surprised.

"You bite your bottom lip when you are deep in thought." he pulled away from her and went back to his chicken. "Care to share your thoughts with me?"

Beth lowered her head. "What is happening between us Domenic?"

Domenic cocked his head at Beth. "What do you mean?"

A typical man, Beth thought. Has no clue on what is going on. "You know what I mean. We barely know each other and we have slept together."

"You make it sound like something dirty." He replied.

"It's not normal. I usually like to date a man a couple of months before I agree to sleep with him." Beth was getting annoyed.

A New Beginning for Beth

"Is that what you want? Do you want to date a couple of months and then we can have sex?" Domenic was being sarcastic and Beth didn't like it.

"Is that how you started dating James?" he asked.

"What does James have to do with it? And yes, as a matter of fact, James and I dated six months before we slept together." Beth snapped.

"And where did that get you?" Domenic asked.

"I'm not enjoying this conversation." Beth stood up and moved away from Domenic.

"I didn't mean it like that, Beth. Have you ever just thrown caution to the wind?"

"Caution to the wind? I bought a farm with a cemetery for Christ sake and I can't even grow a tulip to save me life! I give silk plants silk worm!" Beth was on the edge of hysteria and Domenic was about to push her over.

Domenic shook his head." That's not what I meant. Have you ever just done what your body wanted regardless of the outcome?"

Beth had never led a promiscuous life. She never had a one night stand. As a matter of fact, she had only been with four men including James and Domenic. Not enough to make her a slut but enough to know what made her feel good. The other two relationships were while she was in school. One during the end of high school and they only had sex once. The other was before she met James.

He was the university catch and Beth was his girlfriend. He looked good on her arm but he was as dull as a broken pencil. He was the first to give her an orgasm and Beth realized half way through the relationship that besides his looks, his knowledge in bed was the only thing that kept her from ending the relationship. Then she met James.

He was easy to talk to and they had the same things in common. It was a good relationship during their dating days. But when it came to love making, he was too preoccupied with his own pleasure to even consider hers. She knew this going into the relationship but had an unrealistic idea that he would loosen up once they were married. But things only became worse.

Beth destined herself into believing that her sex life would never be anything more than a few minutes a month without stimulation for herself. That was until she met Domenic. In the short time she had known him he made her feel like a woman again. Not just physically but also mentally. He stimulated her like no one had ever done before. And now here she was, wondering if he was only looking for a good time without the long commitment. But Beth wondered if she was looking for the same thing.

Did she want to jump into a serious relationship so quickly after her separation? If she did, it would certainly be with Domenic. But she was unsure. Unsure of her needs and unsure of what Domenic wanted from her.

After some thought, she knew Domenic was right. "I'm not one of those women who run with scissors and I don't know if I'm capable of doing so." She tried to find some calm and order in her jumbled thoughts.

Domenic studied her face. Unlike himself, Beth was definitely the one man, one woman type. He could deal with that because Domenic was feeling that Beth was worth it. "I'm not going to push you into something that you don't feel comfortable with." He reached out and touched her face. "Besides, I don't think you are the type to be swayed too easily."

He was smiling at her and she was feeling frustrated with him and with herself. "Thanks Domenic, I really appreciate that." her tone hinted sarcasm but Domenic ignored it.

He gently kissed her on the lips. "It's been a long day. Maybe you need some time alone with your pets."

Pickles and claws were curled up in a small pillow that Domenic had placed on the floor. They had become friends while she was out with Peter and she missed it. Beth felt as if she had missed her baby's first steps. "I see they are getting along now."

Domenic looked over at the sleeping animals. "They sure are. But it wasn't easy. Claws wouldn't sit still long enough to get acquainted with pickles."

"I need some time Domenic. I need time to sort out my life before I can devote any time to someone else." Beth didn't look up at Domenic who stood silently beside her.

He nodded his head. "I understand Beth and I won't push myself on you. You decide when the time is right and I will wait."

A New Beginning for Beth

Beth felt a tear roll down her sun burnt cheeks. Domenic saw the sadness in her eyes and wanted to kiss it away but all he could do was kiss her tears away. He made a promise to himself to never let Beth feel sad and confused. He really cared for her and it made his heart ache when he saw her so melancholy.

"I better get going." He said as he walked towards the door.

Beth followed close behind. "Thanks for babysitting for me Domenic. And thanks for understanding."

"Anytime baby." He said leaning in to kiss her.

He called her baby and it sounded so comfortable. Boyfriends sometimes call their girlfriends baby. Maybe Domenic thought of her in that way. Maybe she was Domenic's girlfriend. But Beth thought about that day he had another engagement.

That thought came back to haunt her. One day soon she was going to ask him about that. She was going to ask him about all his past. Even if he didn't want to disclose anything about past relationships with her, she was going to ask just the same. She wanted to know everything about Domenic Ragonese.

"Call me if you need anything." Domenic kissed her once more before he got into his car.

Beth watched him drive down the road and disappear around the corner. She walked back inside the house and locked the door behind her. Pickles and claws had awoken from their nap and were groggily walking towards her.

She scooped up pickles and cuddled him close to her. She rubbed claws behind the ears, taking Sal's advice on not cuddling her. She purred and rubbed against her legs. "I think Mr. Pickles needs to go for a walk." She grabbed his little harness and collar and once pickles was secured in his small harness, she headed out the front door, locking it behind her.

The sun filled the sky with bright reds, pinks and oranges. Another beautiful day tomorrow, Beth thought to herself as she walked pickles to the end of the driveway. As soon as they reach her lawn, pickles plopped him self down and whimpered slightly. She knew how he felt. She was tired also. "Okay boy, that's enough walking for tonight. Maybe tomorrow we can try crossing the street. " Beth carried him back to the front door and back inside the house. She relocked the front door, removed his harness and leash, gathered up claws by the scruff of the neck and carried them upstairs to her bedroom. She placed the pets on the bed and they immediately curled up together and fell asleep. If only life was as simple as that, Beth thought.

She ran the bath and added some bubble bath. Her cheeks were slightly burned from being outside all day so she took care to apply some aloe Vera to her sunburned cheeks. Beth climbed into her bath and closed her eyes as the smell of jasmine filled her senses. She recalled the day's activities then tried to rid her mind of any thoughts.

It was almost nine by the time she slid between her sheets. Pickles and claws hadn't moved from their spot. "I wish my life was as simple and uncomplicated as your lives." She said kissing her babies goodnight. She closed her eyes and her final thoughts for the night were of Domenic. Although having a man in her life was the last thing she wanted, she was glad she had Domenic. And she was glad that he showed her that there are men out there who care more for her feelings then their own.

The sound of an Iron Gate opening and closing woke Beth from a sound sleep. She looked over at her bedside clock. It read twelve thirty five. Her stomach growled and she realized she hadn't eaten supper. She knew she wouldn't be able to go back to sleep on an empty stomach and reached for the light.

Then she heard it. A noise coming from her backyard. At first she thought she had dreamed the sound of her gate opening, but now she was sure it wasn't a dream. Pickles and claws were still fast asleep at the bottom of her bed. She slowly crawled out of bed and moved towards her window. It faced the backyard so she didn't want to warn whoever it was that she was aware of their presence. She slowly opened one of her shutters and peered out into the darkened yard. The neighbors back light reflected on her pool, allowing for better visibility. She looked out but couldn't see anyone. She waited for a moment then after a few minutes, decided that it was her imagination after all.

Then she caught sight of someone. He was standing just below her window looking in through her kitchen doors. Beth felt her heart drop into her stomach. She reached for the phone and speed dialed her grandfather.

"Gramps." Beth whispered. "There's someone in my backyard. Can you send someone over?"

"Where are you right now?" he asked as he motioned for Audrey to phone Domenic and Jack.

"I'm in my bedroom. The sound of the gate opening woke me up."

"Stay put in your room. You grandmother just called Domenic and he is on his way over. She is calling Jack as well. He is trained in this sort of thing."

"Okay gramps." Beth whispered. Her voice trembled with fear as she watched the shadow move from her kitchen door to her family room window. She saw him look inside but the curtains were closed.

"Do you have a lock on your bedroom door?" her grandfather asked.

"No I don't. Should I move something over to block the door?" Beth asked, searching the room for something she could move by herself.

"No, don't do that. If he gets inside he will hear you. It's best if you go to your bathroom and lock the door. Are you on your cell or a land line?"

"The land line and its not cordless." She knew she would have to hang up if she went into the bathroom.

"Okay, then hang up the phone and wait for Domenic and Jack to get there." He reassured her that everything would be alright.

Beth grabbed her pets that had woken up and she went into the bathroom and locked the door behind her. She quietly opened the window and listened for the sound of her gate opening.

Within minutes of the call from Tom, Domenic arrived at Beth's house. He parked down the street as not to draw attention and snuck into her back yard unnoticed. He stood at the gate watching a man trying to open the patio doors that led to Beth's kitchen. When he was unsuccessful, he searched the yard for some sort of tool to pry the doors open. Finding none he noticed the pool shed at the end of the yard and went into the shed in search of something to use.

Domenic stood in the shadows wondering if he should wait for Jack. Jack was trained in this sort of thing and all Domenic had been an orange belt in karate. That only helped him in some situations and prevented him from getting his ass kicked to a bleeding pulp but this was different. This guy could be armed and he could be crazy. Domenic wasn't sure if he should take the chance but he was sure about one thing. If he had to he wasn't going to allow this guy to get to Beth.

Beth had heard the footsteps of someone walking up the side of her house. They hadn't opened the back gate so they must be still along the side.

She went back into her bedroom and peered out the window. She had seen the figure go into her pool shed. Then she saw the gate slowly opened and Domenic step inside her back yard. Fear shot through Beth like lightening. She raced down the stairs and into the kitchen.

When she got to the kitchen doors she slowly unlocked it. Domenic heard the click of the door and turned around just in time to see Beth slip out the door.

"What are you doing?" Domenic whispered. "You're going to get yourself killed."

"I've got your back." Beth whispered back as they moved closer to the shed.

Domenic motioned for her to stay close to the door but Beth was stubborn. She didn't want anything happening to Domenic. This overwhelming urge to protect him filled her body so she searched her yard for something to use. The only thing available was her power washer. Instinctively she switched on the water to the washer and waited behind a bush.

Domenic moved in closer to the shed. He turned his head to see if Beth was behind him and then turned back only to come face to face with the intruder. They startled each other and without thinking lunged at each other. They rolled towards the edge of the pool and the intruder was able to pin Domenic down. Domenic gave a karate kick and freed himself just as Beth hit the switch on her power washer. She aimed the power gun at the intruder and hit him full blast in the face with a forced stream of water.

The forced stream of water knocked the intruder's glasses off and penetrated his eyes. He screamed in pain as he covered his face and tripped over Domenic who was trying to get out of the way. He fell backwards into the pool all the while screaming, "My eye! My eye!"

Domenic jumped in after him but the intruder had managed to climb the ladder and run to the opened gate. He tripped over the lounge chair and rolled towards the gate. Without even stopping, he righted himself and fled out the gate and down the side of the house.

A New Beginning for Beth

Beth turned off the power washer and rushed to the pool ladder, where Domenic was. He climbed out and stood there soaking wet.

"I wasn't planning on getting soaked." He said squeezing the excess water out of his drenched shirt.

"Why did you jump in after him? I had it under control."

"I didn't jump in to get him. I jumped in to avoid getting hit with that power washer." Domenic reached for the pair of glasses the belonged to the intruder.

"Let me get you a towel." Beth said as she disappeared into the house and returned a moment later with two bath towels. "And for the record, I have pretty good aim with that power washer. I never even came close to you."

Domenic removed his clothes and stood there in his boxers, drying his hair. He took a towel and wrapped it around his waist, and slowly maneuvered his boxers off.

Beth gathered up his clothes and hung them on the clothes umbrella to drip dry. She took his runners and placed them upside down on top of the umbrella.

Jack appeared through the opened gate. "I guess I missed all the action." He said at the sight of seeing Domenic naked with the exception of a towel.

"You didn't happen to see another guy soaked to the bone running down the street?" Beth asked.

"Unfortunately no, but I did see a black Honda civic speed down the street." He replied "I was going to follow him but I was more concerned about Beth." He added.

"Thanks Jack." Beth smiled. She invited both men in for a coffee.

Beth went upstairs and left the two men sitting at the kitchen island. A few minutes later she returned with a robe for Domenic. "This was James's. You can wear it until your clothes are dry." she tossed it to Domenic who put it on and casually removed the towel.

Beth sat next to Jack. "I haven't seen you for awhile, Jack. Where have you been hiding?"

Jack was the youngest at the agency. He was in forced retirement since being wounded on duty as a homicide detective. Beth placed him in his early forties even though his full head of hair was Salt and pepper. His face was free of lines and his grey eyes were almost transparent.

Sometimes she found it hard to make eye contact with Jack because his stare was that of someone who would look deep into your soul.

Dressed in a suit he was definitely law, but dressed casually in jeans and a t-shirt, he looked like the guy next door who you would call if you needed something fixed in your house. He stood taller than Domenic but his frame was thin and lanky. He was able to keep fit by running ten miles every other day. He was obsessed with physical fitness and Beth believed that he could have chased the Honda and probably caught it if it weren't for his concern for her safety. He was also a perfect marksman with a handgun and a black belt in karate. Not the kind of person you would want to mess with in a fight.

Jack's stare went from Beth to Domenic then back to Beth. No one had to say anything to Jack for him to know there was something going on between Beth and Domenic. "So how long have the two of you been seeing each other?" He asked trying to make conversation.

Domenic and Beth looked at each other. "We are just friends." Beth replied.

"Okay. If you say so Bethany." Jack sipped on his coffee not believing a word she had said but deciding not to argue the point.

Beth knew that Jack didn't believe her. He always called her Bethany when he knew something was up with her. "We are just friends, really." She insisted. "Isn't that right Domenic?" she turned to Domenic for support.

"Keep me out of this." Domenic said raising his hands up.

Jack stood up and stretched. His long arms reached the ceiling. "Well I'm going to leave you two kids alone." He walked over and put his hand on Domenic's shoulder. "You think you can take it from here?" he gave Domenic's shoulder a squeeze and winked at him.

Beth caught the wink and rolled her eyes in embarrassment. "He's leaving as well." She said. "You can come by tomorrow night and pick up your clothes."

"I guess I'm leaving too." Domenic sighed and followed Jack down the hall.

Beth had retrieved Domenic's keys from his wet jeans and tossed them to him. "You'll need these."

Domenic caught them and blew Beth a kiss. "I'll call you later in the day."

A New Beginning for Beth

After the men left and Beth checked to make sure her doors and windows were securely locked, she crawled back in her bed and closed her eyes. The sound of whimpering came from the bathroom.

"Damn it! I forgot my babies in the tub." Beth jumped from her bed and opened the bathroom door to see claws and pickles still sitting in the bathtub. Pickles had peed in the tub so Beth just washed it down the drain.

"Its okay pickles. Mommy won't leave you alone like that again." she gave him a kiss and carried them both back to her bed. They snuggled with each other on the pillow next to Beth's head and quickly fell asleep. She had wondered if she should call the police about the intruder but quickly decided against it. Jack would let his old colleagues down at the station, know what had happened and they will eventually call her to make out a report.

Then her thoughts changed to Domenic and how he wanted to protect her. James would never have gone to that extreme to protect her. She knew that from past experience when she had the death threat made against her. He couldn't deal with it so he went on vacation without her and left Beth to figure out the threat herself. His parting words to Beth were of her making a choice between their marriage and her career. She chose her marriage which inevitably disintegrated.

But Domenic was different. He was everything that James wasn't. Although she liked that about him, it also frightened her. Her feelings for Domenic were becoming deep and this too frightened her.

Shut up brain, she thought to herself. "Domenic is right, I think too much." Beth mumbled. Pickles head perked up when he heard Beth talking to herself.

Beth reached over and scratched his ears." Don't worry pickles. I am going to stop thinking and analyzing everything and start living. I'm going to grab those preverbal scissors and run like hell with them." She leaned over and kissed her new pets on the head. "And I promise to never leave you in the bathtub again." she said as she drifted off to sleep.

Chapter Six

Beth had just arrived back at her office after spending two hours in court arguing over a set of china dishes. "I can't wait to finish with this case so I can go back to criminal law." Beth said to Mary as she flopped in her leather chair and kicked off her shoes.

Mary handed her some phone messages. "Did you finally get it settled on who was to receive the china?"

Beth flipped through the messages. "My clients getting it, but if I was the judge I would have taken the damn china and threw it out the court house window."

Thank God Beth wasn't the judge, Mary thought. Knowing how Beth had been frustrated with her client and his ex-wife bickering over stupid things for the past year, Beth would have thrown the couple out the courthouse window right after the china.

You can close the case on this divorce." Beth said handing the file over to Mary. "There is nothing left for them to fight over."

Mary laughed. "Sure Beth, that's what you said three months ago."

"If they have anything left to fight about, he can call my replacement. I'm done with family law for good."

Beth sipped on the tea that Mary had placed on her desk and leaned back in her chair as she looked at her messages. There were two from her mother, one from James and one from Domenic. "Hmm, let's see. Who takes precedence? Domenic of course." she dialed his cell but got his voice mail. She left a message in regards to his message and let him know that she was going home and he could reach her there.

She then weighed who was second and after much consideration and reluctance, she dialed her mother's office number.

"Bethany!" her mother cried. "I have been trying to reach you for a week. If I didn't know better I would think you were trying to avoid me."

"No mom. I've just been very busy with work." Beth sighed.

"That's what I wanted to talk to you about. I heard you are switching back to criminal law. Is this so?" her voice was demanding.

Beth could picture her mother tapping her fingers on the edge of her desk. Something she always did when she disapproved of something Beth did or was about to do. "Who told you that?"

"It doesn't matter who told me. What matters is whether it is true or not."

"Yes it is true. And I see that your loyalty is still in tact." Beth felt her anger boil from inside. She knew very well who told her and she was appalled that she was still in touch with James. But inside she didn't seem all that surprised.

"What are you talking about Bethany? You are my daughter and my loyalty is with you." Her mother's voice quivered slightly. Beth knew that sound whenever her mother was caught in a red faced lie.

"Your loyalty is with James. You know it and I know. As a matter of fact, everyone in the free world knows it. I bet you still have lunch with him every Wednesday at the country club. And I bet you have met his new girlfriend the home wrecking whore."

"Don't be silly, he would never dare to bring her."

"Just as I thought." Beth said. Her anger turned to sadness. She felt betrayed by her own mother. "Look mom. I love you. But I can't accept this friendship you still have with James. Especially after what he had done, I would think that you would hate him but not you. It's as if you blame me for what happened." Beth felt the first tears flow down her cheeks. She blinked twice as the tears clouded her vision.

"How many times do we need to rehash the past? He made a silly mistake and you called the marriage off. You never even wanted to give it a chance."

"You're right mom. I did call the marriage off. But the sight of seeing him with his pants around his ankles banging the office tart really made it difficult for me to want to keep the marriage going." Her voice was angry and her words were filled with sarcasm. "I have to go mother." Beth said not giving her mother a chance to respond. "I have one more thing to say to you though. How the hell did my grandparents end up with a child like you?" with that, Beth slammed the phone down.

She picked it up again and rang Mary. "The next time my mother calls, tell her I dropped off the face of the earth and you have no idea when I'm coming back."

"That sounds good to me." Mary replied back and hung up the phone.

Beth took a few deep breaths and went to her bathroom to wash her face. She looked at herself in the mirror and wondered why her mother was the way she was.

Joanna Jackson Bardos was the opposite of her parents. When some girls marry men who are like their fathers, Beth had the misfortune to marry someone like her mother. Joanna looked down at anyone who didn't agree with her even if she were wrong. She always played it safe and didn't accept change very well.

She also wasn't the type to be a mother. That's why she only had Beth. And she was glad her parents took on the responsibility of raising Beth so she could pursue her medical career. Even though she spent most of her time with her grandparents, Beth was more like her mother in more ways then she cared to admit. And they seemed to be the bad parts of Beth. the parts that Beth wanted so much to rid herself of.

Her thoughts were interrupted by a knock on the door. Mary stuck her head in and she was wearing that lusty grin again. That could only mean that Domenic was outside her door again.

"That hunk is outside again. Shall I let him in or can I have him for awhile?" she grinned ear to ear.

"Mary just send him in. and wipe the drool off your mouth." Beth smiled back at her.

Domenic walked into Beth's office followed closely by Mary.

"That'll be all Mary." Beth said. Her eyes widened as Mary just stood there staring at Domenic. She had the look of someone who was starving and Domenic was the hamburger. Beth walked over towards Mary took her by the arm and led her out the door. "Hold all my calls." She said before closing the door on her secretary.

Beth leaned against the door and smiled at Domenic.

"What's up with that secretary of your?" Domenic asked Beth. "Every time I come here she looks at me as if she is mentally undressing me." He blushed slightly and Beth found that a turn on.

"Can you blame her?" Beth asked. "Look at that suit you are wearing. It makes a woman want to take it off you." She purred.

Domenic moved closer to Beth. "Baby, you can take it off me anytime." He kissed her hard on the mouth. "Does this door have a lock on it and have you ever done it on your desk?" Beth clicked the lock on the door. "Yes it has a lock and no I've never done it on the desk. I've never even done it anywhere in this office." She looked around.

"Well we should change that." Domenic picked Beth up and placed her on the desk.

Beth wrapped her arms around Domenic and slowly slid his suit jacket off his shoulders, revealing a neatly pressed white shirt.

"Is this what you call running with scissors?" she whispered in Domenic's ear as he gently kissed her neck.

"You can call it whatever you like." He moaned as he pushed against her revealing what she does to him. He moved his hand between her thighs probing her gently.

Beth moaned as he touched her in her sensitive spot. His fingers moved faster as Beth felt herself come to the edge. She felt a rush of sexual desire fill her body as she came, burying her head in his shoulders as to not be too loud. Her body trembled against Domenic and he held her tight while she trembled from his touch.

Beth unbuttoned her green blouse and lifted her lace bra, exposing her breasts for Domenic. She invited his mouth to explore them as she unbuckled his belt. She wanted him inside her moving in and out. He unzipped his pants and pushed himself gently inside Beth. She smiled and moved her body up to him.

They moved in unison as he cupped her breasts kissing one then the other. She pulled him close, holding him as his body moved with hers.

Domenic moved faster as he felt himself come inside Beth. He fell against her as his knees weakened from the orgasm.

Beth turned him on so much that he found it difficult to control himself. He wanted her every moment of the day. He found himself thinking about her when he woke up in the morning and she was his last thoughts when he went to sleep at night.

Beth held Domenic tight as he quivered from his sexual explosion. "God, what you do to me." He whispered kissing her between words. "I can't get enough of you Beth."

Those words filled Beth's heart and touched her deep within her soul. She had never had a man desire her as much as Domenic did. His words made her forget the problems she had with her mother and her sadness over her failed marriage. Even if it were just a lust relationship between them, it was something Beth realized she needed in her life right now.

She needed to feel wanted and needed and Domenic has given this to her. She cupped his face in her delicate hands and gently kissed his mouth. Her lips moved to his cheeks and his forehead, moving over every inch of his beautiful face.

"Thank you." She whispered."

Domenic looked at her sideways. "Thank you for what?" he asked not quite sure what she was thanking him for.

"Thank you for everything. Thank you for letting me take my hair down and thank you for making me feel like a woman." she smiled at him and for the first time she looked deeply into Domenic's eyes. What she saw in his eyes was his feelings for her.

He truly cared for Beth and this wasn't just a sexual thing between them. Domenic was developing deep feelings for her and this brought happiness to her soul. But she dare not say the love word to him. And part of her wasn't ready to hear that from him. With love came commitment and she wasn't in a position emotionally to commit to anyone.

"I want you to always feel like a woman and I never want to hurt you." He said.

"I believe that you are telling me the truth when you say that." she hugged him close and sighed in his ear.

Domenic held her and stroked her blonde hair. He loved holding her after they made love, even if it was a quick one on her office desk.

"We need to do this more often." Beth giggled. "I guess I will never look at this office the same anymore, thanks to you."

"Is that a good thing or bad thing?" Domenic asked.

Beth's smile changed to a wide grin. "Definitely a good thing."

Domenic followed Beth home and changed into his clean dry clothes from the night before. Beth had taken the privilege of washing and drying them for him before returning them. Domenic was grateful to her for that because he was able to get out of his monkey suit. If he could get away with it, he would go to work in jeans and a t-shirt everyday. But he needed to look the part of a lawyer and part of that was to dress a certain way.

Beth showered and changed into some shorts and tank top and joined Domenic in the family room.

"I hope you don't mind that I went ahead and ordered a pizza." He said as he channel searched for something to watch on TV.

Beth nodded in approval as she watched him flip from channel to channel not giving her enough time to even see what was on.

"Oh the Simpson's!" He said with excitement as he settled in next to Beth to watch the cartoon.

Beth looked at him through the corner of her eye and laughed to herself at the boyish part of him coming out. But in all reality, she enjoyed the Simpson's as well.

"I forgot to tell you. Jack wasn't able to get a lead on those glasses that guy was wearing." Domenic said during a commercial. "Apparently they were a generic brand of glasses and just about every optical store sells them."

"Did they have any records of anyone buying them in the past few months?" Beth asked.

Domenic shook his head no. "They stopped making those a couple of years ago. Who can tell how old they were."

"I guess that lead was a dead end." Beth sighed.

The doorbell rang. "Must be the pizza." Domenic said, getting up to answer the door.

The phone rang at the same time." I'll grab the phone. You get the door." Beth said.

Domenic paid for the pizza and carried it back to the kitchen. He noticed the expression on Beth's face and she motioned for him to be quiet. "Who is this and what do you want?" she asked the caller.

Domenic checked for a caller ID but it came up unknown. Beth motioned for him to pick up the other line and listen.

"That was some stunt you pulled last night." The caller growled. "You almost took my fucking eye out with that power hose."

"What were you doing in my backyard and who are you?" Beth demanded. "And how did you get my number?"

"Look bitch, you listen here." His voice was demanding. "Just shut the fuck up and listen."

"What is it you want?" she asked.

"I want you to tell your boyfriend he still owes my boss. If he doesn't come up with the goods soon his mother will have an accident."

His words scared Beth but she wasn't sure who or what he was talking about. "What the hell are you talking about? I don't have a boyfriend." Her voice got louder but never showed any sign that he was intimidating her.

"Don't lie to me bitch!" he screamed. "I saw you with him at the park yesterday!"

Beth realized immediately he was referring to Peter. She tried to replay all the strangers she saw at the park but came up empty except for his ex girlfriend but she somehow doubted she was behind this.

"I wonder how your boyfriend would feel if he knew you were two timing him with that lawyer dude?" he cooed. "I bet he would go postal on your ass if he knew."

The blood rushed from Beth's face. This guy has been watching her. For all she knew he could be on her street watching her house as they spoke. She felt her knees buckle and she became light headed. Domenic motioned for her to keep talking to get more information from him.

"I bet he's listening in on this call right now." He laughed as if he was daring Domenic to prove him right, but Domenic held his silence.

"Maybe if I knew what it was he owed you I could tell him to pay up." Beth said calmly.

"What do you take me for? An idiot?" his voice became serious and frightening. "Just tell him that if he doesn't give us the goods soon then he can say goodbye to his old lady."

A New Beginning for Beth

There was a click on the phone and the line went dead. Beth hung up the phone and sat back down on the couch.

Domenic immediately pulled out his cell and speed dialed Jack. After informing Jack of the phone call that Beth had just received and asking him to find anything on this guy, he went into the kitchen and pulled a bottle of wine from the refrigerator. He poured two glasses and handed one to Beth. "I think you need this." He said.

Beth took the glass and drank it down fast. She held her glass up and replaced it with his. "What the hell was that all about?" she asked hoping Domenic would have an answer.

But he was as dumbfounded by the call as she was. "What do you think Peter owes this guy?"

Beth shrugged her shoulders. "Whatever he owes him, it could get his mother killed." Then a sad thought came to Beth. Maybe Peter was stealing after all. Maybe this guy paid Peter to steal something from the lab and because of the step up in security he wasn't able to deliver.

The same thoughts came to Domenic. "I think our friend Peter is in deeper than we originally thought."

Beth nodded and sipped her second glass of wine. "I hate to admit it but you're right. Maybe that's why your employees wanted him checked first. They probably already knew he was stealing."

Domenic removed two slices of pizza and placed one piece each on two plates. He carried them into the family room and sat next to Beth. "One thing is for sure, Peter is definitely involved in these thefts but the question is, what is he stealing?"

Beth nodded in agreement as she picked at her pizza. "Whatever it is, it has to be big for this guy to be following us and threatening his mother."

Beth grabbed her purse and searched through it for a piece of paper. Once she found what she was looking for, she took her cell phone and dialed the number on the paper. The voice on the other end answered with a hello. "Hi Alice, this is Beth Singer. Do you remember me?"

"Oh Beth dear, of course I remember you. As a matter of fact I was just talking about you with a friend of mine."

"I hope good things." Beth replied.

"Of course Beth. Only good things." Alice answered back.

Domenic sat in silence, eating his pizza and watching Beth.

Beth got right to the point. "The reason I'm calling is that I noticed my calendar is clear for tomorrow and I thought if you had no plans, we could go out for lunch and then I could drop you off at the senior's center."

"Well that is very sweet of you Beth dear. And I would love to have lunch with you." Alice beamed with excitement.

"I'll be more than happy to drop you back home as well if you like. I have to run some errands in the city and you can call me when you are ready to be picked up."

"I don't want to be a bother, Beth." Alice said.

"It's no bother at all Alice. So I will see you around eleven tomorrow morning?"

"Eleven will be fine. Do you have the address?" Alice asked.

Beth didn't want to let on to Alice that she already knew where she lived so she asked for the address. Beth said goodbye and hung up the cell phone.

"Care to tell me what that was all about?" Domenic asked.

"You have any plans tomorrow?" Beth asked Domenic.

"What did you have in mind?" he asked.

"We are going to snoop around Peter's house." Beth said.

Domenic narrowed his eyes at Beth. "The last time I recall breaking and entry is against the law."

Beth nodded her head and finished off her pizza. She handed her plate to Domenic who went back into the kitchen and put another slice on both their plates.

"It's only against the law if we get caught." Beth said.

"And how do you plan on going in the house without them suspecting anything?" Domenic asked.

"Leave that to me. I will think of a plan." She replied.

Beth showed up a little before eleven and found a parking space in front of Alice's house. She leisurely walked up to the front door and rang the doorbell. She wanted the neighbors to see that she was a friend of the Bucar's as not to draw suspicion from anyone. Alice greeted Beth and welcomed her into her home.

The house was small but quaint. Upon entering the foyer there were a set of stairs that led up to the second floor. To the left was a small sitting room that was filled to the brim with over stuffed furniture. There was an array of throw blankets placed meticulously on the sofas to hide the wear and tear of years of abuse.

The tables were jammed packed with ornaments and dust collectors of all shapes and sizes. Delicate handmade doilies covered the coffee table and end tables. A small television sat below the only window in the room. It seemed out of place with the slightly Victorian décor.

Beyond the sitting room was a small dining room. There were two small china hutches against the left wall. One consisted of china for special occasions and the other was filled with more small statues and ornaments. Beth was beginning to get the feeling that Alice Bucar was a bit of a pack rat.

Off to the sitting room was a hallway that led to a small bathroom and bedroom. Beth assumed the bedroom was Alice's as the stairs in the foyer would be too steep for her to climb everyday. Beyond the dining room was the kitchen.

Beth followed Alice into the kitchen as they chatted about the weather and how lucky they were at bingo the other night. The kitchen was tiny but had enough room for a small table and two chairs. A nice place to have morning coffee, Beth thought.

The counter was lined with small appliances and a bread box. There was a window above the sink that overlooked a small gated fenced in backyard that led to the back alleyway. A small shed sat at the far end of the yard and there was a wooden picnic table with an umbrella stuck through the middle. The cedar wood had turned grey and there were remnants of redwood paint still clinging to some of the wood. Beyond the kitchen was a small utility room that housed the washer and dryer. There was also a set of stairs off to the kitchen that led to the basement.

Beth made a mental picture of the layout of the house as she talked with Alice. "Is there any place in particular where you would like to go for lunch?" Beth asked.

"Just getting out of this house is fine with me, so why don't you decide." Alice said with a smile.

Beth had passed a diner on the way there and had thought that it would be the perfect place for them to have lunch.

"Are you ready to go?" Beth asked as she watched Alice gather up her purse and check her wallet for money."

"In one minute dear. I want to make sure the doors are locked." She said checking the back door. Once the house was secure, they left by the front and Alice locked the door behind them.

Beth helped her into her car. "Very fancy car you have Beth." Alice said admiring the soft leather interior.

"Thank you Alice, I hope you will be happy with the choice of restaurants."

"I'm sure I will." Alice replied.

Fifteen minutes later they were mulling over the menu at the delta café'. Beth decided on a chicken caesar salad and Alice chose the pasta with shrimp.

"How far is the senior center from here?" Beth asked making conversation.

"Not too far. About a ten minute drive up the hill on Gardener Road." Alice said as she sipped on her soda.

Beth knew Gardener Road very well. It was a main throughway that housed several retirement homes and apartments. Most were government run but there were some that were owned by private individuals. Unlike her grandparent's apartment, they weren't as well kept, but they were close to all amenities and there was a large shopping center in walking distance. The senior's center was located between two retirement high-rises and was connected by a common area.

It was obvious that something was on Alice's mind. "Is something bothering you?" Beth asked.

"Actually, there is." Alice hesitated. "Do you remember Agnes from the bingo hall?"

How could Beth forget? "Isn't she the one with the pink hair?"

Alice nodded. "She asked if she could get a ride with us. I didn't think it would be a problem so I said yes. I hope I didn't overstep myself by saying yes." Alice didn't want to bother Beth more than she already did by having her take her.

Beth took her hand. "Of course not Alice. We can pick her up right after lunch."

Relief filled Alice's face. That was definitely a load off her mind.

"What time did you tell her we would come by?" Beth asked.

"I told her to expect us around twelve thirty."

Beth checked her watch. "We better hurry and eat if we are to pick her up at that time."

They arrived at Agnes house at twelve twenty. Beth parked in her driveway, helped Alice out of the car and they walked to the front door. It was a small one story house built just after the war. The lawn and front garden was meticulously kept and the front porch wrapped across the two large picture windows at the front. A few lawn chairs and a small table sat on the porch. It was a perfect place to watch the kids in the neighborhood play or to watch the sunset.

Agnes greeted them as they approached the front door. She was obviously watching for them.

Agnes welcomed them in. "I'll just be a moment." She said, directing them to have a seat.

Agnes disappeared down the hallway as Beth and Alice sat in the living room.

"Don't ask her about Charlie." Alice whispered. "He dumped her for Martha Russell."

"What happened?" Beth asked.

"I'll tell you later." Alice whispered.

Beth nodded and changed the subject. "I see that Agnes likes to collect things as well."

Alice looked around the room. "My yes, she does. I hadn't really noticed until you pointed that out."

Agnes joined them in the living room. "Are you girls ready to roll?" she asked.

Beth and Alice followed Agnes to the front door. Agnes locked the door and Beth held the back door opened for Agnes while Alice made her way around the car and sat in the front seat.

Agnes stood for a moment, hesitant on whether she wanted to get in. "what's wrong?" Beth asked.

"I don't like to sit in the back seat. "Agnes said. "I always ride in the front seat." Her voice was demanding.

Beth looked at her then over at Alice who had already taken her place in the front seat. "I'm sorry Agnes but Alice is riding in the front. If you want you can ride in the front on the way back."

Agnes made a sniffing sound that irritated Beth. "Fine! I will ride in the back seat but I'm not going to be happy about it."

Beth slammed the door shut and silently counted to ten. She climbed into the front seat and started the car. Alice was about to offer her seat to Agnes but Beth gave her a look that told her to not bother.

"Everyone buckled in? Beth asked as she put the car in reverse and pulled out of the driveway.

"Of course we're buckled in." Agnes snapped. "What do you take us for? Old farts or children?"

"I was just making sure Agnes." Beth replied trying to keep her cool.

Beth turned the radio up to listen to the news and Agnes demanded she turn it down. Beth immediately turned it down.

"You're going too fast!" Agnes snort. "If we get into an accident I'm going to sue you."

"If we get into an accident Agnes, I will move a little to my left so I won't block you as you fly through my windshield." Beth responded.

Alice tapped Beth on the knee letting Beth know that it was pointless to argue with Agnes. But Alice did find it amusing as she kept her smile on her face and had to stare out the window to focus on the scenery. She didn't want to break out laughing at Beth's remarks.

"That wasn't very nice." Agnes wailed.

"And you aren't being very nice, considering I am driving you as a favor to Alice."

"Fine! I'll be nice." Agnes sat quietly for a minute until she opened her mouth again. "Alice tells me you are a lawyer." Her tone turned sweet.

"Yes I am Agnes." Beth replied with a much more calming voice.

"That reminds me of a joke. What do you call one thousand lawyers at the bottom of the ocean?" Agnes asked with a giggle.

"A good start." Agnes laughed heartily at her joke.

Beth had heard it before and just rolled her eyes.

"Now that isn't nice Agnes. No more lawyer jokes." Alice insisted.

Agnes pushed the back of Beth's chair. "You have no sense of humor, lawyer girl?"

Beth was boiling inside and wanted to stop the car and drag Agnes out by her hair but Alice flashed puppy dog eyes at Beth and that persuaded Beth to try and be nice.

"Agnes, did you change your hair color? It looks more lavender today." Beth asked.

"Are you being sarcastic?" she snapped at Beth.

"No, no, I really like the color. It's much better than the pink you had at the bingo hall."

She gave a big toothy grin. Her lipstick was a shade darker than her hair and it looked as if it was applied with a crayon. She even managed to get the lipstick on her teeth. This woman gave Beth bad feelings and bad thoughts. She even smelled like moth balls.

Beth smiled back trying to hold back the laughter of having Barney the dinosaur's mother in her back seat.

"So ladies, are you going to meet some men at this seniors center? Or are you finished with men Agnes?" Beth slapped her hand over her mouth as she realized what she had said.

She felt a hand smack the back of head.

"What the hell was that for?" Beth screamed. She wanted to put the car in park so she could turn around and strangle Agnes.

"I don't want you mentioning men to me. Especially that gold digger Charlie's name to me." she growled.

"All he wanted from me was my money. Now I have all these sexy things to wear and no one to wear them for." She wailed.

Beth stared straight ahead gripping her steering wheel tightly. Alice glanced over at Agnes who was sulking like a two year old in the back seat. Then her glance turned to Beth who was turning red with anger. Beth wanted to haul Agnes out by her purple hair and throw her to the curb.

Alice put her hand on Beth's lap again and shook her head no as if she could read Beth's mind.

Beth made a mental note to ask Alice about Agnes' problem later. Until then the only thing Beth had on my mind was getting the old biddy to the seniors club so she can make some other poor souls life miserable.

"Alice tells me you are seeing her son Peter?" Agnes said, her voice turning sweet again.

Beth was getting the impression that Agnes may be bipolar the way her moods flipped.

"We have had a couple of dates. But I do like him." Beth said gritting her teeth and trying to be polite.

"Alice, are you sure this slut is good for Peter? She is tainted with one failed marriage. You know how much of a gentleman Peter is. Why would he want to date a slut unless he was only in it for sex?"

"Agnes!" Alice screamed. "Now that was not nice. Beth was kind enough to pick you up and you say that about her?"

"It's okay Alice." Beth said calmly. "Agnes can't help herself since Charlie dumped her for another woman. She is just upset."

Agnes and Alice gasped together.

"Well I never!" Agnes was shocked to be spoken to in such a manner.

Alice slid down in her seat. She kept clearing her throat to stop from breaking out in laughter.

"And if you dare to hit me again, this slut will drag your sorry ass out of her slut car and throw you to the curb." Beth yelled as she glanced back through the review mirror at Agnes.

Agnes had her hand up in the air. "You wouldn't dare!" Her voice quivered with anger.

"Just try me!" Beth shouted back.

Alice felt as if she were in the middle of a war zone and cowered in her seat.

Agnes sat back in the seat and was silent.

Alice gave a 'would you really do that,' stare and Beth nodded back a 'yes she would' nod.

When they arrived at the center, Beth pulled the car up to the front doors and put the car in park. She got out and walked around the car to help Alice out. She stood at the curb with Alice, waiting for Agnes to get out but she wouldn't budge.

"Now what's her problem?" Beth sighed.

"Be patient with her." Alice suggested calmly. "She is a very lonely woman. She has no family and very few friends."

"With that attitude of hers can you blame anyone for not wanting to be around her?" Beth said.

"Are you getting out or what?" Beth yelled to Agnes.

"Aren't you going to help me out?" Agnes cried from the back seat.

Beth rolled her eyes and slumped her shoulders.

A New Beginning for Beth

"Go help her dear." Alice said putting her hand on Beth's arm. "For me please?"

"Ok Alice." Beth sighed, and went around to the other side and opened the door for Agnes.

"Get out!" Beth snarled.

Agnes looked up at her with sadness in her eyes.

Beth rolled her eyes and blew out a sigh. She was beginning to feel guilty about the way she talked to Agnes, but Agnes had no right to smack her in the head while she was driving.

"Here let me help you." Beth said holding out her hand.

"I can do it myself." she said, slapping Beth's hand away.

Beth pulled her hand away. "Fine! Just close the door after yourself you old coot!"

"Only men are coots." Agnes snapped back, as she slammed the car door as hard as she can.

"Exactly!" Beth said waiting for Agnes to realize why she said it.

"I am not a man, and I don't look like one either!" Agnes screamed.

"You're right Agnes. You don't look like a man. You look more like a wilted flower with that purple hair of yours." Beth laughed.

Alice snickered under her breath trying to keep her composure.

"Well I never!" Agnes wailed.

"Well maybe if you had you wouldn't be such a nasty old lady." Beth yelled back.

Alice sighed. "Do I have to come over to that side of the car and separate the two of you?"

Beth and Agnes stopped their bickering and looked at Alice.

Alice was right. They were fighting over silliness and Beth hated to be nasty to people, but Agnes made it so easy for her to dislike her.

Alice turned and walked towards the front entrance.

Beth and Agnes followed behind in silence.

"Alice did you bring a sweater with you?" Beth asked noting the sweater that Agnes had.

I forgot." She frowned. "They keep the air so cold in there."

"If you want, I can go back to your place and get you a sweater." Beth offered and took this opportunity to get into her house.

Alice hesitated for a moment but then decided it would be okay for Beth to be in her house without her there. "I have a sweater in my bedroom closet. My bedroom is on the first floor. Take the pink one because it will match my dress." She said handing her house keys to Beth.

"I'll bring the sweater back before I do my errands and go and take my puppy out for his walk." Beth said taking the keys from Alice.

"You have a puppy?" Agnes interrupted.

"Yes I do." Beth replied without making eye contact with Agnes.

"I would love to see him." she smiled.

Beth ignored Agnes. "You better get inside before all the seats are taken." She said.

Beth held the door for the ladies and Agnes stopped short of the door. She looked at Beth and handed her a piece of paper. "I'm sorry about the way I acted and if you ever need anyone to look after your puppy you can call me anytime."

Beth looked at the paper. Agnes had scribbled her name and phone number on it.

"Um, thanks Agnes. I'll keep that in mind." Beth wasn't sure if she was sincere or was playing with her.

Agnes leaned over and gave Beth a kiss on the cheek. "Thanks for the ride Beth." she smiled and entered the center.

"I told you she isn't so bad." Alice whispered.

Beth nodded to Alice but still wasn't sure if she should completely trust Agnes. "I'll be back shortly with your sweater."

Beth pulled out of the parking lot. She knew that fifteen minutes wouldn't be enough time for her to look through the house and get back to Alice. She recalled passing a hardware store on the way to the center so she decided to pop in and have a duplicate made. She felt guilty about that but she knew that it was the only way she could search the house thoroughly.

Beth took the house key off the ring and handed it to the sale clerk who quickly made a duplicate key for her. "You sure you only need one key?" he asked.

"Just one key thanks." Beth replied.

A few minutes later Beth was parked in front of the Bucar's house. She had placed the key back in the same place on the key ring and used her new key to gain access to the house. It clicked the door open and Beth stepped inside the small foyer.

"First things first." She said as she went to Alice's bedroom, found the pink sweater in the closet and headed back to the center.

Once Alice had her sweater, she asked her to call when she was ready to go but to give her a fifteen minute warning so they wouldn't have to wait.

Beth was back at the house another ten minutes later. She parked a few doors down and casually walked up to the front door. She looked around to see if anyone was watching. The park was empty of children and parents and the street was deserted except for the few cars that drove past on their way to the main shopping area.

Beth unlocked the door and slipped inside unnoticed. The first place she wanted to check was peters bedroom. Beth assumed it was on the second floor so she quietly climbed the stairs. They creaked under her feet and for a moment fear shot through her. What the hell was she doing? She thought. She felt guilty going through the house like this, but she knew it had to be done.

There were two rooms upstairs. The larger room faced the front of the house and overlooked the park. This was Peter's bedroom. It was painted a marine blue and had a small flowered border that ran halfway across the wall and covered all four walls. There was a small closet that housed Peter's clothes.

Beth looked in the closet but found nothing unusual. She searched his dresser, carefully trying not to disturb the contents of each drawer. She found nothing significant in the drawers either. She looked around the room. The only other pieces of furniture were a small television and a chair.

Yesterdays clothes were draped neatly over the chair. She looked at his bed. She ran her hand between the mattress and box spring. She felt something and took hold and pulled it out.

"Well, well, Peter Bucar. You aren't so innocent after all." Beth smiled as she flipped through the current issue of playboy. "So this is what you do in your spare time." She giggled.

She put the magazine back under the mattress and left the room. She moved to the next room which Peter had converted into an office. If Peter was hiding anything Beth would probably find it there.

A small window overlooked the backyard. Below the window sat a small desk with a computer and monitor. Beth shuffled through each draw. There were the usual things but nothing out of the ordinary. She clicked on the computer and turned on the monitor.

As she waited for the computer to boot up she continued her search through the desk drawers. The last bottom drawer was locked. She looked around for a key but found none. She had thought to try and break the lock but that would tip Peter off to someone being in the house. She decided that the locked drawer could wait.

Just as the computer finished loading Beth caught a glimpse of something on the window ledge. There was a set of keys hanging from a nail behind the curtain. She retrieved the keys and then something caught her eye in the backyard. At first thought she was imagining it so she stood behind the curtain watched. Sure enough she wasn't seeing things as two figures move about the yard. They were wearing hoodies and sunglasses which made it difficult for Beth to get a good look at them. But she was sure of one thing. The two people were women. It was obvious from their small shapely figures. She put the keys in her pocket and went to the top of the stairs to listen.

Within seconds she heard voices coming from the kitchen.

"My god, they are inside the house!" she thought. Her heart beat faster and sweat began to bead on her face. She went back into the office and click off the monitor. She could hear the voices cross the dining room and stop in the living room.

"Should we check the basement first?" one woman said.

"He has an office upstairs. Let's go there first." The other voice said.

Panic filled Beth's thoughts as the voices came closer to the stairs. She managed to duck into Peter's bedroom and squeeze herself into his tiny closet. She moved the clothes in front of her and she crouched low in the dark closet listening as the people came up the stairs. They weren't making any attempt to be quiet. It was as if they knew no one would be home.

"This drawer is locked." One said.

"He has keys around here somewhere. Look for them while I scan the computer."

There was more shuffling around and then one of the women came into Peter's bedroom.

Beth listened as the woman went through his drawers and night table. Beth held her breath as the woman moved closer to the closet.

"I can't find any keys." She yelled to the other woman.

"Don't worry about it. He might have the list on the computer." The other woman replied.

The first woman left Peters room and joined her companion in the office.

Beth waited a moment and slowly opened the closet door. She listened to the two women talking.

"Do you know the password?"

"Yes. It's his niece's name."

"How do you know that?"

"He told me one day when I told him I wanted to check my email. He's not very bright. He uses the same password for his computer at work too."

"When is the old lady supposed to be home?"

"Who knows? She went to that senior's center with Peter's new slut girlfriend. Knowing the old lady, she'll be there for a couple of hours."

There goes that slut word again, Beth thought as she listened to the women type away on Peter's computer.

"Anything yet?" the other woman asked.

"I can't seem to find the folder. He probably has them hidden on here." She clicked off the computer.

Beth slid back into the closet as she heard the women come out of the office.

"Let's take a look in the basement. He might have something on paper down there."

Beth heard them walk downstairs and go through the kitchen to the basement stairs.

She slowly crept out of the closet, moved across the room and waited at the open door. She listened but couldn't hear anything. If they were in the basement then Beth didn't want to take a chance on them finding her by leave the room.

Beth moved back into the room and dialed Domenic on her cell phone. "I'm in Peter's bedroom." She whispered.

"Why are you whispering?" Domenic asked.

153

"Two women broke into the house and they are looking for something." Beth replied in a whisper. She stopped for a moment and listened. She could hear the women come up from the basement and stop in the kitchen. They were talking amongst themselves but Beth couldn't make out anything they were saying.

The sound of a door opening and closing were followed by footsteps leaving through the backdoor. Beth quietly slid into the office and peeked out of the window. She saw the two women walk to the edge of the yard and disappear through the small gate beside the shed.

Beth blew out a sigh of relief. "They're gone now." She said to Domenic.

"You better get out of there before they come back." Domenic demanded.

Beth turned on the computer and noticed that the screen saver had not kicked on yet. She moved the mouse to allow her more time to access the computer. "I will in a second. I need to check out the basement." She said.

"Okay but I want you out of there in five minutes." Domenic was concerned for Beth. If those women came back she would definitely get caught. He decided to go down to the house and plant himself near the back gate. If they were to come back they would most likely use the same route. He could intercept them just in case.

Beth hung up the phone and put it in her pocket. She then realized that she was still in possession of the keys she retrieved from the window.

She tried all the keys in the locked drawer. The fourth key clicked the lock open. Beth quickly opened the drawer and found some medical reports with Alice's name on them. She slipped them in her purse and searched through the drawer for anything else. She came across three memory sticks. She uses them also to store office files when she had work she needed to bring home.

She put one in the computer and it was filled with songs and photos of his family. Beth flipped through some of the photos of his mother, sister and niece. She didn't think there was anything of importance on it so she removed it and moved on to the second one.

On that one there were videos. She opened one video and it was a porno movie that he must have downloaded from the internet. It showed

A New Beginning for Beth

two women and a man in a very compromising position. Beth felt her cheeks flush as she checked out the other videos, all of which were some type of porno. She was definitely getting a different opinion of Peter.

She was satisfied that there was nothing of interest on that stick as well so she moved on to the third one. The third one had folders with medical information on them as well as photos of his mother. Many of the photos showed a deteriorating Alice in different stages of some sort of illness.

Beth searched her purse for her memory stick and found it in the side pocket of her purse. She copied all the folders and pictures onto her memory stick and then put all of Peter's sticks back. She removed the folders she had originally thought to take with her and put it back in the drawer, then locked it up and headed back downstairs.

She checked the back door and found it locked. She inspected the door for any forced entry but Beth came to the conclusion that they must have also had a key.

Beth decided to check out the basement and headed down the stairs. The basement was tiny and had small windows allowing very little light. There was a small storage area and beyond that, a closed door.

Beth checked the door but it was locked. She looked at the set of keys in her hand and tried a key in the lock. The door clicked open and a rush of adrenaline shot through her body. Beyond the door was a fully equipped laboratory. She quickly phoned Domenic back.

"Are you still in the house?" he asked.

"You aren't going to believe this one." Beth said excitedly. "Our friend Peter has a home lab set up in his basement."

Domenic gasped. "You're kidding me?"

"I wish I was." Beth sighed. She was feeling very bad about everything. She was hoping that this suspicion they had about Peter would turn out to be a big mistake. Now she was definitely sure he was into something.

"Don't touch anything. Just get out of that house. I'm in the alley behind the house so come out the back door. I'll be watching for you." Domenic said sternly.

Beth told him she would be out in a minute and headed back upstairs to the kitchen.

Beth slipped out the back door and locked it behind her. She walked across the yard and exited the same way the women did.

Catherine Angelone

Beth looked up and down the back alley for the women but they were long gone.

She spotted Domenic a couple of houses down and quickly walked towards him.

Her face showed disappointment. "I had really hoped that Peter was innocent." She was very upset and Domenic knew it.

He put his arm around her. "I understand, but they must have suspected he was guilty of something if they insisted he be watched."

Beth nodded. "I suppose you're right. Beth reached into her pocket and gasped. She pulled out Peter's keys.

"Damn it! I forgot to put them back." she cried.

"You can't go back through the front door." Domenic said. "You may be seen."

"I could slip them into Alice's purse when I pick her up." Beth suggested.

"Won't she get suspicious?" Domenic asked.

"You're right." Beth thought for a moment. "What if I invite myself in and ask for a tour of the house?"

Domenic thought for a moment. "That could work." He said.

Just then Beth's cell phone rang. "It's Alice." Beth said looking at the number.

She talked briefly with Alice and said she would be there in fifteen minutes.

After she hung up the phone, she handed Domenic her memory stick and removed her house key from her ring of keys. "I want you to meet me at my place and check out the folders and photos I copied from peters memory stick."

Domenic walked Beth to her car. "I'm going to stop at a bakery and pick up some sweets. This way she will have no choice but to invite me in." Beth smiled.

"Smart girl." Domenic grinned. "That's one way to get you in the house." He gave her a kiss and took the key and stick from her. They made arrangements to meet in ninety minutes and Domenic watched as Beth climbed into her car and drove away.

Beth stopped at an Italian bakery and bought a dozen individual pastries. She then went to the senior's center where she found Agnes and Alice waiting outside.

"I hope I didn't keep you ladies waiting too long." Beth said as she got out and helped both the ladies in the car. She noticed that Agnes's mood had mellowed. Beth wasn't about to ask what happened. She was just happy knowing there wouldn't be anymore head hitting.

"What's this here in the box?" Agnes asked as she buckled herself safely in the backseat.

"I wanted to surprise you both with some sweets. Maybe we could all go back to Alice's house for tea." Beth suggested.

Agnes opened the box. "Oh Alice, these are beautiful. Look what Beth bought us." She held the box up to Alice's face.

Alice beamed with delight. "Don't eat any Agnes. Lets wait till we get back to my place and I get the kettle on."

They were back at Alice's house within minutes. Agnes carried the box of goodies into the kitchen while Alice filled the electric kettle with water and plugged it in. she took three cups and saucers out of the cupboard while Agnes placed all the sweets out on a small serving plate.

Beth watched the ladies as she thought about how she was going to put the keys back in Peters office. Then she thought of another plan. "Alice, may I use your washroom to freshen up while we wait for the tea?"

"Of course dear." Alice replied. She showed Beth where the bathroom was and went back to the kitchen.

Beth locked the bathroom door and removed the keys from her purse. She thought about leaving them in the bathroom for Alice to find but she was worried that she wouldn't find them before Peter arrived home.

Beth washed her hands and patted some cool water on her sun burnt cheeks. She dried herself off and took the keys with her out of the bathroom.

Beth walked into the kitchen, holding the keys in her hand for Agnes and Alice to see. "Alice, I found these in the bathroom. Are they yours?" she asked handing the keys to Alice.

Alice looked puzzled. She checked the keys and scratched her head. "They aren't mine."

"Do you think they might be Peter's?" Agnes asked taking them from Alice.

"Of course." Alice lightly smacked her forehead. "He is always forgetting his keys somewhere. I'll give them to him when he gets home."

"I can put them back in his room for you Alice." Beth suggested.

"Oh, would you please?" she pointed to the stairs at the front of the house. "Just put them on his office desk at the top of the stairs. It's the room on the left."

Beth disappeared into the living room and went upstairs to the office. She put the keys back on the nail in the window and returned to the kitchen. Alice was making a pot of tea as Agnes was taking first dib on the pastries.

They took their tea and sweets into the living room and Beth listened as the two women chatted about the people at the center.

Beth looked at her watch. "I didn't realize it was so late." She said, getting up. "I have to take my puppy out."

"Are you sure you can't stay longer?" Alice asked.

"I wish I could Alice but he has been in his training cage all day and it's not fair to him." Beth replied.

"Do you want me to pack up the sweets for you?" Agnes asked with hesitation.

"I bought them for the both of you. Enjoy them." Beth said.

Agnes smiled from ear to ear as she popped another sweet in her mouth. "That's very nice of you Beth." she added.

"I told you she is a nice girl." Alice said to Agnes.

Agnes nodded in agreement.

"Do you want me to drive you home?" Beth asked Agnes.

"Peter will take me home when he gets off work." She said shooing Beth away. "You just get home to that puppy. And don't forget to call me if you need someone to baby-sit." She added.

"I won't." Beth said. She kissed both women goodbye and headed out the door.

Domenic was waiting for her when she arrived home. He had stopped to get pizza and was happily eating in the family room. South Park was blaring on the television while claws and pickles sat nearby eagerly waiting for another piece of crust.

"Please tell me you aren't feeding them pizza." Beth said as she grabbed a slice for herself.

A New Beginning for Beth

"Okay I won't tell you." He laughed as he watched the cartoon.

Beth sat down beside Domenic. They ate in silence while watching the show.

"Did you happen to check out the memory stick I gave you?" Beth asked when a commercial came on.

Domenic shook his head. "I wanted to wait for you." Domenic handed the stick to Beth and she went into her downstairs office to start up her computer.

"Come down when you're ready and bring the pizza." She yelled up to him.

Beth popped the stick into her USB slot and click on the photos. Each one was numbered one through twenty two. The first one showed Alice in a state of confusion. Her eyes were shallow and unaware. With each photo there was less confusion and more awareness of her surroundings. When she got to the last photo, it showed Alice as she is today.

The first few photos looked as if Alice was in some drug induced state.

Domenic joined Beth. "Did you find anything else in the house that might be significant?"

"Peter likes porn." Beth laughed. "But he does have a full lab in his basement." she added, her voice turning serious.

"I'm getting this unsettling feeling that Peter is doing something that is going to get him way over his head." Domenic pulled up a chair next to Beth and studied the photos of Alice.

Beth nodded in agreement. "Based on these photos of Alice and the fact that he has a working lab in his basement, I would bet he is into making illegal drugs."

Beth opened each folder on the memory stick. Each folder contained some type of formula. Chemistry and science was her weak subjects in school so the information looked like chicken scratch to her.

The last folder was titled 'clients.' Beth opened it and found a list of over fifty names and information. It looked as if it were an order form. Each name had an abbreviated word which they couldn't decipher. Beside that was an amount in dollars for each unit. Next to that was a telephone number.

"Peter Bucar is a drug lord." Domenic said. "What do you suppose these abbreviations stand for?"

Beth shrugged her shoulders. "Beats me, but if I were to guess I would think they were the drug of choice for that person."

"There's one way of finding out." Domenic picked up the phone next to the desk and made a phone call. After an exchange of words, he hung up."

"Can you print out a copy of those formulas and the list of names?" Domenic asked.

Beth clicked her mouse and the printer started making copies of the information. "Who was that you were talking to?" she asked.

"Have you ever met Morris Witherspoon?"

"The name sounds familiar. Where have I heard it before?" She said.

"He lives in the same building as your grandparents. He occasionally does some work for them." Domenic said. "He worked in forensics before he retired and he has a chemistry degree. A real wiz with formula's." he added. "He said he will look over the information and see what he comes up with."

"I'm going to have Jack find out about these names and numbers. If Peter is producing illegal narcotics then I'm sure these people have records." Beth said.

They finished their pizza and headed to Beth's grandparents apartment. Domenic called ahead to Jack to meet them there. Twenty minutes later they were gathered around Tom and Mary's dining room table going over the papers.

Morris scanned through the formulas and scratched his head. He was distinguished looking and quite tall given his age of seventy five. He was a doctor of forensic medicine but his specialty was chemicals and drugs. If a cadaver died of some type of drug, he could determine the drug as well as how it was administered. He is still called upon for his expertise when needed. He was needed at that moment.

"These are very interesting formulas." Morris said. "But I'm a bit stumped at what they produce."

"Is there any way to find out?" Beth asked.

"There's always a way to find out. But I need a lab." He replied. "I suppose I could use the forensic lab at the hospital."

"If you were to guess at it, do you think these formulas are some type of narcotic?" jack asked.

A New Beginning for Beth

Morris looked at the papers again. "I would think they were with some of them. But this one has me really stumped." Morris pushed the paper to the middle of the table for everyone to examine. "The formulas don't add up."

Morris stood up and stretched his tall thin frame. "I'm going to take this formula and recreate it at the hospital." He gathered up all the formulas and placed them back in the folder. "Whoever wrote these formulas, I'm sure he had access to lab equipment."

Tom walked Morris to the door and thanked him for his help. Morris promised to be in touch once he had the results, and exited the apartment with the folder under his arm.

"So what do you think?" Domenic asked.

Beth sat stone faced after hearing Morris's opinion on the formulas. She didn't want to admit it but she knew in her heart that Peter was not as innocent as she had hoped. Now she has to face the facts that he may be making illegal drugs and based on the photos of his mother, using her as a guinea pig by testing his drugs on her. She found it so hard to believe that he could be that cold and calculated. She had seen him with his mother. It was obvious that he loved her and she him. Even Alice's friend Agnes never had an unkind word to say about Peter. If he was this horrible of a person, Beth would have picked up on it. Unless he is a very good actor and in that case, he should be nominated for an Oscar.

Domenic sensed Beth was troubled by this. "We'll find out the truth, Beth." he put his arm around her.

"Thanks." She whispered. "But if he is guilty, I will make sure he gets the proper legal advice."

Alice was putting the finishing touches on supper when her son arrived home.

He sniffed the air and a smile formed. "Smells good mom." He kissed her on the cheek and wrapped his arms around her.

"Go wash up dear. Supper will be ready soon." She ordered.

Peter snapped to attention and did as he was told. A few minutes' later mother and son were sitting in the dining room enjoying the fruits of Alice's labor. "How was your day today mom?" Peter asked.

"It was wonderful." She beamed. "Your friend Beth came by and we went out for lunch. Then she dropped me and Agnes off at the senior's center and then came back for us afterwards."

Peter stopped eating and looked at his mother. "Did she ask about me?"

Alice didn't look up. "No but you should give her a call. Maybe she is free tonight."

Peter thought for a moment. "Maybe I can call her and see how she is. But I am too tired to go out. Besides, I have a lot of work to do downstairs."

"She's a nice girl. Even Agnes likes her." Alice said with a smile.

Peter nodded in agreement.

Their conversation was interrupted by the ringing of the phone. "I'll get it." Alice said jumping to her feet. "You finish your supper dear."

A moment later she came back to the table." It's for you Peter." Her face was puzzled.

Peter went into the kitchen to take the call.

"Enjoying your supper?" the voice asked.

Peter's stomach churned as he heard the voice. "How did you get this number?" he demanded.

"I know everything about you Peter. Do you honestly think I would do business with someone if I didn't have any leverage to secure my part?" the person said.

Sweat formed on Peters hands. "I told you I would get you your product, but you have to give me some time. It's not as easy to make as you think."

"Each day that passes is one day closer to death and I'm afraid we are running out of time." The voice turned angry and forceful.

Peter felt his body tremble. "I know, I was going to start on it right after I finished eating. It's difficult to use the equipment at work since they stepped up security. I have to do it the hard way here at home."

"Cry me a river Peter." The voice sarcastically said. "We had a deal and we already paid you half of the money. Now you need to produce the goods for us or else we will have to do something you are going to regret."

"Give me till the end of the week. I'll have what you want by Saturday." Peter begged.

The voice went silent. Peter listened in the phone and could hear a muffled conversation between the caller and another person. "Okay, you have till Saturday. If we don't receive anything by then we will have to take something else." The voice was calm but still demanding. "And it better be the real stuff." This was followed by a click.

Peter stood there shaking still holding the phone. He placed it on the receiver and splashed his face with some cold water. He dried himself off and leaned against the kitchen counter. He knew he was in way over his head but couldn't find a way out. He peeked into the dining room where his mother was enjoying her supper. He loved his mother so much and didn't want to lose her again.

Peter took a couple of deep breaths and rejoined his mother at the table.

She looked up at him and smiled. "Was that one of your friends?" she asked.

Peter nodded. "Yes mom, one of my friends."

"That's nice." She answered as she cut her meat into small bite size pieces.

Peter sat in silence as he watched her, his mind racing. "Mom, I'm going to take my supper downstairs. I really have to get some work done." He went upstairs and retrieved his keys from the windowsill.

He picked up his plate and utensils and leaned over to kiss his mother.

"Don't forget to bring your dirty dishes up when you are finished." She said, kissing him back.

"I promise mom." Peter smiled.

He stood at the top of the stairs and flick on the lights.

"Oh Peter, another thing." Alice yelled to him. "Remember to put your keys back this time. You left them in the bathroom the last time."

Peter stopped. "What?" he asked not really sure he heard her correctly.

"You left them in the bathroom." She repeated. "It's a good thing Beth found them and put them back for you or else they could have been lost."

The sound of a plate falling to the floor filled the air. "What in heavens name was that?" Alice said jumping to her feet and moving in the direction of the crash. She found Peter picking up the pieces of his broken plate and bits of food. "What do you mean Beth found my keys and put them back?"

Chapter Seven

Jack walked with Domenic and Beth to the parking lot. "I want you to take this Beth." Jack handed Beth a stun gun.

Beth took it and examined it. "Do you really think I need this?" She asked.

"No but I don't want to take any precautions. Especially after what happened the other night." Jack said.

Earlier in the day, Domenic and Jack had discussed protection for Beth. they both felt that Peter was involved in something and just the fact that Beth and Peter were seen in a public place, may have made Beth a target as well. They didn't want to tell her to stop seeing Peter. After all, they were the ones who had used her as bait. Domenic felt even more compelled to protect Beth since they had become very close and intimate. If he had his way he would lock her in his house and have twenty four hour guards posted at each entrance. But it wasn't his call and he knew better than to ask Beth to put the case aside. She was determined to get to the bottom of it whether it was out of curiosity or just plain stubbornness. Either way, he knew Beth would finish what she started. So it was his and Jack's job to make sure she stayed safe.

Beth thanked Jack even though she felt strange about carrying a stun gun. She placed the gun in her purse and climbed into Domenic's car.

A New Beginning for Beth

Domenic stood away from the car, talking with Jack. They were too far away for Beth to hear what they were talking about but if she were to guess, she would say that Jack was asking Domenic to keep an eye on her. Domenic was nodding in agreement and every so often they would look over to the car where Beth was sitting.

After an exchange of words, Domenic and Jack shook hands and Domenic climbed in beside Beth. "Ready to go?" he asked.

Beth nodded without saying a word.

Beth awoke to the sound of her alarm. It was just past six by the time she dragged herself out of bed and headed down to the kitchen. She skimmed through the morning paper as she sipped on her second cup of tea.

By the time it was eight, she had showered and dressed in a powder blue pant suit and white blouse. It was very hot and humid and there was a promise of more rain to come. Rain with this heat would be a welcome sight, she thought as she started up her car and rolled down the window. Her cell phone rang and she checked the number.

"Good morning Nancy." She said as she backed out of the driveway.

"Good, I caught you before you were in the office." Nancy replied.

"On my way now. What's up?" Beth asked.

"If you aren't busy tonight, would you like to go out to dinner with me?" Nancy's voice sounded frazzled. Too frazzled for this early in the morning.

"Are the kids getting to you already? School's been out for only a week."

"I know but they are driving me mental. Just say you'll go out with me." Nancy begged.

"Of course I will. What time do you want me to come by?" Beth laughed.

They arranged to meet at the restaurant at five as Beth pulled onto the highway and headed downtown to the courthouse.

It was just after two when Beth managed to return to her office. She was exhausted from being in court all morning and wanted nothing better then to sit in her dark cool office and relax.

Mary's head went up as Beth walked into the office. She jumped to her feet and stopped Beth from entering her private office.

"James's is in there." She whispered. "I tried to get him to sit out here but he insisted on sitting in your office to wait for you."

Beth rolled her eyes. "Now what does he want."

Beth took a deep breath before opening the door. James was sitting on her leather sofa, flipping through a magazine. His eyes went to Beth as she opened the door.

Beth walked around to her desk and put her briefcase down. "What brings you here unexpectedly, James? Don't you need to be at the hospital?"

James was on his feet. "Good afternoon to you too." He said forcing a smile.

Beth sat down at her desk and flipped through yesterday's mail. "James we already agreed on the house. I don't see any reason why you should be here." She wouldn't even look up at him.

He moved closer to her desk and plopped himself down in one of the matching leather chairs. "I didn't come here for that."

"If you have certain things you want to have then just email me a list. You still have my email address right?" Beth glanced up at James who looked very uncomfortable.

She knew that look all too well. He always acted this way when he had bad news for her. The last time she saw this look was when he came to her and told her he was leaving.

"What's wrong?" she asked putting the mail down and giving James her attention.

He lowered his head. "I wanted you to hear it from me first before you found out through someone else."

"Is something wrong with your parents? I know your father wasn't well." Beth asked with concern.

James's shook his head no.

"Then what is it?" Beth insisted.

James hesitated. "Jill's pregnant." He blurted out.

Beth felt as if she was hit with a ton of bricks.

"She's almost five months pregnant." He continued.

Beth was stunned. They had been separated less than three months which means she was pregnant before he left her.

"How long have you known?" Beth asked her voice cracking.

A New Beginning for Beth

"Around the time we separated." He replied. He wouldn't make eye contact with Beth.

Beth's was feeling light headed and her mouth went dry. Her emotions were all jumbled and she wasn't sure how to react to this news. A part of her wanted to leap over the desk and grab him by the throat and choke the life out of him, but her body wouldn't move. Her body felt as if it was being held down by an invisible force.

Now everything made sense to Beth. Now she understood why he so desperately wanted the house. It was the house that they were going to raise a family in. unfortunately for Beth she wouldn't be a part of that family.

Beth searched for the right words to say. She didn't want to show James how hurt and devastated this news had made her. "Well congratulations James. I'm happy for you." It was all she could say without breaking down in front of him.

"If there isn't anything else, I really need to go over a case before I leave for the day." Beth stood up still holding her desk. Her legs were like jelly and her heart was beating so fast and hard that she thought it would break through her chest.

James smiled at her. "I'm glad you are taking it so well. "

"How would you have expected me to take it?" she asked between clenched teeth.

James thought for a moment. "I thought you would rip my face off." He laughed.

Beth chuckled sarcastically, all the while trying to keep her composure. James stood and walked around the desk to Beth. He hugged her tightly and thanked her again for selling the house to him. Beth kept herself ridged and refuses to reciprocate the hug.

She nodded and forced a weak smile. "Can you see yourself out?" she asked James as she pointed to the door.

James walked to the door and turned to Beth. "Thanks again Beth. You are terrific!" He closed the door behind him.

Beth walked towards the door and stopped short of opening it again. She wanted to call him a two timing lying bastard. She wanted to call him heartless and without feeling or disregard for her. But she couldn't get the words out. She couldn't find the door. All she could do was fall to the floor in a heap of overwhelming despair and sadness. She felt her whole life wasting away at that very moment. She lay on the floor sobbing uncontrollably.

Domenic sat in Beth's waiting room as he saw James emerge from Beth's private office. He recognized him from a photo Beth had. He stood up and extended his hand to James.

Mary cowered at her desk pretending to be busy but watched the meeting from the corner of her eye.

"Who are you?" James asked as he reluctantly shook Domenic's hand.

"I'm the new guy." Domenic replied with a smile.

James looked him up and down as if to size him up. "How long have you been dating my wife?"

"You're ex wife, and we've been seeing each other for almost two weeks now." Domenic still had his GQ smile on his face which matched his GQ looks.

"You can go in now." Mary said to Domenic with a smile.

Domenic nodded to Mary and disappeared inside Beth's private office.

"He is so cute and charming." Mary said as she watched Domenic close the door after him.

James stood there in silence.

"He is so perfect for Beth." she added. Mary didn't care much for James. Never did and never will, especially after he dumped her boss.

James mumbled something coherent under his breath and left the office.

Mary felt a small victory for Beth.

Domenic closed the door and turned to find Beth sobbing uncontrollably. She had moved herself from the floor to the leather sofa and had her face buried into the pillow to muffle the sounds of her sobbing.

He rushed to her side. "Beth what's wrong? What did James do?" his voice full of panic.

Beth didn't answer him. She just buried her face further into the pillow and sobbed.

Domenic poured a glass of water and kneeled next to Beth. He rubbed her back and softly asked her if there was anything he could do. He offered her the water but she refused. She didn't want to talk to

A New Beginning for Beth

him or anyone. All she wanted to do was crawl in a fetal position and disappear. She felt her life come to a complete halt and felt even more betrayed by James than before.

Domenic stayed silent. He kept his hand on Beth's back to let her know she wasn't alone.

"How could he do this to me?" Beth cried.

"What did he do, Beth?" Domenic asked softly. "Talk to me please."

"Jill is pregnant!" she sobbed, wiping her tears with her hand. Her mascara left a trail of black streaks down her cheeks. Her eyes and nose were swollen and red and her voice cracked as she tried to speak. "The damn tart is carrying my husband's baby!"

Domenic felt a sharp pain go through him like a dagger. He had thought that Beth had accepted the separation and she had him believing that she had moved on. It was obvious from her reaction that she hadn't.

"I see." Domenic said. His back went rigid and his voice went stern. "Is this why you are crying?"

Beth raised her head to look at Domenic. "You don't think I have a reason to cry?"

"Why should you care that your soon to be ex-husband got his girlfriend pregnant?"

"I don't care about that." she wailed. "Every time I talked to him about starting a family, he gave me excuses."

"So you think that he and Jill planned this pregnancy?" Domenic asked.

"Don't you think so? I guess he just didn't want to have kids with me." Beth was hurting. She had wanted a baby so badly but James never agreed. There was always something in his life stopping I'm from committing to fatherhood. Now it seemed that there was nothing stopping him now.

"Did it ever occur to you that she may have purposely got pregnant to keep him?" Domenic suggested. "I just met your husband in the outer office and believe me when I tell you that he doesn't strike me as the father type. He is too egotistical to put someone else first."

Beth sat up on the sofa and Domenic handed her a tissue and the glass of water. "You think so?" she stuttered.

"Of course I think so, baby." Domenic smiled and brushed a lone tear from Beth's face. "It's his loss if he couldn't see what a wonderful mother you would have made."

Beth thought for a moment. "You're right. Maybe she did it on purpose and now he is stuck with her." the edges of Beth's mouth curled slightly into a smile. Then it disappeared. "The rate I'm going I may never have kids." She sighed.

Domenic took her sad face in his hands and gently kissed her. "What are you talking about? You are still young and besides, you have two babies at home waiting for you." He kissed her again and sat beside her. He wrapped his arm around her and pulled her close.

Beth snuggled under his arm where she felt safe. If anyone would make the pain in her heart go away, it would be Domenic, she thought. He was the bearer of all things good in Beth's life and the giver of love and warmth.

Domenic wanted to protect her from all the evil's in the world. He never wanted to see her cry like this ever again. He wanted to give her everything that she deserved. He even had a fleeting thought of giving her the baby she wanted but fell short of suggesting it. They hadn't known each other long enough for him to ever suggest something like that in such a short time.

"Thanks Domenic." Beth sighed. "I think I need to go home for a bit."

"Do you want me to go with you?" he asked, hoping she would say yes.

Beth shook her head. "I'll be okay. I just need some time alone with my thoughts."

It was past four by the time Beth got home. Pickles was in his training cage and began to whine when he heard Beth come in. She immediately picked him up and brought him outside. She sat in a patio chair watching pickles clumsily walk through the grass. "I need someone to look after you until you get a bit bigger." She said to pickles. He stopped to look at her as if he understood what she said.

He sniffed the grass for a few minutes until he found the right spot, and stood relieving himself as Beth looked on. "Good boy pickles!" she said proudly. "You didn't even get yourself wet this time."

A New Beginning for Beth

Pickles wagged his fluffy tail and ran over to where Beth was sitting. He tripped over his feet and ended up rolling the rest of the way to her. Beth laughed and scooped him up to kiss him. He licked her face and yapped excitedly. "At least someone loves me." She purred as her puppy licked her uncontrollably.

She carried the puppy into the house, retrieved claws from the family room sheers and carried the animals upstairs with her. The animals sat on the bed as they watched Beth changed into a pair of jeans and pink tank top.

She was meeting Nancy at the new Chinese restaurant that opened up on Farmer St. Beth wasn't in the mood for Chinese but Nancy liked it and she would make the sacrifice for her.

Beth went next door to the neighbors and asked if their granddaughter would be interested in making some money by babysitting pickles and claws. She was more than happy to oblige so she left an extra set of keys with her grandmother. Once she was sure that Tara and her pets would get along, Beth said good bye and pulled out her drive.

She was about a mile from the restaurant when her cell rang. "Mrs. Singer?" the voice was slightly frantic.

"Tara, is everything okay?" Beth was about to do a u-turn and head back home.

"Everything is fine. But I'm worried about the kitty. She is stuck in the sheers and every time I take her out of the curtains she climbs back up."

Beth laughed. She forgot to warn Tara about claws. "Just leave her in the sheers Tara. She seems to like being up high."

Once she had assure the girl that claws would be fine, she said goodbye and pulled into the parking lot of the restaurant.

Beth spotted Nancy's car in the lot and parked next to it.

As Beth stepped out of her car, another car pulled in after her and parked a few spaces down on the other side of the lot. Beth noticed a man in the passenger seat and she lost her breath for a moment. At first she thought she was imagining things but then took a second glance at the passenger then felt her heart race as she recognize the person as the man who was caught in her backyard. He was wearing a cap and sunglasses but had a huge white bandage covering his right eye.

She pretended to not notice them and hurried into the restaurant where Nancy was waiting for her in the entrance.

The women greeted each other with a hug. "Good. Now we can be seated." Nancy said waving to the hostess.

"Can we get a seat by the window facing the parking lot?" Beth asked.

Nancy looked at her sideways. "The parking lot? Whatever for?" then she raised her hands in surrender. "Never mind. I have learned never to ask you why when you request strange things."

They were seated at a small table on the other side of the room. There was a large window that gave Beth perfect view of her car.

"I need to use the ladies room." Beth said excusing herself. "Order something for us to drink."

Nancy just stared in disbelief at her friend who disappeared in the ladies room.

Once inside the washroom Beth made a quick call to Domenic, telling him what she had seen and if he could come by and check it out.

"Do you have your stun gun with you?" He asked as he carried his phone to his car and started the engine.

Beth sighed. She hated carrying that thing but she had promised to keep it with her at least until this case was finished. She assured Domenic that it was with her.

"I want you to go back to your table and relax. I'm going to pick up Jack and we will be there within ten minutes."

Beth hung up the phone washed and dried her hands and joined Nancy back at the table.

"I ordered some saki." Nancy said pouring a small glass for her friend.

Beth smiled in agreement and took a sip. The warm alcohol slid down her throat, warming her inside.

She glanced out the window at her car and started to choke. The car with the two men had moved next to her car and she could see the figures talking with each other.

She coughed hysterically and Nancy jumped to her feet and started patting her on the back. "Are you okay Beth?" she asked as she rubbed and patted her back.

A New Beginning for Beth

"This is very strong stuff." Beth managed to say in between coughs. She took a sip of water and was feeling the coughing fit passing.

Her phone rang and she checked the number. "Hi Domenic." She answered.

Nancy's gaze went from the menu to Beth's face. "Domenic? Who is Domenic?"

Beth put her finger up to hush Nancy. "I have the license number." She read off the license plate number of the car and Domenic repeated it to Jack, who wrote it down.

"We will do a check on the plate later. But for now we need to get there and confront the guy." Domenic said.

"Try and enjoy your meal, and don't leave the restaurant until you hear from me." He ordered.

Beth smiled and assured him she would stay in the restaurant until she heard from him.

Beth hung up the phone and looked around the room, trying to avoid Nancy's stares. She didn't feel like answering any questions from her best friend and she knew Nancy would have at least a dozen or so.

The room was decorated in tacky Japanese design, but it was still tasteful. The lamps hung low over each table and were decorated with rice paper and tassels.

"Nice place." Beth said, looking around the room. "I hope the food is good." She added.

"Do you want to tell me what that was all about?" Nancy asked crossing her arms.

Beth brushed her question aside. "Forget about it. Let's just enjoy ourselves."

"So tell me how this new diet is going?" Beth said trying to change the conversation and to forget about the two men in the parking lot.

"Oh, the cappuccino diet." Nancy sighed.

Beth stared at Nancy. "Cappuccino diet? I've never heard of it."

"That's because I discovered it myself by accident." Nancy said proudly. "I drink cappuccinos whenever I feel hungry and it seems to curb my appetite."

"Doesn't sound very healthy and all that caffeine would make one want to bounce off the walls?" Beth commented.

"That's true. The caffeine rush was keeping me awake at night but I was on it for about two weeks and I lost about three pounds."

"That's interesting. So are you still on it?" Beth was curious to know how she could handle being on such a strange diet.

Nancy shook her head. "My skin was breaking out so bad that I had to go off of it. I don't think I will ever lose this weight." she grabbed a roll of fat that was protruding over her jeans.

"You aren't fat, Nancy. You're just right." Beth said trying to cheer up her friend.

"But I'm not like I was before I had kids." Nancy said.

"Exactly, but what do you expect? You had kids and that takes a toll on a woman's body."

The waitress came over to their table to take their order and their conversation about weight abruptly stopped.

Nancy seemed consumed about her weight problem. She didn't look bad yet it was a topic of conversation every time they got together.

They placed their order and agreed to more saki.

"Speaking of kids, I have some news for you." Beth's voice lowered.

"Don't tell me you're pregnant and if you are who the hell is the father?" Nancy shuddered at the thought of her friend getting pregnant by James.

"No, I'm not pregnant but Jill is." Beth's voice was just above disgust.

Nancy broke out laughing. Beth watched her friend as she laughed hysterically at the news. At first Beth found the news hurtful but as she watched her friend laugh uncontrollably at the information, she found herself laughing along with her.

"That is the funniest news I have heard in a long time." Nancy said in between laughs.

"Can you imagine perfect James having baby spit on his Armani suits? It would make him crazy!"

Beth never thought about it like that. James was obsessive compulsive and he hated mess. There were times in their marriage that she wondered if that were the reason why he never wanted kids. "I never thought of it that way."

Nancy raised her glass in a toast. "You know what they say. Revenge is best served cold. And if you could pick out the best revenge on James

A New Beginning for Beth

for breaking your heart, it would be to give him a little bundle of joy with the town slut."

Nancy thought for a moment. "I should add that to make it even more revengeful, the baby would have to be colicky." She clicked her glass against Beth's glass in a toast.

After about fifteen minutes, Beth's cell rang. Domenic told her that they were in the parking lot.

"Can you make up an excuse to go out to your car?" he asked.

"What for?"

"We want to see if the guys in the car would approach you if they see you alone."

Beth agreed without letting on to Nancy and then hung up the phone.

"Was that Domenic again?" Nancy asked.

Beth thought quickly what to say to Nancy. "That was Mary. She asked me to check my brief case for a file. I need to go look in my car."

Nancy's face showed disappointment.

"I'll only be a minute." Beth assures her friend and quickly headed for the front door. She removed her keys and put them in her pocket. She then took out her stun gun and slid it between her purse and her body to conceal it.

She took a deep breath as her stomach fluttered nervously, and walked out towards her car.

The men were parked on the passenger side of Beth's car which gave Beth the opportunity to keep an eye on them as she opened her car door.

Beth had noticed Domenic and Jack standing to the side of the building watching her. She didn't want to draw any attention to their presence for fear that these guys might get scared off.

Beth got into her car and clicked the doors locked just in case one of them decided to try and get in. Beth pretended to be searching for something all the while keeping an eye out for any movement.

She heard the passenger side door open in the other car and saw the man get out of the car. Beth still pretended to be searching for something while the man walked around to her driver's side door. Beth looked up and gasped in recognition of the man. His face was swollen and purple bruising surrounded the white bandage that covered his eye.

Thank god he didn't lose his eye, Beth thought. She wouldn't want to be the one to find it floating around in her pool.

He tapped on Beth's window and told her to get out of the car.

"What do you want? Beth asked trying not to show her nervousness.

"I just want to talk to you so open the door." He replied, his voice sounding more firm.

"You try to break into my house and all you want to do is talk?"

He looked around and then motioned to his friend who got out of the drivers side. He was holding something in his hand.

Beth looked at the long object in his hand and realized he was holding a crowbar.

"I suggest you get out of the car before we drag you out bitch." He ordered.

Beth was shaking and her hands were moist. She knew that one way or another, they were going to get her out of the car. It was better if she did it voluntarily instead of by force so she unlocked her door and opened it. The bandaged man pulled the door open for her and Beth got out.

She stood between the two men, holding her stun gun by her side. Their attention was on her face and they didn't notice her power the gun up.

"What were you doing in my backyard?" Beth demanded. She didn't want to show her fear to these men.

"Let's go for a little ride and I'll tell you everything." The man said, taking Beth by the arm.

"I'm not going anywhere with you." Beth pulled her arm away but his friend grabbed her other arm. He was much bigger than the first man and he gripped her arm much tighter. Beth cried out as his hold on her arm tightened.

Beth reached up with her other arm and stuck the stun into his side. He made a grunting sound and dropped to the ground.

The other man stood there gawking as his friend's body lay on the ground twitching. "What the hell did you do to my friend?" he screamed backing away from Beth.

Domenic came up behind Beth and grabbed her as Jack checked the man that Beth stunned with her gun. Everyone's attention was diverted from the thin man and he was able to hop into the car and peel out of the parking lot before Jack and Domenic could respond.

"He got away." Beth cried as she watched the car pull into the traffic and disappear down the street.

"Don't worry about it." Domenic said. "We will check out the plate number and we'll find him." He put his arm around Beth. "Are you okay?"

"Just a bit shaken but I'm fine." She replied.

Jack made a call to the police as he slapped a set of handcuffs on the man. He laid there in a heap on the ground.

"Is he going to be okay?" Beth asked with concern.

Jack nodded. "You sure got him good." Jack laughed.

"I think that was the idea." Beth said. "I had visions of me being kidnapped and possibly gang raped by these two goons."

"They don't look like gang rapers." Jack smiled. "You probably could have beaten the living daylights out of the small one and this guy seems to be more brawn then brains."

Jack was right. They both didn't seem like professional thugs.

Nancy appeared at the restaurant door. She was about to tell Beth that their food was at the table when she saw the sight in front of her.

"What the hell?" She yelled.

"Go back inside Nancy. I'll be right there." Beth yelled back.

She stood there not sure what to do. Beth gave her the 'get the hell out of here' stare and she instinctively nodded and disappeared back inside.

Beth blew out a sigh. "How am I going to explain this to her?"

The guy on the ground started coming to. He moved slightly, trying to free his arms only to realize that his hands were handcuffed behind his back.

"Can you hear me?" Jack asked the man.

"Did I pee myself?" He mumbled.

Beth glanced down at his pants. "It doesn't look like it, but if you don't cooperate these guys will make sure you pee them next time." she didn't have the heart to tell him that she was the one who zapped him.

"I'm not saying a word." he growled.

"Can I kick him?" Beth asked pulling her leg back in a kicking position. She really wouldn't kick him but she was angry at what he wanted to do to her car.

Domenic pulled her away. "Why don't you go inside with your friend and enjoy the rest of the evening. We can take it from here."

"Besides, you don't want assault charges against you." He added. "I'll meet you back at your place later tonight." He kissed Beth on the forehead and walked her to the restaurant door.

As Beth walked inside, a police cruiser pulled into the lot and park next to the scene. Jack walked over to the driver's door and exchanged words with one of the officers. It was obvious to Beth that Jack and the officers knew each other. The officers got out and shook Jack and Domenic's hands.

They walked over to where the man was sitting on the pavement. He looked like a defeated soldier who was more afraid of being caught with wet pants then with his hands handcuffed behind him.

Domenic glanced over at the restaurant and saw Beth standing at the open doorway. He motioned for her to go back in and she instinctively disappeared inside the restaurant. She sat down across from Nancy who was already waiting in anticipation for the story she was going to tell her. Beth grabbed a large water glass filled it with saki and drank it down fast. She slammed the glass down and ordered another bottle of saki.

Saki must be drunk slowly, the waitress said with a heavy Chinese accent.

"Just keep it coming." Beth responded.

"Are you okay?" Nancy asked concern.

'I will be once I get more saki in me." Beth said filling her glass again and drinking a little bit slower this time.

The two women sat quietly for a few minutes, eating their sushi and all the extra dishes that Nancy had ordered while Beth was in the parking lot.

"Did you order everything on the menu?" Beth asked as she surveyed the half dozen or so dishes that filled their table.

"The waitress suggested a few things that were good and I wasn't sure what you liked so I ordered the best ones."

"I hope this is all of it." Beth said.

Nancy ignored her remark and filled her plate with a little bit of everything. Beth did the same thing and opted for a diet coke instead of more saki. Her head was spinning slightly from the combination of fear and saki.

"Are you going to tell me what happened out there?" Nancy asked.

"I don't know where to begin." Beth said, trying to stall.

"How about at the beginning and what was Jack doing out there in the parking lot? And please don't tell me he was passing by and saw some guys at your car."

Before Beth had a chance to respond, her phone rang. Saved by the bell, she thought.

Nancy sat back in her chair crossed her arms over her chest and gave Beth an annoyed look.

It was Domenic. "All clear out here."

"And the man?" Beth asked.

"The police are charging him with attempted car theft but we are sure he will post bail and be out by tonight." Domenic replied.

Beth knew they weren't trying to steal her car but she didn't want to make a verbal note of that in case she needed to use that story for Nancy.

"When will you be home?" he asked.

"Not for at least another hour, why?"

"I could meet you at your place."

Beth glanced out the window and could see Domenic smiling at her from the parking lot. She knew exactly what he had in mind and that smile made her body heat up.

"I'll see you there." Beth smiled back.

A few more words were exchanged and they hung up. Beth watched as Domenic waved to her and hopped in his car where Jack was already waiting. The car disappeared in traffic and Beth's attention went back to her friend.

"That was Domenic." Beth said.

"I gathered that." Nancy answered with slight sarcasm. "Do you always blush when you talk to this guy?"

Beth put her hands to her cheeks. He did more than make her blush when they talked on the phone. And it was a good thing that Nancy didn't know that.

"I didn't realize I was blushing." Beth said.

Nancy studied her friends face. "If I didn't know you better I would think you were in love."

Beth's eyes widened. "Me, in love? Don't be silly." She tried to brush off Nancy's remark.

Beth nibbled on some chicken as Nancy sat across from her watching her every move. "So are you going to tell me what was going on out in the parking lot or am I going to have to sit here all night wondering?"

Beth raised her eyes to meet Nancy's. Nancy knew when she was lying and she knew that her friend wouldn't accept any explanation but the truth. As much as Beth wanted to tell her everything, she knew it best to give her as minimal information as possible without it being unbelievable.

"I went to get something out of my car and these two men approached me. I had seen them following me here and I had phoned Domenic to tell him what was going on."

"Is that why you gave him the license plate of their car?" Nancy asked. She was sharp. Beth had to give her that. Nancy never missed a beat.

Beth nodded. "Jack is going to trace the number."

Nancy sat silently watching her friend. "Let me get this straight. If you knew these guys were following you, why would you go out to your car when you knew they were out there?"

Beth smiled. "You know I have always been one to run with scissors. I wanted to see what they would do."

"No I didn't know that. But if this is a new thing for you then one day you will trip while running with those scissors of yours and then you'll be in trouble." Nancy said shaking her head. "I also know there is more to this story then what you are saying. And for tonight I will pretend nothing is going on. But when all of this mess is finished with, you need to promise me that you will tell me everything."

"I promise." Beth replied, crossing her heart.

It was past ten by the time Beth and Nancy said their goodbyes. Beth pulled into her driveway and noticed Domenic's car parked in front of her house. Her heart fluttered at the prospect of having him in her bed tonight. Ever since James dropped the new of Jill's pregnancy on her, her thoughts were of having a baby of her own. Although she didn't know Domenic that well, her grandparents adored him and he adored her. Maybe that was enough for her to consider him the perfect man to father her baby. But she wasn't like Jill. She could never live with herself if she purposely got pregnant just to hold on to a man. In her case, it wasn't a question of holding onto a man as it was to have a family. Even if Domenic didn't want to marry her she was sure of one thing. He would never stay out of his child's life.

"Don't be ridiculous Beth." she mumbled to herself. "You are better then that. Forget the notion of getting pregnant. Besides you are still young enough to have children." She shook off the thought and quietly opened her front door.

As she entered the foyer the scent of flowers filled her senses. Down the hall she could see the flickering of candles and Nat King Cole was singing autumn leaves. She kicked off her shoes as pickles clumsily ran towards her. She picked him up and hugged him as he licked her face. Domenic stood at the end of the hall leaning against the wall watching her and pickles. Their eyes met and Beth's heart beat faster at the vision of this handsome man smiling at her. He looked absolutely gorgeous in the candlelight. Beth felt her body heat up and she wanted to jump his bones right at that moment.

"Welcome home." He whispered as he moved closer towards her.

"I have never been as welcomed in my own house as you and pickles have made me feel at this moment." Beth smiled and moved closer to Domenic.

He reached out for her and kissed her gently on the cheek. "Did you have a nice time with your friend?"

"Aside from the attempted kidnapping and being grilled by Nancy, the night was great."

"I have a surprise for you." Domenic said with a smile.

He walked her into the family room and Beth gasped at the sight before her. The fireplace mantle was covered with lit candles as well as the marble hearth. "It's too hot for a fire so I thought I would do the next best thing."

"It's beautiful." Beth whispered.

Domenic handed her a glass of wine. He had a chocolate fondue warming on the coffee table and an array of fresh fruit placed neatly on a tray.

"Where is Tara?" Beth asked remembering the little girl.

"I paid her for her babysitting and walked her home." He said. "I also introduced myself to her grandparents. I didn't want them to worry about a stranger in your house."

"How did you introduce yourself?" Beth was curious to know how Domenic saw himself with her. Was he just her divorce lawyer and part time lover or did their relationship develop into something deeper.

"How would you like me to introduce myself to them?" he asked.

Beth narrowed her eyes at Domenic. He was trapping her and she would have none of that. "Didn't your parents ever tell you to never answer a question with a question?"

Domenic laughed and pulled Beth to him. He kissed her gently on her mouth. "Let's just say that they were pleased with my answer." He kissed her again. "And stop thinking so much. Just go with the flow Bethany."

Beth wrapped her arms around Domenic. She loved feeling him next to her. He gave Beth the feeling of security. A feeling she never felt with her husband. His arms held her tight and they slowly began to move to the soft jazz music that played in the background.

Domenic stroked Beth's silky blonde hair. "I hope you put that terrible incident from today out of your head." He whispered in her ear.

There were a few terrible incidents but the only thing on Beth's mind was the anticipation of the rest of the night. "You mean the James incident?"

Domenic nodded. "I hope I never make you as sad as you were today. And I hope I never see you that sad either."

"At this moment, I don't think it is humanly possible for you to ever make me feel even the slightest sadness." Beth sighed.

Domenic looked into Beth's eyes. He marveled at her beauty and secretly thanked her grandparents for allowing him to meet her.

He had never been in love before but if this was what love felt like then he was sorry it took him so long. In the short time that they had known each other, his emotions were a jumbled mess. His intentions went from wanting to represent her in her divorce to wanting to protect her from the world. Beth had bewitched him and he was her prisoner. If she rejected him he would be crushed. Now he knew why all the women before reacted the way they did when he refused to commit to a relationship. He now understood how they felt and his heart went out to them. For the first time in his life he wasn't in control of the relationship. This tiny women whom he held in his arms was in total control of their relationship and with his emotions.

His body trembled as Beth held him tighter. "I have another surprise for you." He said.

"More surprises?" her eyes sparkled under the candle light.

Domenic led her upstairs to the bedroom. Candles were lit in the bathroom and her Jacuzzi was filled with bubbles that smelled like peaches. It was her favorite scent.

"You relax in the tub while I bring everything upstairs." Domenic said.

He closed the door behind him and retrieved the fondue and fruit from the family room. He blew out all the candles and made sure the doors were locked before he returned to the bedroom. He undressed and joined Beth in the bath.

Beth was laying in the bath and had not paid attention to Domenic's presence. He watched her and marveled at her beauty. His body reacted to the sight before him and he slowly joined Beth in the water.

Beth opened her eyes and smiled. "What took you so long?" she asked leaning towards him to kiss him.

"I had to make sure the babies were fine." He grinned. "They followed me upstairs so I put a couple of pillows on the floor for them to sleep on."

"You're a good daddy." Beth giggled. She motioned for him to turn around. She took a wash cloth, soaped it up and gently washed his back.

Domenic moaned as she moved from his neck and worked her way down his back. "This feels great."

"You are great." She purred as her hands moved around his waist and stopping below his stomach. Domenic leaned against her allowing full access to his firmness.

Beth's body trembled as her hands explored his manhood.

Domenic turned his head towards hers and pulled her mouth close to his. They kissed deeply as Domenic pulled Beth on top of him. Their lips never parted as Beth moved on top of Domenic.

His hands cupped her breasts as Beth moved up and down on his body.

Water splashed on the floor as she moved faster. Domenic held her as he tried to control his orgasm but he was so turned on by Beth's wet body that he could hold on no longer. He pulled her close as he exploded inside her.

Beth slumped against Domenic in exhaustion. "We didn't take precautions." She breathed in his ear.

Domenic nodded as his breathing became steadier and less heavy. "Let's not worry about it tonight."

Chapter Eight

The sound of Domenic's cell phone woke Beth. She looked at her bedside alarm. Four thirty. It was still dark out and Domenic was searching for his phone.

"Hello?" Domenic said his voice husky from sleep.

"Sorry to wake you but I thought you would like to know that I got a lead on that license plate." Jack said.

"That's okay, Jack. What did you find out?" Domenic sat up in bed and flicked on the side table lamp.

Beth made a moan as the light blinded her.

"I guess you aren't alone." Jack chuckled.

"You guessed right." Domenic yawned.

"Should I wait until you aren't so preoccupied?" he asked.

"That's okay. Why don't you come over and bring coffee." Domenic suggested.

"Tell him to bring donuts and muffins if he's stopping for coffee." Beth mumbled as she pulled the blankets over her shoulders.

Jack gave out a grunt. "Don't tell me that you are at Beth's."

Domenic yawned again. "Okay I won't. But when you bring the coffee and donuts, bring them to Beth's place."

An hour later the three of them were sitting in Beth's kitchen sharing donuts and coffee.

"So what did you find out?" Domenic asked as he sipped his Tim Horton's coffee.

Jack shoved a paper in front of Domenic. "Do you recognize the name of the company?"

Domenic scanned the paper and he felt the blood rush from his face. "Are you sure about this?"

"We rechecked it, but it came up the same." He nodded.

Beth watched in silence as Domenic read the report. Her eyes moved from Domenic to Jack who was also studying Domenic's expression.

"What does it say?" Beth asked as her curiosity got the better of her.

Domenic and Jack looked at each other. By the look on their faces it was obvious they were thinking the same thing.

"You're off the case, Beth." Jack said.

Beth looked stunned and confused. "What do you mean that I'm off the case? I'm not off the case." Her voice was stern. Beth grabbed the paper off of Domenic before he had a chance to protest.

She read the paper and her reaction was the same as Domenic's. "Why would the pharmaceutical company have these men on their payroll?"

Jack opened the box of donuts and chose a chocolate donut. "It seems to me that this company is playing both ends against the middle."

Domenic could feel the anger build. He was feeling betrayed by this company that he represented and he wanted to get to the bottom of it. "Maybe they don't think we can do our job."

"Or maybe they know what Peter is up to and if they have their own people looking into it they could avoid the publicity." Beth added.

"There's something else you both should know." Jack said with hesitation. "That guy we arrested was bailed out and he promptly disappeared."

Domenic leaned back in his chair. "No doubt my clients bailed him out."

Jack nodded. Then a smile came to his face. "They don't know we know who owned the car."

"At least we can assume that." Domenic added. "If they know that we know what is going on I'm sure they would contact me today."

Jack went silent. There was something else he had found out and the news confused him.

"Something's on your mind Jack I know that look when I see it." Beth said.

Jack nodded. "We had been doing some asking around with the Bucar's neighbors."

Beth and Domenic looked at each other.

"Did Peter ever tell you what his mother was sick with?" jack asked Beth.

She shook her head no. "Alice told me she was sick but she never went into details. The truth is I don't think she even knew what it was that she had."

Jack stared at Beth. "The story goes that Mrs. Bucar was wandering around in the park naked. She had been living on her own for about a year when her health started going. Peter moved back with her at the insistence of his sister."

"Peter didn't want to move back?" Beth asked.

"According to the people we talked to, Peter didn't want anyone to know about his mother." Jack said.

"Do you think he was into something back then?" Domenic asked.

"It seems that way." jack replied. "Anyway, she was sent to a hospital where she was diagnosed with Alzheimer's."

Beth sat back in her chair. She wasn't an expert in the medical field but she knew there was medicine that can be taken for this. "What type of hospital was she in?"

"It was long term care for people who were suffering from her type of illness as well as dementia."

"But there is medicine that can be taken for that." Domenic added.

Beth listened to the two men. Her gut was telling her that there was more to this then what Domenic was told. She wanted to get to the bottom of this case and being off the case wasn't the answer. She was even more determined to get closer to Peter.

"I'm not off the case and nothing you both can say will convince me to give up on this." Beth sipped the tea that Jack brought her. "Besides you both need me. I'm the only one who has contact with Peter. And it's obvious that they know about me because they were following Peter."

As much as Domenic and Jack hated to admit it they knew Beth was right. They knew that if Beth dropped out of sight now Peter would be suspicious and he might realize that the company was aware of his theft.

Nothing was making sense to Beth. It was almost surreal the way this case was playing out. She was sure Peter was doing something illegal. She also knew that his employer hired Domenic and her grandfather's agency to tail Peter yet they had someone from inside the company tailing him as well. But then there was the question of the women that broke into Peter's house. What was their part in this and who were they?

"I think for now, we need to keep all of this quiet. It seems that we can't let on to anyone outside the agency what we know." Beth said. "I also think that I need to give our friend Peter a call." She added.

Domenic didn't like the idea but he knew there was no way Beth would listen to him. "If you do arrange a date make it in a public place."

Beth agreed and promised the men that she would take all the precautions necessary to keep herself safe.

Jack checked his watch. The sun was up and he hadn't even been to bed yet. "I better get going."

Domenic saw Jack out as Beth went back upstairs. A minute later Domenic joined her.

Beth had snuggled back in bed. "I have nothing booked today." She said closing her eyes.

Domenic moved to the other side of the bed and climbed in beside her. "I wish I could say the same but I have court at ten."

Beth moved closer to Domenic and he instinctively wrapped his arms around her. "It's only six so you have a couple of hours before you have to leave." Her eyes were closed and her voice was soft.

Domenic immediately responded to her touch. "You are too much Beth." he whispered as he kissed her.

Beth smiled as she brushed Domenic's hair out of his eyes. She watched his face as his hands explored her body. She gave out a moan of pleasure as his fingers touched her sensitive spots.

Domenic was pleased with himself. Beth easily responded to his touch and this made him feel wonderful. He loved the way her cheeks would redden when she was aroused. He loved the way she arched her back when she climaxed. He loved feeling her legs wrapped around him and he loved the way her body felt against his.

Domenic Ragonese, you are definitely crazy about this woman, he thought as he disappeared under the covers.

Peter was busy in his office when he was interrupted by his cell phone. He normally wouldn't take a personal call unless it was his mother or sister calling, but this time was different. This time it was Beth. He didn't want her to know that he was unsure about her. "Hello Beth, it's so good to hear from you."

"How did you know it was me?" Beth said with surprise.

"I have you in my cell phone so your name came up." He replied. "I've been thinking about you a lot." He added.

"I'm sorry I haven't called you but work is crazy. Today I'm free and I thought maybe we could meet up for lunch."

"Sounds great but I won't have much time. We are working on a big project and I don't want to spend too much time away from the lab."

"That's too bad Peter. I really wanted to see you." Her voice sounded disappointed.

"I'd like to see you too Beth." he was also disappointed but for different reasons.

Beth thought for a moment. "I could always bring food for us to share in your office if you want." She held her breath hoping he would agree.

After a short silence Peter thought it would be a great idea but suggested they take their lunch in the cafeteria.

They agreed to meet in the lobby of his office building for eleven thirty which gave Beth a couple of hours to prepare. "I can't wait to see you." She said.

"Me too." Peter said.

They exchanged a few more words then said their goodbyes.

Beth had no plan but rather to take things easy. If a window of opportunity opened up for her to get some information, she would jump at it. But she didn't want to push it.

Peter on the other hand had a plan. He didn't completely trust Beth. Ever since his mother told him about her finding his keys in the bathroom something didn't sit right with him. He knew there were times he was being followed and he wanted to see if Beth had something to do with it. He felt his life was spiraling downward and he was getting nervous. He knew how to beat the system at work but how was he going to get his contacts off his back? He worried for his safety as well as his mothers. She had been through enough with losing a year of her life. He even had to deal with Amanda's constant harassment. He thought of firing her but she had enough on him to make his life even more miserable.

Now he had a new problem in the form of Beth. What did she want from him? Was she involved with the people who were following him or was she just an innocent bystander? He just couldn't bring himself to believe she wasn't aware of what he was up to. Especially since she put his keys back on the nail in the window. How would she have known about that?

It was just before noon when Beth stepped into the lobby of the medical building. There was a reception and information desk to the right of the entrance. Beyond that was a security area that housed metal detectors and conveyor belts with x-ray machines. Three guards were assigned to this area. You had to pass this area to reach the elevators and again when you were leaving the building.

Beth hiked her purse high up her shoulder and walked over to the reception desk. A guard sat watching the monitors, unaware of her presence.

Beth cleared her throat and the guard glanced up at her.

He pointed to a clip board. "Sign in please." He said, his eyes moving back to the monitors.

Beth wrote down her name, office address and cell number on the paper and handed it back to the guard. He placed it back on the ledge without taking his eyes off the monitors.

"I'm here to see Peter Bucar." Beth said.

"You need a visitors pass." He handed Beth a laminated visitors pass which she clipped onto her jacket pocket. He pointed to the entrance without looking up. "Once you go through security, take the elevators to the fifth floor. His office is room fifty eight."

Beth smiled and nodded a thank you even though the guard didn't notice.

That was easy she thought. It was obvious that he didn't see her as a terrorist or any type of threat. Either that or he had some soap opera

A New Beginning for Beth

on those monitors and didn't want to miss a beat. Either way, he didn't seem too interested in who came and went.

Beth walked over to the security entrance and placed her bag on the conveyer belt. She waited for the guard to motion for her to walk through security as another guard examined the contents of her purse on the x-ray machine. She knew to expect the security so she left her pepper spray and stun gun in her car. The least attention she drew to herself the better.

"I'm here to see peter Bucar." she repeated to the guard on the other side of the security entrance.

He nodded as if he understood but didn't respond except for handing her, her purse and pointing to the elevators.

Beth was getting the impression that this security feature was just as annoying for the guards as it was for the employees, not to mention what visitors had to go through.

She dismissed his lack of interest and pushed the up button on the elevators.

The door opened and Peter stepped out, almost butting heads with Beth.

"Peter! I was just on my way up to your office." Beth said with surprise.

"I know. Bernie called me and told me you arrived." he pointed to the guard at the information desk.

"How nice of you to meet me in the lobby. Should we go up to your office?"

Peter shook his head. "I thought we would go to the cafeteria." he ushered Beth into the elevator before the door closed and pushed the button for the second floor.

Beth was disappointed. She was hoping to have a look around his office but now she had to rethink her plans.

"That would be great." Beth smiled hiding her disappointment. "I hope you will show me around the building before I leave."

Peter glanced at Beth, studying her face for any hint of deception. Beth's smile was innocent and warm. Just like it had been each time they were together. Maybe he was wrong about Beth. Maybe she really did find the keys in the bathroom. He has had a lot on his mind lately so it would have been very easy for him to forget them. But the fact that she placed them back on the nail kept gnawing at him. He couldn't shake that thought.

"In due time." he replied taking Beth's hand and gently kissing it.

Beth blushed at his public display of affection even though they were the only ones riding the elevator.

Peter moved in closer to Beth, pinning her against the back of the elevator. Beth knew what was coming next and her mind was spinning thoughts of how to get out of this situation. The ride to the next floor seemed to be taking forever.

Beth gently pushed him away. "Eyes are on us." she whispered as she pointed to the camera. The red light was blinking and she knew that Bernie was amusing himself with their display.

"You're right." Peter said as he moved away. "We can always wait till later." His smile hid the uncertainty that he felt with Beth. His sexual advances were a test to see Beth's interest in him but unfortunately he wasn't able to come to a conclusion.

Beth felt a rush of relief wash through her body as the elevator came to a stop and the doors opened. They stepped out into a large corridor and followed the signs that read cafeteria.

They arrived at two large metal doors that were wedged opened. The scent of cooking food drew people from every corridor and they were moving quickly through the opened doors. Each person grabbed a blue plastic tray and took their place in line at the long counter of foods. There was everything from fresh fruit to hot meals to a selection of desserts. No desire or craving was overlooked.

Peter ushered me in front of him as he placed a tray on the metal bars and slid it to each display of food.

"They seem to have everything here." Beth said, as she examined each window that housed the food.

"The company wants to keep us happy so we will be more productive." Peter replied grabbing an apple.

Beth opted for a chicken salad with blue cheese dressing and a large Perrier to drink.

"That's all you're going to have to eat?" Peter asked as he looked at Beth's choices.

"I don't usually eat a large lunch." she answered.

Peter shrugged his shoulders and ordered a hamburger and fries. He paid for the food and they found an unoccupied table near the entrance.

Beth unloaded the tray and placed Peters food, drink and plastic utensils, in front of him.

"I didn't know you ate in the cafeteria." Beth remarked.

"Not usually but I thought it would be something different so you could see a little of where I work." He smiled.

"Does that mean you're going to give me the grand tour after our lunch?"

"Maybe even more than a tour." Peter grinned as he studied Beth for any hint of doubt.

Beth didn't falter. Being a lawyer you spent a lot of time performing in front of a mirror before a big case. She had to be convincing to a jury or judge that her client was either innocent or deserved the house and car in the settlement. She also knew she was good at her deception. If she ever wanted to quit her day job she could easily become a good actress.

"Sounds intriguing." Beth purred, moving closer to Peter.

"Hi Peter. I didn't know you were eating here today." A voice said.

Peter looked up and his face went from warm and inviting to total disgust. His eyes darted to Beth as Beth turned around and was face to face with the red haired woman she had seen in the parking lot.

"Aren't you going to introduce me?" The woman asked.

"Hi I'm Amanda, and you are?" The woman asked before Peter had a chance to respond.

"Beth, a friend of Peters." Beth stuck out her hand as a friendly gesture but Amanda paid no attention.

"You don't mind if I join you both." She placed her food down next to Peter's and pulled up a chair.

"So how long have you two known each other?" Amanda asked Beth. Her face held a smile but her eyes showed jealousy.

Beth watched Peter out of the corner of her eye. It was obvious he was unhappy with Amanda's presence. Although she wanted to know more about this woman, she knew that this may be her only chance to get a look at Peter's office.

"We've been dating only a short time." Beth said.

"Dating?" Amanda turned to Peter. "You didn't tell me you were dating her. I thought you were just friends?" Her voice became louder with each word.

"Maybe Peter didn't feel it was any of your business." Beth said answering for Peter.

Beth reached for Peters hand and he instinctively allowed her to hold it. She gently squeezed his hand to let him know of her feeling of awkwardness and his face softened at her touch.

Amanda sat back in her chair with shock on her face. The anger was building inside her body. She wanted to leap across the table at Beth and rip her hair out and then finish off her lunchtime by beating on Peter for twenty minutes.

"As a matter of fact, Peter and I were just leaving. We want to eat out lunch in privacy and he suggested going to his office." Beth gathered up their food and placed it back on the tray. Peter immediately got to his feet and picked up the tray.

"I guess he is going to have you for dessert by fucking you on his office desk." Amanda said sharply.

Beth turned to Amanda and then directed her stare at Peter. His face was red with embarrassment as Amanda sat there stone faced, arms crossed over her chest in victory.

It was apparent that Amanda and Peter had done just that. There was more to their relationship than colleagues.

Beth waved her hand in the air. "Peter wouldn't do that with me. He knows I have too much class for that."

"It was nice meeting you Amanda." Beth stood and turned on her heels.

Amanda's blood boiled as she felt the pangs of defeat and humility.

Beth stopped and turned to Amanda. "I have a suggestion for you Amanda."

Amanda raised an eyebrow. "And what would that be?"

"Your milk would taste much better for you if you drank it from a saucer instead of a glass."

Peter broke out laughing and almost dropped his tray.

They hurried out of the cafeteria before Amanda lost total control and they ended up in a food fight.

"That was too funny." Peter laughed as they rode the elevator up to the fifth floor.

He was having difficulty holding onto the tray of food as he recalled the look on Amanda's face when they exited the cafeteria.

"I hope you don't mind eating in your office." Beth said. "I knew that if we stayed there any longer it might have become ugly between the two of us and then where would we be."

Peter smiled. "Not at all. I know Amanda and she wouldn't have thought twice about beating the crap out of you right there at the table."

Her suggestion was also another way of her getting into his office undisturbed. As for having access to his computer, Beth would wing it and see what happens.

They walked down the hall towards Peter's office. He took out a set of keys and unlocked the door while Beth held the tray of food. They walked into the office and Peter flipped on the lights then took the tray from Beth. He placed the tray on a counter that was lined with computers and different types of equipment that Beth was not familiar with.

"What do all these machines do?" she asked.

"These analyze all the results and tests that are done in the labs." He replied pulling up two chairs and removing the food from the tray.

Beth turned to Peter. "You do all the testing for everyone else?"

Peter nodded as he pulled a chair out for Beth and motioned for her to sit.

"I'm impressed." She smiled.

Peter returned the smile. "That's my desk over there." He pointed to a desk that was a far cry from the organized one he had at his house. This one was covered with stacks of folders and papers. Pens were tucked inside a coffee mug and underneath the entire mess sat a computer with monitor. Wires were tucked through a hole in the desk and puddle on the floor in a huge heap.

"Looks like the cleaning crew missed your desk for the past six months." She laughed.

Peter looked over at his mess and frowned. "I know it looks bad but I know exactly where everything is. I have to paste a note on the front of my computer to instruct the cleaners to not touch anything except the waste basket."

Beth took her place next to Peter. "Which project are you working on today?"

"There isn't one in particular. We have many different things we test each day."

Beth nodded as if she understood.

"After we eat, I will show you my lab." He replied.

Beth put the plates and cups back onto the tray to bring back to the cafeteria. Peter took her hand and led her behind the filing cabinets where there was another door with a smoked glass insert. Beyond the door was a laboratory that had several counters with beakers and test tubes. The room reminded Beth of science class in high school.

Science scared her ever since she was paired up with Michael Aston in high school. Unbeknown to Beth, he made a stink bomb that not only gave off a smell that was worse then a dead skunk that was left on the side of the highway in one hundred degree heat, but he managed to take out half the desks in the explosion. It took most of the school year to get rid of the smell. She remembers walking into the class and seeing dozens of car air fresheners hanging from the ceiling. That was one of the reasons why she didn't pursue a medical career.

Beth gave out a shudder.

"Are you okay?" Peter asked.

"I'm fine. I just don't like laboratories." She replied.

Peters face showed disappointment. "I thought you would be interested in my work."

"I am interested. I just have this phobia when it comes to science labs." She replied. "Can we go back into your office?" Beth was already through the door before Peter could reply.

She boldly sat at his desk and this move caught Peter by surprise. "So this is where you spend most of your time during the day." She smiled moving the mouse around to open the screen.

Peter watched her for a moment then moved behind her to watch what she was doing. There was a password on his computer so he knew she wouldn't see anything.

Beth did however; notice the external hard drive sticking out of the USB port. It looked like the same one that Peter was wearing around his neck the day she first met him.

Peter swung the chair around and moved in closer to Beth. He leaned over and kissed her passionately. This caught Beth off guard and she pulled away from him.

"What's wrong?" Peter asked.

Beth thought of a quick and convincing answer. "I'm sorry Peter. I just feel uncomfortable getting romantic in your office."

Peter dismissed her concerns. "I locked the door behind me and I'm the only one with a key, except maybe the cleaning crew, but they aren't here till five."

He moved in again to kiss her but Beth once again pulled away. "Now what's wrong?" Peter was becoming annoyed.

Beth stood and moved to the other side of the desk. "Sorry Peter but I don't want to be like Amanda and do it on your desk. I'm not like that."

She moved closer to the door and Peter followed close behind. "I don't think of you like that." he apologized. "Besides, I never did it with Amanda on my desk."

Beth turned to Peter. She studied his face for any hint of dishonesty. "Why would she say that if it weren't true?"

"Because she can't get over the fact that we are no longer a couple." He replied.

He moved closer to her and gently cupped her face in his hands. Beth didn't try to pull away. In spite of her true reasons for being there, she liked Peter. He was sweet and caring and he loved his mother. It was a shame that he was doing something that he shouldn't be doing.

They looked into each others eyes as their lips met again. This time the kiss was gentle and was less lustful. This time the kiss was romantic and caring. They held the kiss for a moment until a knock on the door broke their embrace.

Saved by the bell, Beth thought as she felt herself being pulled in by his charm. She grabbed a hold of her feelings and rubbed her hands down her skirt as she felt her palms become moist.

Peter opened the door and Beth almost choked seeing Jack standing there dressed in a UPS uniform.

"I have a delivery for Joseph Pavone." He said staring at his clip board.

"You have the wrong office." Peter replied, with slight annoyance in his voice. "You even have the wrong floor. He's on the eighth floor."

Jack glanced over at me. "Well it says this office and this floor. Are you sure this isn't his office?"

"This is my office so I would know if Joseph Pavone was here."

Jack shrugged his shoulders. "Okay but I still don't understand how they got this wrong."

Beth looked at her watch. "I better go Peter." She said stopping him from closing the door.

Peter's face showed disappointment. "Can I see you tonight?"

Beth thought for a moment. "Why don't you call me later when you get home and we can arrange something?"

Peter moved in closer to Beth until her back was against the wall and he was inches from her. "I hope we can pick up where we left off." He whispered.

Beth swallowed hard. "I will look forward to it."

Jack was outside the building standing next to Beth's car as she approached. "Thanks for saving me."

"It sounded as if he was getting too friendly with you." He nodded.

"How did you know that?" Beth was confused.

"I put a listening device in your purse the other day." He smiled.

Beth thought for a moment. "Which day was that?"

"Don't worry. I only listen in when I know you are on the case." He said reassuring her that her privacy was still private.

She narrowed her eyes at him. "Somehow I am finding that hard to believe."

Jack smiled and held her car door open for her. "Go home to Domenic. I'm sure he is missing you."

"I'm not even going to dignify that with a response." She said climbing in and starting her car.

"I see your girlfriend left." Amanda said to Peter.

Peter looked up from his computer and glared at Amanda. "Why do you have to be such a bitch? I gave you what you needed so why can't you just leave me alone?"

Amanda moved around the desk towards Peter. "I know what you are up to Peter and I think I should get a cut of the money."

Peter closed off his screen. "You don't know what you are talking about."

"Do you honestly think I don't know about your list of contacts?" her voice was angry.

Peter felt his heart fall into his stomach. He had enough problems to deal with now he had to worry about Amanda keeping her mouth shut. How a good deed could get so out of hand was beyond him. All he wanted to do was make his mother better and now he had threats on his life and his mothers. Now this problem with Amanda was going to push him over the edge.

He felt his face redden and his anger come to a boil. Amanda put her hand on his shoulder. "so what about it Peter? Are you going to count me in?"

Peter grabbed Amanda's hand and squeezed it until she cried in pain. "Listen to me Amanda, I'm not including you in anything, you got that? If you ever snoop through my private files or property again I will kill you!" he screamed, his voice echoing through the office.

He pushed Amanda against the wall behind his desk. She hit the wall with a thud, knocking the wind out of her. She instantly fell to the floor gasping for air.

Peter raised his hand to strike her but held himself back. By the look of shock and fear on Amanda's face, he felt sure his message was heard.

Air filled Amanda's lungs and she scrambled away from Peter, hitting her knee against the leg of the desk. She cried in pain as she quickly got to her feet and ran to the door.

She flung the door opened as Peter moved closer to her. He pulled her away from the door and slammed it shut. "I'm not finished with you." He growled.

"What do you want from me?" She cried as he yanked her head back with her hair.

"I want to make it perfectly clear that there is nothing else between us except for a working relationship. I want you to stay away from me and my mother and Beth." he demanded.

"Okay, okay! I will become invisible, just let go of my hair!"

Peter released his hold on Amanda and moved towards the door. Amanda gathered herself up and slowly moved towards the door. She was shaking and forcing herself not to cry. Peter was always such a calm and gentle person. She had never seen this side of Peter and it frightened her to the point that she thought he would really kill her.

Peter opened the door allowing Amanda to leave. She quickly exited the door. "I don't want to see your fucking face the rest of the day." He snapped as he slammed the door on her.

Amanda didn't wait around to see if he would open the door again. She left the building without signing out. she stood in the parking lot catching her breath when she noticed Beth standing by her car talking to the UPS man she had seen come out of Peter's office.

"Don't they look friendly?" she said to herself.

She watched as Beth climbed into her car and left the man standing there. She felt her sixth sense kick in and tell her that something wasn't quite right with this woman.

"I think I need to find out a little bit more about this woman." she muttered as she beeped her car open and climbed in. she started up the car and drove slowly towards the UPS man. She stopped a distance from him and waited to see him climb into his truck. But there was no truck in the parking lot. Instead she watched him climb into a black equinox and drive out behind Beth. She jotted down his license number and followed him for a distance until she felt sure he would realize he was being followed. She pulled off the next street and stopped at the corner. She watched him pull onto the highway so she turned around and headed for the highway. After about a mile she spotted the equinox take the next turn off. She slowed down to allow herself some distance between the truck and her car, and then exited onto the same ramp. By the time she got to the top of the ramp the equinox had disappeared. She looked up and down the street but the car and its owner was no where to be found.

She looked down at the license number she had written on a piece of paper and quickly made a call on her cell.

"Hey, how are you?" she said in the phone.

There was a pause on the phone as the person on the other end spoke.

"That's great to hear. I have a favor to ask. Can you look up a license number for me?" she asked. She read out the license number. "I will meet you tonight for the results. If you can find out anything else about the person who owns the car, let me know." A few more words were exchanged and Amanda hung up the phone, turned her car around and headed for home. Her next plan was to find out more about this Beth person. Who ever this guy was, she was sure he would lead her to Beth.

Pickles was at the door just as Beth opened it. His tail was wagging wildly as she bent down to pick him up. Claws followed close behind, stopping every so often to chase her tail. "Isn't this a pleasant greeting?" She said with a smile as she scooped up claws and gave her pets a kiss.

Domenic followed behind waiting patiently for his kiss. "How did your lunch turn out?" he asked.

"It was interesting to say the least."

Domenic kissed Beth on the lips. "Interesting how?"

"Our lunch was interrupted briefly by his ex girlfriend." Beth removed her shoes and slipped her feet into some soft slippers. She put the pets on the floor and everyone followed her into the kitchen. She took two soft drinks from the fridge and handed one to Domenic.

"Do you have any information on this Amanda woman?" Beth asked.

"The only thing we know is that she's been working at the lab for a little over a year. Shortly after working there she hooked up with Peter but it didn't last more than two months."

Domenic studied Beth's face. It was obvious to him that she had something on her mind.

"I think we need to find out a little more about this woman." she said.

Domenic took a sip of his soda. "Do you think she has something to do with this case?"

"My gut tells me she isn't entirely ignorant to what Peter is up to." Beth replied.

"You could be right."

"There's something else that is bugging me." Beth added.

Domenic sat silently.

"I may be wrong in this but I don't think I am, but her voice sounded like one of the people who broke into Peter's house that day."

"Are you sure about this?"

Beth nodded. "I'm as sure as I could be. I knew something was familiar about her voice and I thought about it all the way home. Then it dawned on me where I heard her voice before."

Domenic took his cell phone out of his pant pocket and made a call. He asked the person to look up any information they could find on Amanda. He gave the person Beth's home fax number and instructed them to fax over all the information as soon as they got it. A few more words were exchanged then Domenic hung up the phone and stuck it back in his pocket.

He turned his attention back to Beth who was sitting quietly at the kitchen island. A smile formed on his face. "My secretary will fax over the information as soon as possible."

Beth nodded as she noticed Domenic's eyes twinkle.

"It may take awhile, though." He added.

Beth felt her palms moisten as Domenic moved closer to her. She saw that look in his eyes before. It was a dangerous look and she knew it was hard to resist. "I suppose you have an idea how to pass the time while we wait."

Domenic moved one hand around Beth's waist, pulling her off the chair. "I have a few ideas." He whispered in her ear.

He kissed her neck, making Beth moan with pleasure. He knew exactly how to make her feel good which made it difficult for her to resist him.

Beth closed her eyes, allowing herself to become victim to the pleasure she was feeling, until her pleasure was interrupted by the sound of the phone ringing.

"Saved by the bell." She sighed.

Domenic gave her an odd look. "You think you need to be saved?"

Beth gathered her thoughts and buttoned her blouse. "I have found in the short time of knowing you that any woman who comes in contact with you, needs to be saved from your charm."

Domenic's face formed a frown. "Do you think I'm a womanizer?" he asked.

Beth held up her finger to shush Domenic as she answered the phone.

"It's about time I got in touch with you." The voice said.

A New Beginning for Beth

Beth closed her eyes tight. Damn! She thought she had done well avoiding her mother. She made a mental head slap as she realized she didn't check the number first. "Hi mom. How are you?"

"Don't try and be nice." Her mother snapped. "You have been avoiding my calls!"

"Not at all mom. I've been really busy at the office." She replied making a slight strangling sound.

"I want to see you soon and talk to you about your marriage."

"Mom, my marriage is over so there isn't anything to talk about."

"There is always something to talk about and I want to know what you are planning on doing about getting your husband back."

Beth felt the blood rush from her face and the anger billow up from her belly. Was this woman serious? Did she actually expect her to try and get James back? "Mom I caught James doing it with Jill on the office desk! Do you actually think I would want to go back to that cheating bastard? Think about it!"

She heard her mother snap her tongue against the roof of her mouth. Something she did when she thought Beth was being dramatic or overly sensitive. Beth hated when she did that. "One simple mistake. A man is entitled to one mistake." She said.

Beth sighed. "You're right mom. Everyone is entitled to one mistake. But given the fact that Jill is pregnant with his child would make it two mistakes. And for that I would rather stick hot pokers in my eyes then take that son of a bitch back." Her voice got louder with each word.

She heard her mother gasp.

"Now mom, I don't like hanging up on anyone, but I really must go. I will call you when I'm ready."

She hung up the phone and took a deep breath.

"That went well." Domenic said sarcastically. "Are all your conversations with your mother so volatile?"

"Actually that was a pretty civil conversation." Beth laughed. "That woman drives me to drink."

A smile formed on Domenic's face. "Speaking of civil, Jack told me how you caught James and Jill. Is it true you hired your grandparent's agency to follow him?"

Beth shook her head. "I talked to my grandmother about it and she suggested it. It wasn't something I wanted to do but I knew something was going on and I needed to find out for sure."

"Jack also told me what you had said when you caught them." He chuckled.

Beth thought for a moment and broke out laughing. "I almost forgot about that."

"Tell me about what happened. I want to hear it from you." He asked.

Beth took her place back at the kitchen island. "He was performing oral sex on her. He was never very good at it. I always had this over whelming urge to ask him if he was going to continue doing that I wasn't going to come."

They both broke out laughing.

"Anyway, Jack and I walked in and we stood there watching for a moment." She continued.

"Is it true that Jill actually looked up and saw the two of you standing there and she just smiled?" Domenic asked.

Beth nodded. "The bitch looked me right in the eye and smiled as if she was proud of what she was doing."

"What did James do?"

"He didn't know we were there until I cleared my throat. He jumped up and stood there in shock. Then I calmly said, no wonder you never want to eat at home. You're eating junk food at the office." Beth laughed loudly. "I can't believe I said that to him!"

"I can't believe it either." He smiled. "I would have beaten the crap out of him and then dragged Jill off the table and down the hall to the elevators and pushed the down button to the lobby."

"Well that's the difference between you and I." she smiled. "I don't let my emotions get the better of me. But to be honest, I had thought about doing just that."

"So what stopped you?" Domenic asked.

"I think the fact that if I started pounding on James, I might not have stopped until he was dead." Her voice became serious. "It was the most embarrassing moment of my life not to mention the saddest."

Domenic wrapped his arms around Beth and held her close. "You can forget that time now. You have a great future to look forward to. a new place, a new puppy and kitten and a new man."

Beth looked up at him. "A new man? Does that mean you have moved in as the main man in my life?"

"Only if you want me to be, but I would be happy just being a part of your life."

Beth's head was spinning. She hadn't expected this. When they first met it was solely for professional reasons. Within a short time he was sharing her bed and her life. Did she really want to jump back into a relationship so fast?

Beth had to admit that she enjoyed being with him and when she wasn't with him, she look forward to the next time they would be together. She also liked coming home and finding him there to greet her. This was something James never did. Beth also knew that if he was gone from her life, she would miss him. But getting serious wasn't in the cards for her. At least not at the moment.

Beth took Domenic's hand. "I have enjoyed the time we have spent together."

Domenic's face turned serious. "Why do I feel there is a '*but*' in there somewhere?"

Beth shook her head. "The only 'but' I have is that I want to keep things as they are. I'm not ready to get serious with anyone." She looked up at him and his expression softened. She felt tears forming as she saw the affection in Domenic's eyes. "I can tell you one thing. I would miss you even if we never met." She added.

Her words brought a smile to Domenic's lips and warmth in his heart. He had known many women in his lifetime but none had touched him so quickly or as deeply as Beth had. He kissed her with passion and she reciprocated. He liked the way things were also and he wasn't about to do anything to upset this harmonious balance they had between them. "Then for now, we will keep things as they are." He whispered.

Domenic and Beth sat in the family room taping up boxes. They had spent the evening packing up some of the smaller items that Beth wanted to take with her. They shared a pizza and downed a couple of beers by the time they were finished. "that clears out the second floor." Beth said as she took notice of the piles of boxes.

"Maybe you should hire the moving company to pack the rest." Domenic suggested.

"I think you're right. I dread going through the kitchen and basement."

Their break was interrupted by a call from Domenic's legal secretary. Domenic exchanged a few words with her and then closed off his cell. "She's faxing over the information on Amanda that we are looking for."

They moved downstairs to Beth's home office just as the fax came through. Beth retrieved the information and read it over. "There isn't anything unusual about her." Beth said as she glanced over the information. Then she paused as she read about her mother.

"What is it?" Domenic asked.

"It says here that before she started working in the lab, she was a nurse in a nursing home."

"That is a bit odd but not unusual. She is still working in the medical field." Domenic said.

"What was the name of the nursing home that Peter's mother was in when she was sick?" Beth asked.

Domenic knew right away where Beth was going with this so he retrieved the folder from his truck and searched through the information on Alice Bucar. "It says here she was at Master's nursing home." He read aloud.

"Bingo!" Beth handed the paper to Domenic who immediately glanced through the information.

"She was a nurse in the same place." Domenic said.

"Read the rest of it." Beth suggested.

Domenic read on and stopped at the part regarding Amanda's mother. He looked up at Beth and she was grinning. "It seems that her mother was also in the same nursing home during the time Alice was there." He said.

"I think we need to pay a visit to this nursing home." Beth said.

Beth and Domenic pulled into the parking lot of Master's nursing home. They scanned for visitor's parking and found the parking lot almost empty.

"Either they don't have many patients or no one wants to visit." Beth said.

They walked up to the front entrance and went straight to the information desk.

A woman in a nurse's uniform sat behind the desk. Her hair was pulled back in a tight bun and a small nurse's hat was pinned on the top of her head. She was finishing off a powdered donut and wiped her face and hands free of the powdered sugar, as Beth and Domenic approached.

"May I help you?" she asked. Her voice was cheerful and welcoming.

"We would like to get some information about having our father admitted here." Domenic said.

The woman looked at him and then at Beth.

"My father has been diagnosed with dementia." Beth added. "This is my husband."

The woman nodded and her smile returned. She pulled an application form out of her desk and pinned it to a clip board. She retrieved a pen from a jar and handed everything over to Beth. "You need to fill out this application and we will get in touch with your doctor for any medical records. Then once we have all the information his name will go on a waiting list. Unfortunately the waiting period is quite long so it is best to get his name on there as soon as possible."

Beth took the application and looked over at Domenic for support.

"How far along is he?" the woman asked.

"He's just been diagnosed." Beth replied.

"So he is still capable to live at home?"

"Yes but my mother is finding it difficult." Beth said.

"You came at the right time." The woman said. "Most people wait until the patient is so far gone that they can't look after them anymore. They think that they can just walk in here and there would be an opening." She shook her head in disbelief.

"I never realized that there was a waiting list." Domenic said.

"Oh my dear, it could take up to a year before there would be an opening. The problem is that patients can live a long time with this disease. This makes it difficult to find a nursing home that is available."

"What if an opening comes up and my father is at the top of the list but we can still look after him? What happens then?" Beth asked.

"If that happens then his name will stay at the top of the list but we will take the next person who needs to be admitted. When you are ready to admit him then we will find the next available bed for him." she assured Beth.

Beth stood there holding the clip board. "Would it be possible to have a tour of the rooms and floors?" she asked.

The nurse's expression changed. "I don't think that would be possible."

"I will need to have my mother fill out the forms but she wont do so unless I can assure her that you can supply the best care for her husband." Beth insisted.

Beth threw in a few sighs and a sad expression just for the hell of it. Domenic put his arm around Beth to comfort her.

The nurse watched intently as he tried to calm Beth. "I guess it would be okay to go to the floor."

She pointed to the elevators and took the clip board and pen from Beth. She removed the forms and handed them back for her to bring back at another time. "Take the elevators to the eighth floor and when you get off turn right and the nurses station is just down the hall. Ask for Gladys. She's the head nurse and has been here forever."

Domenic and Beth thanked the woman for her help and they rode the elevator up to the eighth floor. As the doors opened the smell of urine and pine sol hit them like a ton of bricks. The walls were a dull yellow and the floor had been poorly washed. There were a couple of patients laying on gurneys outside their rooms as nurses busily changed their bedding.

"Oh my God!" Beth gasped. "How can someone leave their loved ones in a place like this?"

"No wonder there were no visitors. Who could handle the smell?" Domenic added.

They walked up to the nurse's station and asked to speak with Gladys.

"What is it in regards to?" she asked.

"We wanted to take a short tour of the facilities." Beth said.

The woman frowned. "This really isn't a good time for a tour. As you can see we are under a crisis with some of the patients."

"Yes we can see that. What happened?"

"The usual. Sometimes our patients soil themselves and if we don't get to them right away, they remove their diapers." she sighed.

"This explains the smell." Domenic added.

The nurse looked agitated at his remark. "Um, yes that's why it smells here. But you get used to it."

Beth wasn't buying a word of it. The smell was too strong to be caused by a couple of patients. She made a mental note to report the home for a surprise inspection, as soon as she got back into the office.

The nurse paged Gladys, and within minutes Domenic and Beth were greet by a large black woman who looked as if she used a shoe horn to get into her uniform. She waddled towards them, hands on hips, as if she was annoyed at the whole concept of being there.

"What is it?" she demanded.

The nurse cringed at the tone in Gladys's voice. "These people came up for a tour."

"You're not from the health department are you? You people are supposed to call before you come. This really isn't a good time because a couple of our patients decided to strip."

"No we aren't. We have a loved one who is suffering from dementia and we are looking into nursing homes that specialize in the condition." Domenic said.

Gladys blew out a sigh. "That's a relief. If you don't mind the smell we can start at the other end of the hall."

They walked down the hall and entered a small room with faded green sofa's and office chairs. There was an outdated television in the far corner and faded flowered curtains hung from the dingy window. The room looked as if it had been decorated in the late sixties.

"This is the visiting room." Gladys said.

Beth and Domenic just nodded. The smell was less noticeable in the room. This may have been due to the location of the room or all the air fresheners strategically placed around the room. Either way, Beth and Domenic wanted to linger there for a few minutes to get away from the smell.

"I know the décor is a bit out dated but funds are minimal and used for the care of the patients rather then the decorating." Gladys said in an apologetic voice.

They continued back towards the nurses station as Gladys explains the protocol for each day. Meals were served at seven in the morning, noon till one in the afternoon for lunch and supper was brought in around five. They encouraged loved ones to come during the meal times to help feed their family members but that rarely happened.

"People have good intentions when they bring their family members here but after a few weeks the visits become fewer and far between. Eventually they limit their visits to a few minutes on the patients birthday or Christmas." Gladys said.

Her face became sad. "Eventually they stop showing up at all. We have a staff of four per shift and twenty patients. It makes it difficult to give the proper care that each patient requires." She continued.

"What about volunteers?" Beth asked.

Gladys snickered at Beth's question. "We can't even get new nurses to stay on longer than a year before they quit and find a new job. And they get paid for being here."

"Well noted." Beth remarked.

They came to the end of the tour and Beth needed to bring up Amanda's name to Gladys.

"Can we go back to the visitors room the talk about the procedure to getting our loved one in here?" Beth asked.

Gladys looked at her watch then looked around. "I suppose I can spare a few more minutes. I think the girls have everything under control."

They walked back towards the visitor's room and made themselves comfortable.

"How did you hear about our home?" Gladys asked.

"From a friend who used to work here. Maybe you know her. Her name is Amanda Lott."

Gladys thought for a moment. "Oh yes I remember her." The tone in her voice was obvious to Beth and Domenic that she didn't think highly of Amanda.

"Well she's not a good friend. I met her through another friend." Beth said.

"She worked here for about six months and her resignation came at a very bad time." Gladys said.

"Why was that?"

"One of the nurses on the same shift as Amanda, was killed by a hit and run driver."

Domenic and Beth look at each other. "That is terrible. Did they ever catch the person?"

Gladys shook her head. "It happened right outside in the parking lot."

"They must have been going pretty fast because she was killed instantly."

Gladys continued. "Two days later Amanda up and quits for no good reason. But I wasn't surprised. She complained about everything here. We all knew it was a matter of time. I just wished she would have waited until we could find a replacement for Roberta."

"Was it true her mother was a patient here during that time?" Beth asked.

"As a matter of fact she was." Amanda removed her the same day. We didn't think it was a good idea because her mother was pretty bad but what could we do?"

Beth started to feel bad for Gladys. Her first impressions were all wrong. Gladys seemed dedicated to her job and the patients but funding was low so they had to make due with what they had. She made a promise to herself that she would talk to her mother about holding a fund raiser. In spite of the differences she had with her own mother, they did agree on one thing. And that was her grandparents. Her mother would die first before putting them in a home. If she knew the suffering that was going on in this place, she would surely want to help. Being a doctor she would even devote her own time to come in and examine the patients.

For a brief moment, Beth was beginning to feel closer to her mother. But those moments always disappears as soon as they got together.

They thanked Gladys for her time and rode the elevator down to the main floor. They walked out into the parking lot and looked around.

"Did you find anything unusual about the story of that nurse being struck by a speeding car?" Beth asked.

Domenic nodded. "How can a car be speeding in this parking lot?"

"I know what you're saying. There is no way the lot is big enough for a car to get up to that kind of speed to cause the kind of damage that Gladys said." Beth said.

They climbed into Domenic's car and he started up the engine. The air conditioning blew out warm air so they cranked the windows until it cooled off.

They sat there in silence as they waited for the air to cool off. "My gut is telling me that some how Amanda is involved in this." Beth said.

Domenic glanced over at her. Beth sat staring out the front window. "Don't ask me how but it just seems very strange. And I don't think the woman was killed by accident. It sounds deliberate to me." Beth added.

Domenic put the car in drive and drove back to Beth's house. "We'll ask Jack to find out the full name of the Roberta and to see if she has any family in the area." He said.

It was past eight in the evening by the time the information of the accident victim came through on Beth's fax machine.

"Her name is Roberta Smythe and she left behind a husband and two small children." Beth read aloud.

The information gave her last known address. "I'm sure her husband still lives there." Domenic said. "Do you want to pay him a visit?"

Beth agreed and they hopped into the car and drove to Roberta's husbands' house.

They pulled in front of the small ranch style house. There were toys and small bikes scattered around the front lawn. They walked up to the front door and rang the door bell. There was yelling in the house and the door was opened by a four year old girl. She was dressed in a nightie and she smiled up at Beth and Domenic. "Daddy, there's some people here." She yelled.

Her father was close behind. "Jennifer, I told you to never open the door." He scolded her as he picked her up in his arms.

"Are you Paul Smythe?" Domenic asked.

Paul looked at Domenic then at Beth. "Yeah, what do you want?" his voice seemed guarded.

"We want to ask you a few questions about your wife and her accident." Domenic continued. "Can you spare us a few minutes?"

He opened the screen door. "Sure I have a few minutes."

Beth and Domenic entered the doorway and immediately stepped into the living room. There were toys scattered all over the floor. A laundry basket of unfolded clothes sat next to the sofa.

Paul put his daughter down next to a pile of dolls. "Play for a bit Jennifer while I talk to the people."

Jennifer picked up a doll and pretended to have a conversation with it.

A New Beginning for Beth

Paul sat down next to the laundry basket and motioned for Beth and Domenic to take a seat. "So what's this about?" he asked as he began folding clothes.

Beth instinctively grabbed a few clothes piled them on her lap and began to fold them. Paul and Domenic looked over at her. "Sorry, it's a force of habit." She said as she continued with the folding.

Paul stopped folding and pushed the basket over to Beth. "Knock yourself out." he smiled, then turned his attention towards Domenic.

"So what can I do for you?"

"First off we want to say how sorry we are to hear about your wife's accident."

Paul nodded in appreciation.

"Can you tell us anything that happened to your wife before the accident?"

Paul thought for a moment. "Nothing that I can thing of. Everything was about the same as always."

"What did the police say about the accident?"

"They said that it was a hit and run and they still haven't caught the bastard that ran her over."

Paul was angry as he spoke but who could blame him?

He looked over at his daughter who was playing quietly on the floor. "There was something that I read in the autopsy report that I found unusual." He said.

"You had a copy of the autopsy report?" Beth asked.

Paul nodded. "I'm a nurse as well and I wanted to read exactly how my wife died."

Beth and Domenic found this odd considering it was cut and dry.

"Why would you want to read this when it was a hit and run?" Beth asked.

Paul leaned back in the couch. "Just a feeling I got. I just didn't think it was so cut and dry."

"Something must have happened before this that made you feel this way." Domenic remarked.

"If you can think of anything that happened or something that your wife may have said before this, would shed light on this accident." Beth added.

Paul looked over at Beth and studied her face. "Do you think it wasn't an accident?"

"Do you think it wasn't?" Beth asked.

Paul stood up and went to a desk near the front door. He opened the top drawer, pulled out a folder and handed it to Domenic. He sat back down on the sofa as Domenic read through the report. Domenic finished and then handed it to Beth.

Beth read through the report. "It says here that they found two sets of tire marks on her body."

Paul nodded. "The police think that the person's front and back tire ran over her."

"She would have had to be lying on the ground for that to happen." Beth said.

"She was found at the side of the road with head injuries that indicate she was thrown at impact. " Beth read aloud.

"Can we keep this?" Beth asked.

"Be my guest. I was keeping it in case someone would take an interest in my wife's death and realize that it wasn't a simple hit and run accident." He said.

"Can you recall anyone that Roberta may have not gotten along with? Maybe an ex-friend or coworker?" Beth asked.

"She was well liked. She had quite a few friends. Everyone liked Roberta. But come to think about it, there was a nurse she worked with."

"What did she say about her?" Beth asked.

"She called her a B.I.T.C.H. and said she was a pain to work with." Paul looked over at his daughter who briefly looked up when he spelled the word.

"Do you recall the woman's name?"

Paul thought for a moment then shook his head. "It started with an A but I can't remember the name."

"Would it be Amanda?" Domenic asked.

Paul looked over at Domenic. "Yeah, I think that was her name. Amanda."

"Roberta said she had to report her. She was spending too much time with one patient and ignoring her other ones including her mother. Her mother was a patient there as well. Roberta had enough to deal with

A New Beginning for Beth

without having to do someone else's job." He shook his head in disbelief. When our son Cameron was born she only took three months maternity leave because they were so desperately understaffed. She was entitled to at least six months."

"Who was the patient Amanda spent her time with?" Beth asked.

"She never mentioned the name, but I'm sure they would have a record of it at the nursing home." He said.

Beth looked over at Jennifer who was laying on the floor sound asleep. "We have taken up enough of your time. If you can remember anything else, please call me." She took one of her business cards from her purse, wrote her cell number on the back, and handed it to Paul.

Paul took the card from her and read it. "You're a lawyer?"

"We both are." Domenic said. "We are investigating a case and your wife's accident came into the picture so we are following every lead."

"You think my wife was involved in something?" Paul asked.

Beth shook her head. "She may have been without even knowing it. That's why it is important that you remember any conversation you may have had with her. Even something you don't think was important."

Paul walked them to the door. "Let me know if you find out who killed my wife."

"We will." Domenic said.

They climbed into the car and Domenic backed the car into the driveway to turn around. Beth looked over at Paul who came rushing up to the car.

"I just remembered something." He said with excitement.

Domenic popped the car in park and they climbed out to talk to Paul.

"Roberta told me that the woman who Amanda was spending so much time with wasn't a normal patient."

"What do you mean?" Beth asked.

"When she was first admitted she was in the third stage of dementia but within a few months of being there she was able to do everything for herself."

"You mean she was cured of it?" Beth remarked.

"That's what Roberta thought. She said it was very strange but then figured that the woman may have been misdiagnosed."

"Do you think it was possible that they made a mistake about her condition?" Domenic asked.

Paul shrugged his shoulders. "It's very unlikely but not impossible."

Beth and Domenic looked at each other. "Thanks for remembering this information. It has really helped us out." Domenic said, shaking Paul's hand.

He stepped away from the car and waved goodbye to them.

Domenic and Beth rode for a few miles without saying a word but they knew what each other was thinking. "This case is getting stranger by the minute." Beth said, breaking the silence.

Domenic nodded in agreement. "You got that right."

"I think it's time that I pay a social visit to Alice.

Chapter Nine

The rain on the window woke Beth. She buried her head in the pillow. She hated waking up to rain because it was difficult for her to get motivated. She would rather stay in bed and sleep all day.

The sound of pickles whining at the bottom of the bed got her attention and she jumped out of bed and carried him to the back door.

She put him down on the grass and he cried as the rain soaked him. "Hurry and do your business pickles before we both get soaked."

He finally squatted and did what he had to do then clumsily ran up to the steps where Beth was waiting. She scooped him up and carried him into the laundry room to retrieve a towel for both of them. "You're a good boy pickles. At least you didn't do it on my comforter." She said, rubbing him dry with the towel.

She carried him back to the kitchen where claws waited patiently for breakfast. As she scooped out food for her pets, she noticed a note from Domenic. Jack phoned me early this morning and told me he had some information about Alice. I'll call you later when I talk to him, the note read.

She made herself a cup of tea and made a call to Mary. "Anything happening today?"

"Nothing that needs your immediate attention." She replied. "I will call you if something comes up."

Beth hung up and took her tea into the family room. It was full of packed boxes which made it difficult for her to move around. She flopped down on the sofa and flipped on the television. She was enjoying the slack time while she made the transition from family law back to criminal law. But she knew that it was a matter of time before she would be up to her armpits in cases again so she was going to take full advantage of this free time.

She flipped through the channels and decided on an episode of Jerry Springer. It was trash and she knew it but his guests always made her appreciate her life and how normal it was compared to the people who entertained the audience by stripping and fighting.

Somewhere between the toothless trailer trash twins who wanted to marry each other and the man who wanted to marry his horse, Beth had fallen asleep. She was awakened by the sound of her telephone ringing.

"Hello?" she said her voice still groggy from sleep.

"Is this Beth Singer?" the voice asked.

"Who is this?"

"I am phoning to warn you that if you don't keep your nose out of our business you won't be breathing through that nose of yours."

The voice said calmly but forcefully.

Beth felt herself spring awake. "What business are you talking about?" she asked trying to hear more of the man's voice.

"Listen to me bitch! Peter owes me and I know that you are investigating him. He needs to finish a job for me and when he does you can do what you want." The voice demanded.

Beth felt her heart drop in her stomach and her pulse raced as she felt herself exposed.

"Does he owe you money?"

The man laughed. "Better than money."

"Well maybe if you tell me I can help you."

"You think I'm so stupid? I know who you and your boyfriend Domenic are. You just need to back off until Peter is finished then you can have him and everyone else you are investigating."

"I bet you are the guy that tried to attack me in the parking lot and who tried to break into my house." Beth was toying with him. She was trying to get information out of him. As far as she knew he didn't know that they traced the car he was in.

"I should never have sent him to do a man's job. The guy screwed up too many times."

"So you fired him and now you are doing the job yourself?"

More laughter from the man. "Let me put it this way, he won't be screwing up anymore."

"Did you kill him?" Beth knew he wouldn't answer but she had to give it a shot.

"Just keep your nose out of the business until Peter finishes his job. If you don't, you will be joining my ex- employee."

There was a click and Beth felt the blood rush from her face. She grabbed her cell phone and called Domenic. "Can you come over?" she asked.

He knew by her voice that something happened. "Are you okay?"

"I will be. I just need to have someone here right now."

"I'm scheduled for court in twenty minutes, but I will call Jack to come sit with you."

Beth agreed and hung up the phone.

Jack arrived within fifteen minutes and they sat together in the family room.

Jack had made a fresh cup of tea for Beth and a coffee for himself. He listened in silence as Beth told him what the person had said to her.

"If the man employed this other guy then he works for the same company that Domenic represents. Why would he want Peter to continue doing what he is doing if they are investigating him for theft?" Jack asked.

Beth shrugged her shoulders. "This is getting more bizarre everyday."

Jack sat silently mulling over all the information. "I wonder if Domenic has a list of the top brass in the company."

"Do you think it could be someone in the company?" Beth said.

"We have taken every precaution to hide our existence, yet this guy knows about you and Domenic and I'm sure he knows about the agency being involved. There are only a small handful of people who know of us and they are all top people in the pharmaceutical company that Domenic represents."

Beth sipped her tea, mulling over the information they had so far. None of which had a simple conclusion. Every time they found a new lead, that lead just made the case more confusing and each lead led back to Peter and his mother. Now there was Amanda. She was involved in something and Beth felt that Amanda knew Peter was up to something. To what degree was uncertain, but these people had the answers to the dozens of questions that were flooding her mind.

"Maybe we should pay a visit to Amanda's mother." Beth suggested.

Jack nodded in agreement. "She may be able to shed light on some of this."

Jack leaned back in the leather chair. A smile formed on his face. "Not to change the subject but I'm curious about something."

Beth looked over at Jack. "Curious about what?" she asked.

"What type of relationship do you have with Domenic?"

Beth was surprised at the question. "He's helping me with my divorce."

Jack's eyes twinkled. "Since when does that involve spending the night?"

Beth laughed. "If I didn't know you better I would say you are jealous."

"You're like a little sister, Beth and I am just looking out for you."

"He's your friend, so I suppose you would know better than me if I need to watch out."

Jack shook his head. "I didn't mean it like that. I just don't want to see you get hurt again. I know how difficult it was for you to have your marriage end."

"I'm a big girl, Jack, but thanks for being concerned." Beth assured.

"I do have one question for you in regards to Domenic." Beth said.

"What would that be?" he asked.

"Do you know anything about why Domenic left family law for corporate law?"

The smile left Jack's face. "That is something you should discuss with Domenic. I am in no position to divulge that information to you."

"So you do know." She said. "I don't like the sound of this." She added.

A New Beginning for Beth

"Let's just say that I understand why Domenic changed over to corporate law. But I think you should really discuss that with him." Jack looked at his watch. "I better go. Will you be okay until Domenic gets here?"

Beth nodded in assurance and showed jack to the door. "Thanks for sitting with me." She said, hugging him.

"Anytime hon." Jack replied, hugging her back.

Beth was busy cleaning up her home office desk when the sound of the telephone broke her concentration.

"Hello is this Beth?" the voice asked.

"Yes, who is this?"

"I don't know if you remember me but I'm a friend of Alice's. You gave me a ride to the senior's center." The voice said.

Beth rubbed the back of her head in memory of the whacking she received that day. "Agnes, how are you?"

"I'm sorry to disturb you dear but I was wondering if you needed anyone to look after your pets anytime soon?"

"How did you get my number?" Beth asked although she had a suspicion as to who gave it to her.

"I hope you don't mind me calling. I was just worried about your babies since you are single and you work."

"That's very kind of you Agnes and yes I could use your help since I will be moving in a couple of weeks."

"Give me your address and I will be over in a flash to give you a hand." she said with excitement.

Beth gave her the address exchanged a few more words and hung up the phone. She stood there for a moment wondering what just happened. "Did I just agree to have that crazy woman in my house?" she said out loud. She slapped her forehead with the palm of her hand when reality jumped up and bit her on the ass.

"Get a grip of yourself, Beth. This could work in your favor." She thought. "After all, Agnes is a good friend of Alice's and she might shed some light on this case."

Twenty minutes later, a taxi pulled up into her driveway and Agnes stepped out of the back seat. She was dressed in a purple pant suit to match her lavender hair. Agnes handed the driver some money and Beth watched as the taxi backed out of the driveway and drove away.

Gino, who lived across the street was watering his lawn and stopped in midstream when he saw Agnes standing in Beth's driveway.

Gino was newly retired and spent his days tending to his garden and to everyone's business. He was also henpecked by Maria who watched his every move. Gino waved a hello Beth's way as she walked out her door to greet Agnes.

Agnes had noticed Gino too and she had that look of hunger in her eyes. "Is he married?" she asked as she met Beth on the front porch.

"For over thirty five years." Beth replied.

The hunger left Agnes eyes. "That's too bad. He looks like he still has some life left in him."

Beth now understood what Alice had told her about Agnes and her past boyfriend. She must have been one sex pistol when she was younger.

Agnes followed Beth into the kitchen. She squealed with delight at the sight of pickles and claws sleeping together on the pet pillow in the family room.

"Be careful of the kitten." Beth said. "She hasn't been declawed yet and she likes to climb the curtains as well as humans."

"Nonsense." Agnes sniffed. "You just have to learn how to hold onto to her." She picked up the kitten and laid claws in her arms like you would a baby. Claws laid perfectly still as Agnes rocked her back and forth and sang softly to her.

"Well, how about that!" Beth said in amazement. "Who knew that claws liked to be treated like a baby?"

"That's because she is a baby." Agnes responded.

"Too bad Sal didn't figure that out when he babysat them."

Agnes's attention turned to Beth. "Who is Sal?"

A smile formed on Beth's mouth. "Someone who would be perfect for you."

"Does he have a car?"

Beth shook her head. "He isn't allowed to drive anymore because he had an accident."

Agnes moved her dentures around in her mouth. "I can relate to that. I have to cab it or catch a ride with someone anytime I want to go out. I lost my license the same way."

A New Beginning for Beth

Beth thought it best not to ask how. If it was anything like Sal's reason, she thought it best not to know.

Their conversation was interrupted by the door bell. Beth was greeted by the sound of Domenic's voice from down the hall.

"Who's that?" Agnes asked.

"A colleague of mine." She replied.

Domenic appeared in the kitchen with Sal close behind.

"I hope you don't mind but I took the liberty of inviting Sal along." Domenic said.

That look of hunger appeared in Agnes's eyes again as she looked Sal over. He was a little shorter than her and about thirty pounds lighter but he was dressed for a date and he didn't have a walker. This was all good in Agnes's eyes.

Sal took a step back as he noticed Agnes was holding claws. "Be careful of that little dickens. Her claws are like razors." He said to Agnes.

Claws slept quietly in Agnes's arms. "She's not so bad. You just have to learn to hold her the right way." Agnes said.

Domenic and Sal peered over at the sleeping kitten.

"Well how about that! Who would have figured that the little thing liked to sleep on her back?" Sal said with amazement.

Beth glanced through the menu until finally deciding on chicken wings and spinach dip to start. Everyone ordered the same.

"So how do you know Beth?" Agnes asked Domenic. She had been a bit suspicious of Domenic since they left Beth's house. After all, she is supposed to be dating Alice's son, Peter.

"We are both lawyers and I'm representing her in her divorce." Domenic replied.

Agnes fell silent for a moment as she mulled over his response. "And how do you know Beth?" her attention turned to Sal.

"I'm her real estate agent." Sal responded.

Agnes nodded her head. "How is that business going? I was thinking of selling real estate myself but I don't drive so it would be difficult to get around."

"I don't drive either so I usually have the clients drive or I take a cab." Sal sighed. "Because of that it makes it difficult to sell anything."

Again Agnes nodded. "Ever been married?" she asked Sal.

"Nope. Never found the right girl."

That hungry smile returned to Agnes's face. "That's good. I would hate to have someone else's sloppy seconds, not to mention extra baggage in the form of children."

"Have you any kids that I need to worry about?"

"Same as you. Never been married."

Sal sat back in his chair and studied Agnes's face. "I'm surprised that a hot chick like you hasn't been caught yet."

Agnes's giggled like a school girl. Beth and Domenic sat there in silence listening to the flirty conversation between the two seniors.

"Aren't you the flatterer?" Agnes giggle, fanning her hands in Sal's direction. "I bet you are a real lady killer too."

"I'm a one woman man when I find the right woman to be with."

Beth looked at Sal then at Agnes. "Domenic, tackle the waitress when you see her and order me a double amaretto sour."

Domenic was enjoying the talk between Sal and Agnes. "Who says love has an age limit?" he whispered in Beth's ear.

Beth ignored Domenic's words. "Agnes goes to this senior center on the other side of town, Sal. Maybe you could join her one day."

Sal and Agnes were too involved with each other to notice Beth. She chose to just keep quiet. She did plan the meeting between Sal and Agnes but didn't expect it to be so successful so quickly.

If Agnes knew anything about Alice and Peter, Sal would find out.

Domenic paid the bill and they all hopped into his car. "Where to?" he asked as he started the engine.

"I'm a bit sleepy so maybe I will call it a night." Sal said with a yawn.

"Maybe I will call it a night also." Agnes said following suit.

Domenic watched the two love birds through his rearview mirror, as they cuddled into each other. "So whose place are you both going to?"

"My place." Sal replied. "Unless we need to stop at Agnes's place first to pick up some things."

They made a quick stop at Agnes's place so she could pack an over night bag. Sal went with her to give her a hand, while Beth and Domenic waited in the car.

"It was your idea." Domenic said.

"I know, but I didn't expect the two of them to hit it off so quickly."

"I guess at their age the first date lasts the first five minutes." He laughed.

"I just hope Sal can find out something and isn't using her for sex just to get the information out of her." Beth snapped.

"Relax. Let them have some fun." Domenic said, rubbing Beth's shoulder. "If you're good I can continue this massage at your place." His voice lowered to a whisper.

Beth leaned back in the seat and closed her eyes. That was an offer she couldn't refuse.

They dropped Agnes and Sal off at Sal's apartment then headed back to Beth's place.

They were inside the front door when Domenic's cell rang. He checked the number. It was Jack.

He flipped the phone open." What's up?"

Beth turned on the lights in the kitchen as Domenic continued his call with Jack.

After an exchange of words, he hung up. "Jack's coming over so that massage will have to wait." His voice turned serious.

"What's going on?" Beth asked.

"I think we have a break in the case." He replied.

Ten minutes later the three were sitting in Beth's kitchen sipping on beers.

"I found out some interesting information about our friend Amanda." Jack said. He pulled out three files and handed one to Beth and one to Domenic.

They opened the folders and read through the information.

"The night that Roberta was killed, she decided to stay a little longer. Our informant remembered that because Amanda made a fuss on how one of the nurses was caring for her mother."

"Was her complaint unfounded?" Beth asked.

Jack nodded. "Amanda's mother was getting better care than some of the other patients because Amanda was staff. They always treated the staff's family a little better."

"It sounds to me like she deliberately drew attention to herself." Beth suggested.

"Or maybe she wanted to rule herself out as a suspect." Jack added.

"We all know that based on the examiners report, that this was no accident, so who would have wanted to see her dead?" Beth asked.

"Amanda has a sister and this girl isn't what you would call an upstanding citizen." Jack said.

They read the report on Lydia. She had been arrested for assault three times. Two of which she served time for.

Beth leaned back in her seat. "Do you think that the other voice I heard that day in Peter's house was Lydia?"

"It all makes sense." Domenic added. "Who else would have any knowledge in what Peter was up to other then someone close to the situation?"

"If we draw our conclusion on Amanda and Lydia as being the two women who broke into Peter's house, it still won't answer who else is after Peter." Beth said.

Jack shook his head in disbelief. "In all my years as a detective and then working as an investigator, I have never encountered a case that has so many questions as this one." He ran his fingers through his salt and pepper hair as he mulled over any thoughts of a possible lead.

Jack stood and stretched the stiffness of sitting for a long time, out of his long lean body. "I'm going to call it a night." He yawned.

Domenic and Beth walked Jack to the front door. "Tomorrow morning I'm going to call in a few favors from downtown to look into Amanda and Lydia." Jack said as he kissed Beth good night on the cheek. He gave Domenic a strange handshake that only men do and disappeared into the darkness of the night.

Beth locked the front door. "Are you staying the night or do you have to get up early in the morning?" she asked turning her attention to Domenic.

"I can still get up early in the morning if I stay here." He grinned. "But I need a change of clothes and I know come the morning I won't be thinking about going home to change." His smile turned serious. "Would you mind if I call it a night as well?"

Beth kissed him gently on the lips. "I need to get up early as well so it's okay with me if you want to go home."

After saying good night to Domenic, Beth went back to the kitchen to tidy up before bed. She sat at the kitchen island looking over the information on the case when the sound of the phone broke the silence.

"Beth, did Domenic leave?" Sal whispered.

"Yes Sal, what's wrong?"

"I can't speak long because Agnes is in the other room but I found out something very interesting about Peter and his mother."

"Give me the information and I will relay it to him."

"It seems that Peter was coming into the nursing home where Alice was living and giving her injections. Apparently these injections were supposed to be vitamins but whatever they were it cured Alice of her illness. Within a couple of weeks, Alice was back to her normal self. Everyone thought she was misdiagnosed but Agnes knew that wasn't true. Agnes used to be a nurse and when she had visited Alice in the home right after she was admitted she had read her chart. There was no question as to what Alice was suffering from."

Beth sat in silence as Sal continued telling her how Agnes witnessed Peter giving his mother an injection one day and how she asked what it was.

"Peter told Agnes it was just a series of vitamins to keep her healthy but Agnes didn't believe it." Sal said.

"What made her think it was something else?" Beth asked.

"Because within two weeks Alice was back to her normal self. Agnes said that no vitamins could have helped Alice." Sal replied.

"Maybe he was giving her a shot of that drug they use to help with Alzheimer's." Beth suggested.

"I asked her the same thing, but she said that Alice was too far gone for that to help her. And besides, that drug you are referring to, doesn't cure it. It just prolongs the inevitable."

Sal made a shush sound in the phone. "I have to go."

He hung up before Beth could say another word. She hung up the phone and sat down on the sofa. Her body was numb from the information that Sal had given her. Her thoughts were running rampage. Each thought drew the same conclusion. She knew what Peter was stealing. Why didn't she see it? Maybe she knew it all along but didn't want to believe that Peter was playing God with his own mother's life.

Beth checked her watch. It was just past eleven but she knew Peter would still be up. She grabbed her cell phone and made a call to Peter.

"So nice to hear from you." Peter said as he answered the phone.

"I know it's late but do you think we could meet up for lunch tomorrow?" Beth asked.

There was a brief pause in the conversation. Beth listened in the phone and could hear Peter whispering. He had placed his hand over the receiver but Beth could make out two voices. One was Peters and the other was another man's voice. It was too muffled to understand what they were saying but she wasn't getting a good feeling about it.

"I'm taking the day off of work tomorrow but maybe we can meet for supper tomorrow night." He suggested.

Beth agreed and made a date to meet at eight the next evening at a restaurant on the outskirts of town.

She phoned Domenic and gave him the information that she had on Peter and told him of her plan to meet with him the next night. "I wish you would have called me first before you did that." his voice serious with concern.

"I'll be fine." She assured him. "Besides, I'm sure you and Jack will be lurking nearby to make sure nothing happens."

They exchanged a few more words and said their goodbyes. Beth gathered up her two pets and carried them up to bed.

"I hope I can finally lay this case to rest." She yawned to pickles who was cuddled up next to her. She flipped off the light and let her thoughts of the case, leave her as sleep took over.

Jack pulled into the parking lot of his apartment. He had been up for almost eighteen hours working on several stake outs. His body was stiff and exhausted from sitting all day and most of the evening, in his car watching husbands and wives coming and going in different motels with someone other than their spouses.

He stepped out of his car and walked slowly to the back entrance towards the building. He was too busy fumbling with his keys to notice the car heading straight for him.

The lights momentarily blinded him as the car clipped him in the hip and knocked him towards the side of the lot. He lay there for a moment stunned from the impact but relatively unharmed. He looked up and saw the lights coming towards him again and in his basic training at the police academy, pulled out his gun and fired into the light.

A New Beginning for Beth

The first bullet took out one of the headlights, giving Jack a better view of the driver. The second bullet hit the windshield, leaving a large hole in the passenger side. The car swerved away from Jack as the bullets made contact, and it side swiped a car that was parked next to Jacks.

It came to a stop then quickly reversed towards Jack who had managed to get to his feet and get inside the building lobby. He was on the phone to the emergency as he watched the car arch forward and disappear out of the lot only after Jack was able to repeat the license number to the emergency operator.

Within minutes two cruisers and an ambulance were on the scene. Tom and Mary were in the lobby tending to Jack who was annoyed at all the attention. "I'm okay." He said to the paramedic as he tried to strap on a blood pressure band.

"We would like to take you to the hospital to do some x-rays on your ribs to be sure." The paramedic insisted.

"Go with them dear." Mary said. "Tom will follow behind to bring you back."

After some more convincing, Jack finally agreed to being checked out. "Don't mention anything to Beth." he said to Mary as he climbed into the back of the ambulance.

"I wont, I promise." She assured him.

"Hey Jack, I'm coming with you." One of the detectives said as he climbed in behind Jack. "I have some questions for you in regards to this license plate number."

It was obvious that they knew each other. "Sure Mike. What do you need to know?" Jack asked as the paramedic climbed in and insisted Jack lay on the gurney so he could do his job.

Jack and Mike Scott had worked in the same division before jack was wounded in action and was forced into retiring. They still remained friends and mike went as far as to invite jack over for family functions.

"Are you sure this number is correct?" Mike asked.

"As sure as I'm laying here in the back of this ambulance." Jack replied. "You can't find a trace on it?"

"We know who owns it but by the description you gave of the car, it's not the car that the plates belong to."

Jack looked puzzled. "The car I saw was a light colored, four door corolla."

"That's just it. The car that these plates belong to is a Toyota. And it belongs to an Alice Bucar."

Jack felt the hairs on the back of his neck stand up and the color rush from his face."

"Are you sure about that?" jack asked, taking the pad from his fellow detective and reading what was written.

"As sure as you are lying in the back of this ambulance." Mike replied with a snicker.

Beth was busy making calls to different moving companies to secure movers for her upcoming move. She had gone through each room, deciding on what was going and what she wanted to leave behind.

Beth had two houses to furnish and decided to take everything except the kitchen sink. She would take that too but the cost of a plumber on a Saturday would put a dent in her budget. Besides needing everything, she couldn't bare the thought of Jill and James using the things that she had bought and paid for. Or at least contributed to purchasing them.

After several calls, she finally was able to secure a company. The owner arranged to come over that day and inspect the amount of furnishings and belongings in order to know the size of truck to reserve for her move.

She spent the rest of the morning going through her office and boxing up files and equipment she wouldn't be using till after she was settled into her new house.

Pickles and claws had followed her down to her office and they were busily amusing themselves with a piece of paper that was on the floor and some dust bunnies that floated out from under the desk.

Beth would every so often, stop what she was doing and watch them with amusement. "If only life were that simple?" she said out loud to no one in particular.

The sound of the doorbell broke the silence. Saved by the bell, she thought as she made her way upstairs to the front door.

Domenic stood on the other side of the door, carrying a bag of fast food and a tray of drinks. He must be a mind reader, Beth thought as she realized she hadn't eaten all day.

They greeted each other with a kiss as Beth took the bag of food from Domenic and he followed her into the kitchen.

"I was packing up my home office before you came." She said as she removed the hamburgers and fries from the food bag.

"Any success in getting it all finished?"

Beth nodded. "Yep, and I even have an appointment with a moving company today. They are coming in to give me an estimate."

"How much are you taking with you?" Domenic asked as he sipped his cola.

"Everything." Beth replied.

Domenic stopped in mid sip. "Are you sure you need everything? This house is pretty big and you have a lot of furniture."

"I don't need everything. But I'll be damned if I'm going to let James and the tart have it."

Domenic shook his head in disbelief. "Beth, you really need to come to terms with this divorce and learn to move on."

Beth looked at him. Surprised at what she had just heard him say. "I have come to terms with it. I'm sleeping with you, aren't I?"

"That's not what I meant."

"I know what you meant. And it will take more than a few rolls between the sheets for me to forget the pain I went through with him." Beth snapped. She was hurt by his callous remark and it made her lose her appetite.

She put her hamburger back on the plate and pushed the food away.

Domenic sat watching her. He knew that she was hurt but he was tired of how she was acting when it came to her soon to be ex husband. Secretly he felt jealousy towards him. He had her for so many years and treated her as if she were a second class citizen. She deserved so much more and Domenic felt that he was just the man to do that. But his mouth had a way of making her feel bad, even if he meant well.

"Don't you like your hamburger?" Domenic asked, knowing that it wasn't the food.

"I'm not hungry and I really need to get back to work." She replied without making eye contact. She left him sitting in the kitchen as she went back to her office and locked the door behind her.

Domenic sat dumbfounded and alone in the kitchen. He wasn't sure what had happened or whether he knew how to fix it. Although he knew a lot about Beth, there were still some aspects of her that were a mystery to him. This attitude and her sudden silence, was one of those mysteries. He didn't know how to respond. Should he follow her downstairs and insist they talk about it or should he just leave and let Beth lick her wounds until she was ready to come around?

He gathered up the leftover food and threw it in the garbage. Then he positioned himself on the sofa and with the remote in hand he flipped through the channels until he settled on CSI in Miami.

Beth sat at her desk, fuming over what Domenic had said to her. It wasn't so much what he said as it was that he was right in what he was saying. She knew she had to get over this James and Jill situation and try to look at it in a more positive light. Maybe Jill did her a favor by taking James. It wasn't as if she and James had been blissfully happy. When you get right down to it, Beth was pretty miserable the last two years of her marriage. She knew that the divorce was the best thing for her. But the last thing she needed was some man pointing this out to her. She had spent many years being unhappy in her marriage, and she was entitled to be angry over how the marriage ended. The years she wasted with James and the time and money she spent putting him through medical school gave her the right to be angry and bitter.

She didn't want James back. All she wanted was to go through the anger that she suppressed throughout her marriage. She wanted to express it and get the last word in before they signed on the dotted line. And if taking everything that she paid for away from James was her way of doing all this, then she was entitled to do so. Domenic just didn't understand that. Instead of arguing the point with Domenic, she chose to dismiss his remark and change the subject.

"I am meeting up with Peter tonight." Beth said as she placed a box filled with files on the family room floor. "I think you should be there as well."

Domenic stared with a surprised look on his face. "I know you were planning on meeting with him but you never told me what the meeting is about."

"I want to get to the bottom of this case. I'm tired of pussy footing around. We need answers and Peter is the only person who can give us those answers." She replied.

Domenic wasn't too sure about Beth's idea of putting all the cards on the table. There were still some things he wanted to find out before everything was brought out in the open. One being who in the company was involved. He knew there was someone higher up that had an interest in what Peter was doing and in order to find this out he needed more time to investigate. He didn't want anyone tipping off this person before he had a name. "Do you think that is a wise idea? After all, we still need to know all the players in this."

Beth looked at Domenic. Their eyes met for a moment and then she turned back to her packing. "The only way we can get any names is if Peter will cooperate. And if I tell him that we have enough evidence to press charges he may just cave in and tell us what we want to know."

"We need to put our cards on the table and see what happens." Beth added.

"You seem preoccupied today dear." Alice said to her son.

Peter sat staring at the food that his mother made for him. He wasn't hungry and had not heard her comment.

"Peter? Are you okay?" Alice asked as she snapped her son out of his deep thoughts.

Peter looked up at his mother who was sitting across from him at the table. "I'm just thinking of work." He replied softly as he reached out and patted her hand.

He loved his mother and would do anything for her. But how was he going to protect her now? Her life was in danger and she wasn't even aware of it. He was at a crossroad in his life and each path was equally dangerous. Whatever path he chose his mother would end up the victim.

He had very little sleep and had called in sick. He knew he had no choice but to give the man what he wanted. He also had the threat of exposure from Amanda. He had thought of talking to Beth about it but decided against it because he felt he couldn't fully trust her. The episode with the keys still haunted him.

Alice placed some Tylenol in front of him and insisted he take them.

"I had plans to go shopping today but I could cancel them and stay here with you." She said.

Peter shook his head and held the Tylenol in his hand. "Don't worry mom. I have a lot of work to do today so I will be busy downstairs. You keep your plans."

Alice looked at her son. She knew something was bothering him but he was always so tight lipped about what was going on in his life. Especially the past few months. Alice knew better than to ask questions.

She managed a smile as she stood to go get ready for her friends. She stopped at the doorway of the kitchen, turned and hugged her son.

"I love you mom." Peter whispered as he felt his mother's arms around him. "Always remember that."

Alice kissed him on the top of his head. "I love you too dear. No matter what, that will never change."

Peter closed his eyes and blew out a sigh as Alice disappeared down the hall.

"I know mom." He whispered to himself.

Beth checked her watch as she drove to the restaurant. Domenic and Jack were going to arrive thirty minutes after Peter arrived. This would give her time to talk to Peter before bringing them in. she felt her stomach flutter as she pulled into the parking lot. She looked around the lot as she parked her car. She didn't see Peter's car anywhere.

She had rehearsed her lines as if she were auditioning for a part in a play. She knew she had to tread carefully so she spent the day searching for the right opening line. Unfortunately there was no way she could open up the conversation without upsetting him. So she decided to just tell him what she knew and that for his and his mother's protection he needed to come clean.

She sat in the car for a few minutes then decided to wait for Peter in the restaurant. As she walked towards the entrance of the restaurant, Peter pulled into the parking lot. He had not noticed her as he parked his car. Another vehicle followed closely behind and parked next to Peter. She watched as Peter got out of the car and approached the driver. There was an exchange of words and the by the on Peters face, he was not happy to see this person. Beth tried to get a glimpse of the driver but the car had tinted windows which made it almost impossible to see inside the car.

She watched unnoticed as they continued their conversation. She hoped the driver would get out of the car but the driver started the car and backed out of the parking spot and sped away, leaving Peter standing there. Beth ducked into the restaurant before Peter noticed her.

A New Beginning for Beth

She was waiting to be seated when Peter finally walked into the restaurant. "Oh Peter, you're here. I'm still waiting for a table." She said acting surprised but happy to see him.

He smiled and kissed her on the cheek. The waitress seated them in a quiet booth with a view of the main street.

Peter glanced through the menu. "Why the urgency to see me tonight?"

Beth looked up from her menu. "Why would you think it was an emergency? Can't a girl have dinner with a special friend?"

Peter smiled at her but his eyes told a different story. Beth couldn't help but get the feeling that Peter had his guard up. Either that or he was preoccupied with something.

"You seem tense tonight, Peter, is there something on your mind?"

Peter shook his head. "Actually there is but it isn't something you could help me with."

"Try me. Maybe I can help." She insisted.

Peter sat across from her, studying her face. Should he ask her about the keys and his suspicions? What if he was wrong and he actually did leave them in the bathroom? He has been preoccupied with all the things going on in his life that it could quite possibly be that he did forget them.

Peter took a deep breath and blew it out in a long sigh. "There has been something bothering me."

Beth leaned towards Peter. "Tell me please. I want to help you if I can."

Peter proceeded to tell Beth about the keys. After he finished he waited for her reaction.

Beth knew she was busted but she was a good lawyer and sat stone faced. She didn't want to let on that she had been in his house.

"How did you know to put them back on the nail in the window?" he asked.

Think Beth, she thought to herself. "I didn't." she replied.

"What do you mean you didn't?"

"I put them on your desk. Maybe someone else put them on the nail." She said nonchalantly.

Peter sat back in his chair and stared at her. "You mean to say you didn't put them on the nail?"

"That's exactly what I'm saying, but I don't see the relevance here. What are you trying to say to me Peter?" Beth was turning the tables on him.

Peter's face went red and beads of sweat began to form on his forehead. He took his napkin and wiped his face as Beth stared at him. She didn't change her expression.

"I'm sorry. I have been under a lot of pressure lately." He said apologetically.

She reached out and took his hand. A smile formed on her face as their eyes met. "I know you have Peter and that is one of the reasons why I wanted to see you tonight."

Beth looked over at the door just as Domenic and Jack came into view. Peter followed her stare and immediately recognized Jack. "Isn't that the UPS driver that came to my office the other day?"

Beth nodded as they walked up to them. "Yes but he doesn't really work for UPS."

Jack sat down next to Peter and Domenic scooted in next to Beth. "This is Jack and Domenic." She said introducing them to her date. "Domenic is a lawyer and colleague and jack works for my grandparents as a private investigator."

The color drained from Peters face. He shook his head in disbelief. "This cant be happening. You can't take me in now. I have to finish my work." He mumbled.

"They aren't here to take you in, Peter. They are here to help you." Beth assured Peter.

"Peter looked over at Beth and the fear in his eyes was evident. This meeting has put the fear of god in Peter and she needed to find out what he was into.

"Tell us about your work, Peter." Jack asked. "What is it you are working on?"

Peter lowered his head. "I can't tell you or they will hurt my mother."

"Jack can protect your mother." Beth said. "We can help you but you need to tell us what you have been doing."

Peter's eyes went from Beth to Jack then to Domenic. He realized that they were aware of what he has been doing. What did he have to lose? He looked around the restaurant. It was empty except for a couple of tables and the staff.

"Would you feel better if we went somewhere else to talk? Beth asked.

Peter nodded. "Would it be okay if we pick up my mother first?"

"If you want, I could send over a black and white to sit with her." Jack suggested.

Peter hesitated then agreed on the police. "I think that would be okay but they are to just sit outside watching the house. I don't want my mother to know anything."

Jack made a quick call and relayed the orders. "Let's roll." He ordered as he hung up the phone.

They all walked out of the restaurant towards Domenic's truck. The sun had set and the parking lot was dimly lit as they crossed the lot. A car entered the parking lot and sped up, heading right for them.

"Here we go again." Jack yelled and pulled Beth out of the way of the oncoming car.

Domenic grabbed Peter just as the car reached them. They both ran towards the entrance of the restaurant as the car made a quick U-turn and headed back towards Jack and Beth.

There was only one way out of the parking lot so Beth jumped into her car and quickly backed out blocking the car inside the lot. The car was able to avoid hitting Beth's car but lost control and ended up sideswiping three parked cars, crushing the driver's door in the process. The driver popped the car in reverse and backed down to the end of the lot. The bumper had dislodged from the front of the car and scraped against the pavement creating sparks that lit up the darkness like sparklers on the fourth of July.

It jumped the curb and crossed the grass, taking out a few small bushes. Once it was on the side road, the driver put the car in drive and headed down the road. Everyone had piled into Beth's car and was already out of the lot and turning the corner in pursuit as the car sped down the street in a stream of flying sparks. Halfway down the road the bumper dislodge and got trapped underneath the car.

This caused the driver to lose control and jump the curb. It came to a rest by hitting a large maple tree on the boulevard.

Beth pulled her car in behind the car and Jack jumped out, gun drawn, and cautiously approached the driver's side. The driver was frantically trying to free herself from the wreckage but with no success. The impact in the parking lot left the drivers door too damaged to be opened.

"Let me see your hands!" jack demanded as he pointed his revolver at the driver.

Everyone moved towards the driver side and Peter immediately recognized the driver. "That's Amanda's sister!" he yelled. "What the hell was she thinking?"

"She was thinking of finishing the job she started when she tried to run me over last night." Jack said.

Domenic and Beth looked at each other then turned their attention back at Jack.

"She tried this last night?" Domenic asked.

Jack nodded. "I guess this old guy is still pretty quick on his feet."

A black and white pulled up and had guns drawn as they approached Lydia's car. She was cursing up a mean streak as one of the officers yanked the passenger side door open and ordered her out of the car.

"It was all Amanda's idea." She screamed as the officer handcuffed her hands behind her back. "I wasn't going to hurt you. I was just supposed to scare you."

"It didn't seem that way last night." Jack said.

Lydia flashed him a puzzled look. "What are you talking about?"

Jack stared at her in disbelief that she would deny being the driver who almost ran him over the night before. "Are you trying to tell me that you weren't driving the car that almost killed me last night?"

Lydia's face went red. "That bitch!" She screamed. "I can't believe she is going to pin everything on me!"

"That bitch! That bitch!"

"If it wasn't you then who was it?" Jack asked trying to calm Lydia.

"I want to tell you everything. I'm not going to jail again for her." Lydia cried.

One of the officers reminded Lydia of her rights to an attorney but she dismissed his advice. "Peter, Amanda is crazy. She wants a cut of the money you are making off of your sales and she won't stop until she is satisfied."

Peter flushed red and sweat beaded down his face. "I don't know what you're talking about. What money?"

Lydia looked at Peter. She knew he was lying and so did everyone else. She shook her head and slid in the backseat of the cruiser.

Jack leaned in to speak with Lydia. There was a short exchange of words between them. Jack looked back at Peter then drew his attention back to the backseat. He nodded to Lydia before closing the door.

Jack walked over to Peter who was standing close to Beth and Domenic. His color changed from red to ash white. "I think you have some things you need to talk to Domenic and Beth about." Jack said to Peter.

Peter lowered his head. "You promised protection for my mother." He whispered.

"There is a cruiser parked in front of your house as we speak." Jack assured him.

Jack turned to Domenic. "Take Peter to Beth's place. He has some things he needs to tell you. I'm going to have a chat with Lydia at the station."

Domenic handed Jack his keys and they all piled into Beth's car with Domenic behind the wheel.

Peter sat in the backseat staring out the window. It was obvious that he was deep in thought.

"Peter, we want to help you." Beth said.

Peter glanced over at her and then back at the window. "You have no idea how powerful these people are."

"I represent the company that you work for." Domenic said. "We are aware that someone from the company has been in contact with you. If he is trying to blackmail you then you need to talk to us so we can fix the problem for you."

Peter shook his head in disbelief. "You obviously aren't that in tune with the company if you think that they are trying to blackmail me."

"Isn't that what is happening here?" Beth asked.

"Why would they want to blackmail me? They have all the power. There is no reason for them to use blackmail to keep me in line."

"If a company is blackmailing you or using force to keep you in line, the government will close them down." Domenic said.

Peter gave out a menacing laugh. His laugh made the hair on Beth's arms stand up. Beth had not known Peter long but she had a different opinion of him. He never came across as someone bad. Not at all like the person she was witnessing in the backseat of her car.

"You aren't listening! They are the government! They control everything. Everything we have come to believe is all lies!" He cried.

Domenic pulled the car into an empty parking lot. He found a spot out of sight of the main traffic on the road.

"What are we doing?" Beth asked curiously.

"He turned the car off and turned to Peter. "Why don't you tell us what you mean by that remark?" He insisted.

Peter stared at Domenic, unsure if he was going to pull him from the car any moment and beat him to a bloody pulp. He then turned to Beth who had shrugged her shoulders in uncertainty about Domenic's motives.

Peter put his hands to his face and sighed deeply. "Let me ask you something. If you wanted to start a business that tax payers would happily contribute to and the government would give a tax break for, would you? Not only that but you would have total control over everyone's lives and no one would complain if you increased your prices?"

Beth studied Peters face. "There's no such business."

Peter again blurted out his menacing laugh. "Are you kidding me? Of course there is and I work for them!"

"Even the pharmaceutical companies have certain laws they have to abide by." Domenic said.

"True but we aren't talking about rule and regulations. We are talking about dollars." Peter replied.

Peter blew out another sigh. "When I was hired by the company I had to sign a confidentiality form. Regardless of how long I am employed I can not ever talk about my work in the labs. Everyone has to sign one."

"In some companies that is mandatory." Domenic said.

Peter nodded his head in agreement. "True, but only to protect their secret recipes from being stolen. What if you have to keep quiet about having products that they don't want the public to be aware of because this knowledge wouldn't be profitable?"

A New Beginning for Beth

"Why don't you just tell us what you are talking about?" Beth insisted. She was getting annoyed by all this cloak and dagger talk and wanted to get to the bottom of this.

Peter continued. "So much money has been raised for cancer, and AIDS and different illnesses. Do you ever wonder with all this money why we haven't found at least one cure? We made incredible strives in technology the past twenty years yet we haven't come up with a cure for diabetes. Why is that?"

Beth thought for a moment at what Peter was saying. "Maybe these types of illnesses are more complicated then one would think and that's why there has been no cure for it. At least they have been able to control it with insulin."

Peter smiled at Beth. "Now you are getting it. The whole idea is to create something that is profitable for the company. And what better way then to create something that would keep the illness under control without curing it?"

There was silence in the car. What Peter was saying was just too surreal for Beth to understand. "If these companies have the cure for diabetes then why not get it approved? This could save so many lives."

"What is the profit in curing people?" Peter asked. "Do you know how many people in North America alone have diabetes? Do the math Beth."

"What I'm trying to tell you is that they have the cure for so many illnesses but what would be the point in curing people? What is the profit in that? So they come up with something that will keep the illness under control. That way these sick people have to rely on the medicine to keep them alive."

"They have a cure for them but instead use the sickness to make money." Domenic added.

"Exactly!" Peter replied.

"Makes perfect sense to me." Domenic said. "There's no profit in healthy people."

Beth leaned back in her seat absorbing all the information. "Isn't the government aware of this?"

Peter laughed. "Beth, you haven't been listening to me. They are the government. They run the country. The people that represent our country are puppets. They aren't the true government. The pharmaceutical companies rule this country and every other country. The funny thing about this is the puppets and the people are quick to give these companies money to find cures for diseases and illnesses that they already have cures for. What a business!" he finished his speech with a huffing sound of disgust.

"Is that what you have been stealing?" Domenic asked. "Did you steal the cure for what your mother was suffering with?"

Peter's attention turned back to Domenic. "Wouldn't you? If you saw your mother slowly disappear in front of you, wouldn't you do what you could to save her?"

"But you used her as a human guinea pig." Domenic said.

Peter nodded in agreement. "It was the chance I had to take to help her. I couldn't watch her fall deeper into her own world not knowing me or my sister or her own grandchildren. I hated watching her lose her independence and dignity. She had become nothing more than a shell of a woman who had no control over herself including her own bowel movements. Especially when I knew there was a chance to bring her back."

Beth weighed the information. She knew legally what Peter did was wrong but was it morally wrong? Were the pharmaceutical companies guilty as well? Corruption was all too familiar to Beth. She had experienced that as a defense attorney and this whole scenario reeked of it. She knew that if she were put in Peters place, she may have done the exact same thing. The thought of anyone she loved going through such a devastating illness as Alzheimer's or dementia was bad enough. But to stand by and watch when you could give them a new lease on life was even worse.

"I understand what you are saying but there is one thing that has me confused. Who is this man that has you so scared?" Beth asked.

Before Peter could answer his door was yanked open and a gun was pointed at his head.

They were so deep in conversation that they hadn't noticed the car pull into the parking lot.

"Get out of the fucking car." the man ordered.

The three of them did as they were told. Beth walked around to the driver's side with her hands in the air.

The man she had encountered in her backyard and again in the restaurant parking lot stepped out of the driver's side of the van and grabbed Beth's arms and handcuffed them behind her. He then proceeded to do the same to Peter and Domenic.

"Times up, Bucar. Do you have what I want?" the man growled as he waved the gun.

"I have it but it's not with me." Peter said.

The man turned to Beth and Domenic. "I think we should introduce ourselves." He smiled. "I know who both of you are but you don't know who I am."

He paused, waiting for a reply but Beth and Domenic stood in silence.

"I'm Peter's new business partner, Sam. And this idiot over here is my driver and comedy relief Winston."

Winston made a sound of annoyance. It was obvious he didn't like to be referred to in such a manner.

Sam walked over to Beth and put the barrel of the gun to her hair and lifted a curl from her shoulder. "I have to hand it to you Ms Singer. You certainly did a number on Winston's face with that power washer. Who would have figured it could do so much damage?" he laughed with a snort.

Winston placed the keys of the cuffs in his pocket. "Can we get this over with? I hate the idea of standing out in the open like this."

"Relax Winston. This will be over with soon enough." Sam snapped. "You are getting too paranoid." Sam shook his head.

"I thought you got rid of your comedy relief after he screwed up?" Beth asked Sam.

Sam shook his head. "I need someone to clean up the mess when I'm finished."

"Where are you going to take us?" Domenic asked.

"Well first we need to pick up our parcel from Peter. After that will be up to Winston." Sam shrugged his shoulders.

A smile came across Winston's face. "This will be fun." He said, grabbing Beth and pushing her into the back of the van.

Beth pulled back trying to resist but this just angered her captors even more. Winston slapped her across the face and pushed her to the floor of the van. Beth hit the floor of the van with a thump, banging her head against the back seat.

"I'm going to pay you back for damaging my face, bitch." He snarled at her as she scrambled to regain her composure.

Sam motioned for Domenic and Peter to get into the back of the van. Winston pushed Peter in. he fell against Beth as she tried her best to make room for him. They both found it difficult to keep themselves upright while their hands were cuffed behind them.

Domenic reluctantly made his way to the van as a set of headlights pulled into the parking lot and headed towards the group at high speed.

"What the hell is this, a parade?" Sam yelled as he aimed his revolver at the on coming car. He fired off a couple of rounds at the car, hitting the front fender as the car made contact with his body, throwing him to the side of Beth's car. Domenic instinctively body slammed Winston against the side of the van knocking the wind out of him. Beth scrambled out of the back of the van and plopped herself on top of Winston, holding him to the ground as Domenic searched his pockets for the cuff keys. He managed to find the keys and remove his cuffs while Beth kept Winston from getting to his feet.

Domenic unlocked Beth's cuffs and handed her the keys, instructing her to do the same to Peter.

She climbed back into the van and removed Peter's cuffs just as the car hit the van and jolted them forward towards the front seats. Domenic had managed to grab hold of Winston and throw the cuffs on him just as the car made contact with the van a second time. They jumped out of the way as the impact of the car pushed the back of the van in their direction.

Sam lay motionless on the ground as the car reversed then started back towards them. Domenic grabbed Sam's revolver which was lying on the ground next to him, and fired at the headlights of the car as it made another approach in their direction. He took out one of the lights and hit the roof of the car with the second shot. The car swerved away from Domenic and turned towards the exit of the lot.

Once he was sure the car was leaving he took a set of the cuffs and cuffed Sam's hands behind him. He checked him for broken bones even though he wouldn't know a broken bone from a hole in the wall. Sam moaned as he regained conciseness.

"What the hell?" he mumbled as he tried to free his hands.

"The police are on their way." Beth yelled from the van. "I also requested an ambulance just in case our friend here needs it."

Sam struggled with his hands, trying to free himself. "I'll be out in one hour." He laughed as Domenic helped him to his feet and placed him inside the van. He sat down with a thump, next to Winston who was none too happy about going to jail.

"Maybe so, but we will bring charges of attempted kidnapping and attempted murder against you." Domenic said as he slammed the door on the two men. "No judge will give you bail on those charges."

Domenic turned his attention to Beth and put his arms around her. "Are you okay honey?"

Beth snuggled in his embrace. Her heart was racing a mile a minute but his arms made her feel safe. "I'm okay now." She whispered.

They held each other unaware that Peter was watching them in disbelief. It finally hit him that there was something between them and he felt his heart ache. He realized at that moment that his suspicions about Beth were true. She only pretended to like him in order to get close enough to find out more information. He turned away as Beth glanced in his direction.

Realizing the situation, Beth pulled away from Domenic and walked towards Peter. "I'm sorry Peter. I never wanted to hurt you." She put her hand on his shoulder but Peter pulled away.

"That's okay Beth. I knew it was too good to be true that you would ever be interested in someone like me."

"That's not true Peter. I really do like you. I agree that my intentions at first were to make contact with you and win your trust but after getting to know you, I have seen a different side of you."

Peter looked at Beth and briefly made eye contact with her.

"You are a wonderful person and I will help you to get out of this mess." Beth continued.

"There is no mess, Beth." Peter said. "What are they going to charge me with?"

"You have a point there Peter. If they want to press charges against you then the company will expose the truth and they certainly wouldn't want to do that." Beth replied.

Peter nodded in agreement.

Beth thought for a moment as she looked at the two men in the van. "One thing that I'm puzzled about. What does Sam have to do with all this?"

"Sam is an executive with the company. He got wind of what I was doing and decided to do some investigating himself. He found out about my mother and he approached me with an offer." Peter said. "He offered me money and no harm to my mother if I were to make the drug again for him."

"Couldn't he just get it himself?" Domenic asked.

Peter shook his head. "He is an executive but on the bottom of the totem pole. He doesn't have that kind of access. Besides, he needed to be sure that it would work before he made contact with me."

"How did he know about you?" Beth asked.

"I have no idea. I suppose it was a lucky guess." Peter said shrugging his shoulders.

The three of them watched as an ambulance pulled into the parking lot, followed closely behind by a police cruiser.

The same officers stepped out of the car and walked up to where the three were standing. "It's a busy night for you three." One of the officers remarked.

Domenic pointed to the back of the van as one of the paramedics opened the doors to look in at the wounded. "Which one was hit by the car?" he asked.

"I am and take these cuffs off of me!" Sam yelled.

"Shut the hell up." Beth yelled back. "You're lucky I don't give you the same thing I gave your comedy relief."

Domenic and Peter looked at each other and smirked. "Yeah you wouldn't want to tangle with her. She's a wild cat." Domenic laughed.

"What took you so long?" Domenic asked one of the officers.

"We passed the other car on the road. It had been pulled over and the driver was injured. The ambulance had to take her to the hospital."

"Her?" Beth asked.

A New Beginning for Beth

The officer looked at his note pad. "Yeah. And would you believe it was the sister of that other woman we arrested earlier? Running people over with their cars must be a family trait."

"The guy is okay." The paramedic said to the officer. "He won't need to be taken to the hospital."

Beth handed the keys to the cop. "you'll need these."

He took the keys from her and he and his partner placed Sam and Winston in the back of the cruiser. "The three of you will need to come in to make a statement."

"We'll do that first thing in the morning." Domenic promised. "If there isn't anything else, we need to go."

Once their assistance was no longer needed, the three of them climbed into Beth's car and pulled out of the parking lot.

Peter sat in silence in the back seat wondering what was in store for him now that the truth was out. "What is going to happen to me?" he asked.

Beth glanced over at Domenic. "We are going to take you to your car and you are going to go home and take care of your mother." She said.

"Aren't you going to tell the police about me?" he asked.

"As you said before, no one will press charges against you without revealing the truth. So I think you are safe."

"What about Amanda?" Peter asked.

"What about her?" Domenic replied.

"What will happen to her?" Peter asked with concern.

"She and her sister will have charges brought against them for attempted assault. If they have no records they may get away with probation and community service." Beth said. "But I'm sure your bosses will get them off especially since they are aware of what the company has been doing."

Peter leaned back in his seat, relieved that they wouldn't be going to jail. "I know that Amanda and Lydia wanted to make money with this cure but they only did it to help their mother out. She had a rough life and they wanted to give her a comfortable life in her old age."

"It still doesn't make it right." Domenic said as he pulled into the parking lot of the restaurant and parked next to Peter's car.

Peter lowered his head. He knew that Domenic was right about what they did. He also knew that what he did for his mother may have been legally wrong, but he would do it all over again. He loved his mother and wanted her final years on earth to be full of love from her children and grandchildren. He wanted her to cherish these years. Not have them slip away from her memory like everything else had.

Peter climbed out of the car and turned to Beth and Domenic. "Thanks for understanding and helping me."

"What are you going to do now?" Beth asked.

"Well first, I'm going to go home and give my mother a hug and tell her I love her. And then tomorrow I am going to look for a new job."

"They could always use your expertise at the police department." Domenic suggested.

Peter thought for a moment and smiled. "I may just mull over that idea."

He leaned into the car and kissed Beth on the cheek. "I hope we meet again Beth."

"Quite possibly." She replied with a smile.

Peter waved to them as they pulled out of the parking lot and turned onto the main street and merged with the traffic. He got into his car and pulled out shortly after them. He was very lucky tonight thanks to Beth. His heart still ached when he recalled watching her and Domenic embracing but he knew that she was out of his league. "Maybe one day I will find someone like you Beth." He said out loud.

Beth and Domenic drove in silence back to Beth's house. "Do you want company tonight?" Domenic asked, breaking the silence.

Beth closed her eyes. "That would be nice." She whispered. She moved her hand and gently placed it on Domenic's knee. He smiled as he felt the warmth of her hand on his lap.

"What are your plans for tomorrow?" he asked as he pulled into her driveway.

Beth looked over at him and kissed him deeply on the mouth. "I'm going to give my mother a call and invite her out for lunch."

Pro Bono

Chapter One

Beth stood at her window watching all the commotion as she quietly sipped her tea. Pickles whined at the door, wanting to join in on the Halloween festivities that was happening at the main farm house but Beth thought it best that he stay put. He was only five pounds of puppy and could easily get trampled by all the visitors.

"Sorry baby. You can't go out yet." She said as she reached down and rubbed him behind the ear.

Beth had bought the farm in July and moved in a month later. Her soon to be ex husband had made her an offer on their matrimonial home that she couldn't refuse. He also gave her the offer to stop making her life miserable by ending their seven year marriage.

Now here she was a new owner of twenty five acres of farm land as well as a beautiful farmhouse and converted barn. At first she thought about living in the house, but it was too big for one person. So she decided to live in the converted barn. Who knew she would end up living in a barn not to mention owning a working farm? She had tried growing a vegetable garden one year. That was a total bust. If she couldn't grow anything in a five by ten foot plot of ground how the hell was she to manage twenty five acres?

She shook off her negative thoughts as she watched Agnes greet more children who came to pick out a pumpkin for carving. She had met

Agnes through Alice Bucar and in turn introduced Agnes to her friend Sal. They hit it off so well that within weeks of knowing each other they decided to get married. "I guess love has no age limit." Beth thought.

She smiled as she watched Agnes move around the cemetery, dressed in a black grim reapers robe. She dyed her frizzed hair a bright orange and used a can of hair spray to stick black felt triangles on her head. From a distance she looked like a carved pumpkin on a black post. Up close she looked funny and this brought amusing giggles from everyone who encountered her.

Her grandparents and their friends had taken over the main farm house which gave Beth a sense of security without intruding on her privacy.

They had made plans to section off part of the land for the seniors to grow their own vegetables. They also have plans to have inner city families do the same. Most of the land Beth had leased to local farmers in need of more land for crops. This gave Beth some extra money and kept the farm from going to hell in a hand basket.

The seniors use the house for canning and baking pies from the fruit they harvested from the abundance of trees. They had set up a sign at the side of the road to invite customers to come and pick their own fruit. They also sell their home made goodies, using the profit to help pay for the monthly bills on the house. They also use the house for parties and gatherings. Agnes and Sal have planned a summer wedding next year and it will take place right next to the pool.

Today was Halloween and to Beth's surprise, the previous owners had planted a pumpkin patch. Grandpa Tom had a great idea to scatter the pumpkins around the cemetery and allow visitors to walk through to pick out their own pumpkin.

When Beth bought the farm a family cemetery was included with the deal. At first she shuddered every time she looked at it but after awhile it grew on her. Who would have guessed that it would be such a big hit with visitors? They loved reading the old tomb stones that dated back to the late eighteen hundreds.

A familiar vehicle pulled into the driveway and Beth's body immediately heated up. She was all too familiar with the driver of the silver BMW and seeing the car make its way up the long drive made her body tremble with delight.

She met Domenic through her grandparents when they felt she needed the best to represent her in her divorce. Although Beth thought her divorce was cut and dry her grandparents were right about one thing. Domenic was just what she needed and not just in a professional manner.

Shortly after they met they became lovers and he was the best lover she had ever had. Not that she was an expert in the field but Domenic certainly made her toes curl and her body shake with pleasure. Even the sight of his car made her erroneous zone heat up ten degrees.

The BMW slowly drove past the main house, continuing up to where Beth resided. As it got closer Beth could see Domenic behind the wheel. A smiled formed on her face as the car came to a rest next to hers.

Domenic cut the engine and piled out of the car. He popped the trunk and dragged out two large garment bags. Beth sighed knowing it was their costumes for the party that the seniors were having tonight. She really didn't want to dress up but Domenic wouldn't take no for an answer. She reluctantly left him in charge of picking out a costume for her and by the size of the bags she had a feeling that she would be dressed in some over stuffed barnyard animal costume.

She opened the door before Domenic had a chance to knock and pickles made a bee line for the main house. "Pickles! Get back here!" Beth yelled. But the dog had no intentions on returning. There was food cooking at the main house and he wanted to make sure he got his fair share of cookies and treats.

"Let him have fun." Domenic said as he greeted Beth with a kiss.

"It's easy for you to say. If he doesn't get trampled he'll get fat from all the cookies." Beth sighed.

Her attention was diverted to the two garment bags that Domenic had laid across the sofa.

"Do I dare ask what kind of costume you picked out for me?"

Domenic ignored Beth's question and unzipped the first bag. "What do you think?" he asked as he pulled a pirate costume out of the bag.

"Cute. I gather that ones yours."

Domenic nodded as he unzipped the other bag. "And this ones yours."

Follow Beth's adventures in the second addition entitled 'PRO BONO.'